DARK HEART

A B Endacott

Cover designed by Marcus Moltzer
Cover illustration by Nicole Sizer
Map illustration by Ellen Liu

This book is a work of fiction. Names, characters, places, and incidents either
are products of the author's imagination or are used fictitiously.
Any resemblance to actual persons,
living or dead, events, or locales is entirely coincidental.

ISBN 978-0-6487299-0-7

For my wonderful bookstagrammers.

In no particular order, Blue, Mel, Jayse, Nat, Madi, Sam, Kat,

Jess, Jem, Tay, Julie, Laura, Jess, Abi, Teagen, Laura.

I'm sure I've forgotten people...forgive me!

Your hearts are among the wonderful that I have come to know.

Thank you for your support, your enthusiasm

And for being part of such a wonderful community.

This book very well may not have come into being without you all.

Thus conscience does make cowards of us all

Shakespeare, Hamlet

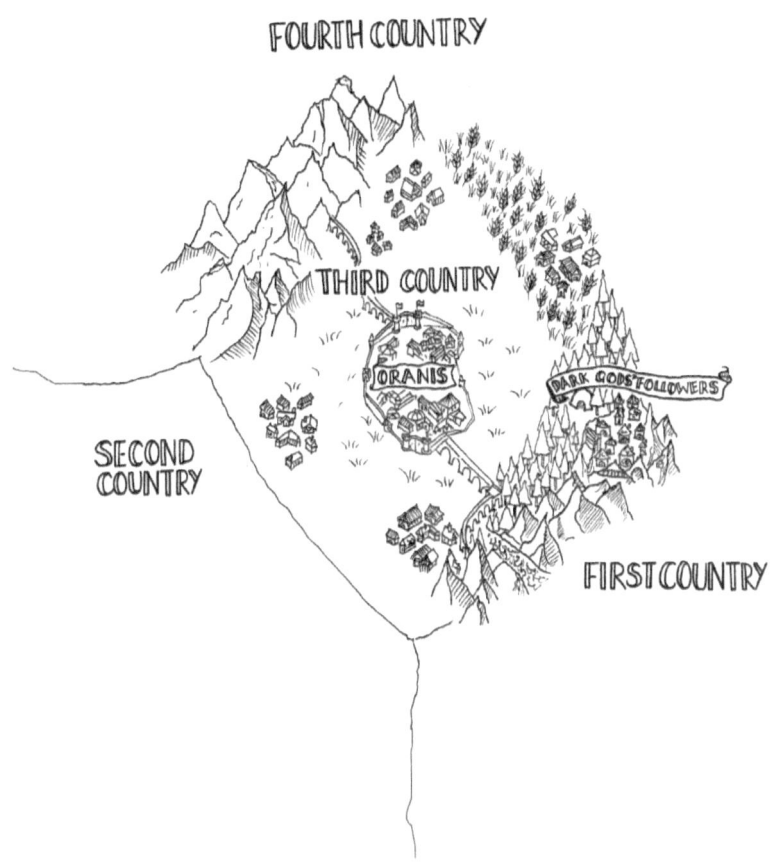

Third Country

ONE

At a glance, the woman in the cell didn't look as though she had been someone important. Certainly, she didn't look dangerous. Her robes held the dirt of a garment worn unceasingly, only betraying glimpses of their original pristine white. Snatches of purple, blue and crimson peeked through the grime at the hems. The woman's pallor was the sickly hue of someone who had not seen the sun in quite a stretch of time.

She reposed on the room's solitary bench, her eyes closed, as though her time imprisoned had imprinted her with a bone-weary fatigue.

But at second glance, the way she held herself apart from the filth of her dingy surrounds made it apparent this was not a woman to be trifled with. Indeed, the line of her posture was not that of exhaustion but of anticipation. Care was needed when dealing with her – a lot of it.

It was for this reason that Councilwoman Freyanna Kuch stepped into the cell with extreme trepidation. It was for this reason too that the door was closed behind her with a rapidity that made her very aware that she was, to all intents and purposes, on her own.

At her entry, the eyes of the Chief Healer – former Chief Healer, to be precise – snapped open and the battle between the two women began.

Any observer would have seen nothing beyond the way the two women seemed locked in a state of intense concentration. This fight took place between the phenomenal abilities of the two greatest healers the city had ever seen. Both possessed the ability to heal with merely a thought. Both possessed the capacity to use that power to instead tear flesh and bone apart. Both were trying now to use that power on the other.

For long minutes the two women remained locked in their invisible battle, seeking to extinguish each other's life. Freya felt the strain on her heart, elongating the pauses between each beat. The edges of her thoughts took on an insubstantial quality and sensation on the left side of her face began to elude her. It took a supreme effort of will to rally her strength and pull her injuries back into the correct harmony of her lifesong. Her desire to live gave her the strength she needed to push back, to feel for the melody and harmony of the Chief Healer's body and push against her lifesong with every part of her will. For a time, she could hear the distortion in the other woman's body, but then her efforts were repelled and the damage reversed. It was clear that their skills were evenly matched. Whenever one managed to make some kind of incursion, the other was able to heal the damage without relinquishing her own attack. Bones cracked but were immediately healed, ruptured arteries were re-formed instantly. The breath driven from lungs as airways constricted rushed back in as those same airways were eased. Neither could best the other. The fight ended as abruptly as it had begun in mutual recognition of the stalemate.

Freya did not move, did not so much as adjust her feet. She gave no sign of any discomfort or unease as she regarded the woman who until only a few cycles before had been one of the most powerful individuals in the city of Oranis. She felt an echo of the respect and, yes, fear the woman's presence had always inspired in her; even in filthy clothes in this dark, cramped cell, the Chief Healer kept her composure. But Freya had been forced to turn into something new by the uprising against the Kade. The old fears that had restrained her had been burned away and she was still discovering the person who had been freed from those shackles.

The Chief Healer broke the silence. "So." There was a hint of cold amusement in her voice.

"Indeed," Freya replied, her voice level. She watched warily for any sign of movement. A physical attack could be just as dangerous as one from the mind.

"I must congratulate you, Freya. You surprised me."

Freya raised her eyebrows in lieu of requesting elaboration. The strangeness that she and the Chief Healer were talking with such intimate candidness only served to make her more curious about what the woman would say.

"I didn't actually expect you to support rebellion."

"Why not?"

"Because it would ask too much of you."

"I made the decision that I would be willing to die, if it came to it," Freya countered.

The older woman laughed softly. "What makes you think I was referring to your life?"

A sense of déjà vu swept over Freya. Something in the Chief Healer's manner reminded her of the time she had spent tending to Zarech, the enigmatic leader of the Followers of the Dark Gods. He too had seemed to possess a greater understanding of the world around him. He had even revealed the reality of the Gods' existence and the abilities that the truly faithful possessed – the fact that true and ardent belief meant one was able to actually touch the gods themselves and was left with an echo of that god's power. But although he had revealed so much to her, he had kept even more from her. She hadn't liked the way he had toyed with her then and she didn't like the way the Chief Healer was toying with her now.

"I'm not here to play games," she snapped, her temper freeing itself.

The Chief Healer raised her eyebrows, cool surprise on her face. Freya's outburst had done nothing to break her composure. "So why are you here?"

"Because you killed the first three people who tried to speak with you."

"You know, the first thing you need to moderate in leadership is your temper," the Chief Healer remarked.

With no small effort, Freya reined in her anger. "What makes you think that I'm in a position of leadership?"

"I have done this before, you know. I just happened to be on the other side of this conversation the last time I was involved in it," the Chief Healer replied.

"I know that you may think I betrayed the Kade—" Freya began, but the Chief Healer cut her off.

"You didn't betray the Kade, Freya. You betrayed me." For the first time, there was a crack in the composure of the older woman and genuine emotion slipped through.

"You wanted me to be Kade!" Freya retorted.

"I wanted you to be one of us," the Chief Healer corrected her.

"Why? Why me?" Freya was being drawn to a line of discussion far from her purpose, but a compelling combination of anger and curiosity wouldn't let her allow these questions to remain unanswered.

"Because you were special." The other woman's eyes glittered with restrained anger. "I must admit, I thought you would never become aware of your abilities and would simply remain a superb healer, willing and happy to be one of us."

Something in the Chief Healer's comment brought to mind a claim Zarech had made — that many Kade had supported the Rebellion to empower their own gods and by extension, themselves. Freya wondered if that had motivated the woman in front of her. Somehow, she doubted it.

"Why did you support the Kade takeover?" Freya asked.

"Why do you think?" The Chief Healer's smile was smug.

Again, Freya's temper rather than reason drove her response. "Don't play games with me."

"What do you want me to say? Some were involved out of a genuine desire to empower the Kade gods. After they saw what could be attained with deep, devout faith and powerful gods, a great many sought to further their own position. And some simply wanted power." She smiled, although there was nothing humorous in it.

"And you?" It shouldn't have been important to Freya, but it suddenly was.

"Why do you think?" The question was thrown at her. Another test? Freya had no idea.

Freya took the time to form each word before she spoke, her voice slow and careful. "I think you genuinely believe."

The way the Chief Healer inclined her head was an invitation to continue.

"But you're a healer. So how were you comfortable with people being hurt, and so senselessly?"

"How were you?"

Despite Freya's best efforts to remain control of her emotions, anger and frustration bloomed inside her, but and she found herself giving words to the accusation which thundered through her mind. "Because you and your people started it."

She received no outward sign that her comment had made any impact.

"Before you decided to topple us, the city was peaceful. There was almost no unrest. How many people died during your gambit for power? How many have died in the cycles since you claimed power? How many will die in the coming days as you try to maintain your hold? Can you really justify that much death and suffering by simply saying that we started it?"

"You're avoiding the question," Freya pointed out. "You supported the Kade takeover."

"Did I?"

Freya opened her mouth to reply and closed it again. The truth was that she had no idea what role the Chief Healer had played during the Kade takeover. The limit of her knowledge was that once the takeover had been successfully completed, the Chief Healer replaced the old head of the Healers' Guild. There had been few famous figures of the takeover. The Kade governance had announced itself as a fact, as though it had always been there and always would be. Figureheads might have been a rallying point, or fed into claims of Kade supremacy, but figureheads were also fallible. If they fell, so too could the Kade's authority.

"I was approached when the takeover was all but a sure thing. I was told that I had been chosen. What would you have had me do, Freya?" Iron was in her voice as she spoke, and rage, too. "I was given an opportunity to make a difference – a real difference, to use my talents and abilities to actually help people. And as time passed, I saw that the takeover had brought peace, security, prosperity. I was given a chance to change the system of healers – to save *more* people. The takeover gave that to me. But to answer your question, if I had been given a say, no, I would not have supported the takeover. But I wasn't. Can you say the same?"

Freya fought the impulse to take a step back, away from the accuracy of the quietly delivered accusation.

"The uprising took the city back for its people," she insisted.

"So you'll reinstate the Dual Accord?" The other woman's smirk gave away the fact that she knew the Pious Resistance was going to do no such thing.

"That's not something over which I have a say," Freya said.

"Ah, I see. Of course you don't." The Chief Healer's smirk widened. "Uprising, takeover, rebellion...they're all the same thing, really."

"But we did it for the right reasons," Freya insisted, her voice verging on petulant.

"Most of the Kade who were behind the uprising eight years ago believed that too." The Chief Healer shrugged.

With great effort, Freya held herself back from being drawn further into this discussion and away from the purpose that had brought her into the room in the first place. "I'm here to ask if you will co-operate with us."

The harsh sound of the Chief Healer's laugh echoed discordantly off the stone walls. When she finished, she fixed Freya with that unsettlingly incisive gaze. "Co-operate how?"

"You were a prominent member of the Kade governance. If you tell the Kade that we want to look after them, too, we think it would help restore order more swiftly."

"And why would I do that?" The Chief Healer shifted again so that she could look more directly at Freya. Freya had always felt uncomfortable under the older woman's scrutiny. The Chief Healer had a way of looking at a person and making them feel as though she were gleaning insights from the very depths of their soul. It felt no different now.

"Because you're a healer. You don't believe in allowing needless harm to take place," Freya told her, refusing herself to be rattled by the weight of the woman's direct gaze which had once so terrified her.

"According to you, I'm a member of a group who only care about self-empowerment," the Chief Healer replied.

"Can you blame us for what we did?" Memories of the fear, abuse, violence, and repression that had characterised the Kade's rule over the Third Country flickered through her mind. They stoked Freya's rising anger.

"Absolutely."

"And for that you'll let more people die?"

"Once you've seen enough of that sort of violence, it stops affecting you." For the first time, the Chief Healer sounded tired, old.

"How did you learn to live with it?" Freya's question was soft, a guilty admission of her own complicity in the violence that had plagued the streets in the Resistance's bid to topple the Kade and the subsequent assertion of its hold over the country.

Defiantly, the Chief Healer raised her chin, her eyes filled with malevolence. In that moment Freya knew she would never do anything to help the Pious because of what Freya had done in betraying her.

It was the suddenness of her attack that gave her the edge. Freya didn't think the Chief Healer expected Freya to try to kill her again. It was over almost immediately. The woman's body fell sideways with a thud that seemed too soft for a body, especially not the body of a woman as formidable as she had been. Yet no lifesong coursed through Freya's mind, confirming the truth of the Chief Healer's death.

Freya left the cell. The guards outside hovered in obvious anxiety. She gave curt instructions for them to deal with the corpse before she went to find Makkyd. They asked no questions about the circumstances in which the Chief Healer had died, and wouldn't, even when they found no mark on the body. Freya knew Makkyd would have chosen who stood outside the cell with extreme care.

It was only a short walk to the rooms of the leader of the Pious Council. The irony did not escape Freya that she had rescued Makkyd from the very building in which the Chief Healer had been kept. While there was a perversity about a school in the heart of the city being turned into a prison, it was certainly practical.

The door to the Pious Council leader's rooms was open and Freya entered without knocking. Makkyd looked up from the report she was reading, her expression holding the question she did not bother to put into words.

"Dealt with, as you asked," Freya said. "One way or another."

TWO

Light streamed into the room. Located on the uppermost floor of one of the city's administrative buildings, its windows offered a peaceful picture of the city, but few of the eight people in the room were looking at the view.

Freya entered, taking in everything with a glance. It was a skill she had been required to perfect as a Master-ranked healer; even wasting a second could cost lives. That capacity to look, assess, and act in the same instant had served her well as a member of the Resistance. The room was obviously one accustomed to housing powerful people. It was obvious in the rich carpet underfoot, the carefully rendered paintings on the walls, and of course the large table which dominated the room. To produce something of that size, let alone that quality, several craftsmen must have been involved – it all spoke of power. A figure by the windows caught her attention. Even rendered a silhouette by the bright light, she knew instantly it was Ashtyn. As she walked to him, she tried to still the familiar way the sight of him made her pulse flutter by wondering why there were no curtains. It wouldn't have surprised her to learn someone had ordered them removed. The Kade often decorated their rooms in the blue, scarlet, and purple that represented their gods. After the briefest hesitation, she came to stand beside Ashtyn. He acknowledged her presence with the upward curve of his lips.

"Worth it all for the view," he joked quietly.

"That was my reason for joining the Resistance. I wanted better rooms," she returned.

His shoulders lifted in silent mirth. With the sunlight sinking into his dark hair and catching amid the green of his eyes, he looked unfairly good.

"You've been well?" he asked softly.

She nodded. "You?"

"I'll be better once we get this meeting over with. I'm sick of meetings," he grumbled.

She agreed. They had barely won the city – it had been only a handful of cycles. Yet every day had been filled with at least one meeting – to determine where the final pockets of struggle within the city were following the capture of the Kade's highest members, to sit with individuals in the city's key sectors to acquire their co-operation, to decide how to proclaim the new order, to re-assess the situation. They were seemingly never-ending. It had kept them apart.

"Perhaps we should have a meeting about how many meetings we're having," Freya suggested, keeping her face straight despite the mirth which spilled into her voice.

Ashtyn's snicker broke her restraint, sending her into uncontrolled giggles.

It was a moment of levity that she appreciated for more than simply the fact that it brought respite to the seriousness of the previous few fivedays. It was also a demonstration of how far she and Ashtyn had come. Following her discovery that he had been sent to recruit her into the Pious Resistance, she had felt a sense of betrayal that cut to her core. The fact that they had been lovers – in an adulterous relationship no less – had made everything a thousand times worse. Even after she had returned to the Resistance, it had taken her a long time to be able to speak with him, let alone do so comfortably. There was still much left unsaid between them, such as why he had not conveyed the request that she be on the frontline of the uprising's final battle. They had crossed paths briefly over the time since their victory, but each time had been fleeting. Nevertheless, there had been a mutual cautious delight in their brief exchanges, even if they were always called away on more urgent matters before they could have a meaningful discussion. She hoped that one day the weight of everything unsaid between them could be lifted. The reality was that she cared about him far too much. That had been forcefully driven home to her when news he had survived the battle had reached her. The manner in which relief had become a physical presence, coursing through her veins and driving her to her knees as soundless sobs wracked her, had been the final, undeniable proof of just how powerful her feelings for him were. But she had no idea how to take that first step with him. Perhaps it was why she had not challenged the convenience of the excuse that she was too busy to seek him out.

Makkyd's entrance brought her back to the present, also forestalling any further conversation with Ashtyn. Everybody drifted to the central table and took a seat. Makkyd sat at the head.

"Now. We need to talk about how we've been going about things, how we should and could better structure our administration," Makkyd said with her usual lack of preamble.

Beside her Ashtyn muttered, "Oh Goddess. A meeting about meetings."

Freya bit her lip as her body shook with laughter.

Makkyd gave them a cool stare. For a moment, Freya thought Makkyd was about to reprimand them, but instead she merely turned to Lyssa as though she had seen nothing. "Are you ready?"

The beautiful artist nodded, throwing a look of her own in Freya's direction. Freya returned the stare with vague amusement. She had long since given up trying to understand why Lyssa disliked her so much. Her suspicion was that the artist had an interest in Ashtyn and was jealous that Freya had, for a time at least, been involved with him.

Writing began to appear on the paper placed in front of each seat as Makkyd spoke. Lyssa's ability was to manipulate ink on paper. It had proved useful for conveying messages when secrecy was paramount before and during the uprising.

"At the moment, we're plugging leaks more than we are looking at the larger strategy of governing," Makkyd said. A murmur of agreement greeted her words.

"Unfortunately, Astrom's death has left us a person short. While all of the city's sectors are under our leadership, coordinating what we've got and what we know is that much more difficult."

Silence met those words. Almost certainly everybody was thinking about Astrom – Makkyd's second-in-command. She had died in the final battle of the uprising. Astrom had been brought to where Freya was overseeing the treatment of the wounded. Freya's skill as a healer, even without her ability, was remarkable. Indeed, that night she saved dozens of lives both through her direction to others, and through her own talents. But she couldn't revive the dead. Freya shivered as she remembered the shock that had engulfed her when she realised that the person who had trained her how to fight, who she considered a friend, the person who had effortlessly pulled skeins of admiration from those who surrounded her and wove them into an unbreakable loyalty, was dead, and there was nothing she could do to fix it. It hadn't seemed fair then and it didn't seem fair now.

Makkyd's voice strode into the silence. "The most pressing thing is to have a service for those lost in the uprising – on both sides."

"How are we even going to have Pious ceremonies?" asked Oltrem, the head of the mason's guild.

"Which brings us to the first problem," Makkyd replied. "All of the Goddess' Children were slaughtered six years ago. Because, like the Kade's Ordained, they were so secretive, much of the detail of the Pious religious practices is lost to us."

"Did none of them survive?" Ashtyn's voice balanced incredulity against heartbreak.

"Not that we know of," Makkyd said. The bluntness with which she spoke made the truth even harder to hear. Given the brutal efficiency with which the Kade had dismantled so much of the Pious identity, it was hardly surprising that important knowledge had been lost, but it was still shocking to hear the truth voiced like that. The Pious Council had been avoiding addressing this issue, busying themselves with other matters. It was far easier to deal with the need to repave the roads or find the last pockets of Kade loyalists than it was to face the truth of what had been done to the Pious. But it was an unavoidable reality that much of their religious culture had been decimated and they couldn't distract themselves from it for any longer.

"Most people still remember the prayers," Freya pointed out.

"You're correct, Freya. Our greatest asset here is collective memory. We don't even have a significant number of Pious texts – the Kade were characteristically thorough in their efforts to find every last one and destroy them." Makkyd sounded tired and bitter. Freya was right there with her.

"What about the Kade texts?" asked Grat, the slender man who had assumed the leadership of Oranis's scholars.

"What, you're suggesting we burn them in retaliation?" Bardan asked icily.

"That's not what we stand for," Ashtyn said.

Grat cleared his throat. "I was actually suggesting that they may make reference to some Pious religious practices."

Freya looked at Bardan. The portly man who now led the merchants' guild was the first friend she had made in the Resistance. She adored him for his gentle warmth. It surprised her that he had assumed Grat was proposing such a nasty retaliation, even if he opposed it. The years of persecution and the years of subversive rebellion had unquestionably changed the heart of every person in the room in some way. Except perhaps Makkyd. Freya could believe that Makkyd had always been that way.

The redheaded woman was looking thoughtfully at Grat. "It's a good idea."

"What about the Kade Ordained we have imprisoned? Do you think they may know anything?" Freya suggested.

"It's worth asking them." Grat scribbled something on the margin of the paper in front of him.

"The Head of the Ordained would likely know the most," Makkyd added.

"She may not want to be of any help." Freya's thoughts slid with no small measure of discomfort to the Chief Healer.

"Well, that actually quite neatly brings me to another issue," Makkyd said. "What are we going to do with the Kade leaders who are still alive? The Chief Healer died two days ago while in prison, but if her actions prior to her death were any indication of how the other leaders may behave, they won't be particularly co-operative."

The change that swept through the room was a tangible thing. Every person's face showed shock in its purest form. Even in a regime that didn't have figures, the Chief Healer had been an imposing figure on the landscape of the city's leadership during the Kade's rule.

"What happened?" Bardan asked.

Freya's mouth went dry. Her eyes darted to Makkyd, but her leader looked as calm as ever.

"She was found dead in her cell," Makkyd said.

"Really?" Bardan's incredulity rang through his voice and in the expression across his face.

"Really. At this stage, it looks as though she took her own life." Makkyd's voice was unyielding, daring Bardan to challenge her further.

Freya could feel Ashtyn's eyes on her but she kept her face carefully neutral. Nobody knew about the role she had played in the death of the Chief Healer and she wanted it to remain that way. Although she and Makkyd had agreed it was a necessary course of action, it had been decided without the knowledge of the rest of the Council.

"So what will we do with them?" Sek asked. Freya remembered the night she had accompanied him and his twin, Ellan, to rescue Makkyd following her capture by the Kade – from the same building in which the Chief Healer had been held. Both twins were terrifyingly effective killers. The presence of the pair, who now held joint control of the weavers and tailors, had ensured the success of their mission. At the time, Freya had been afraid of them. In truth, she still was a little. She couldn't imagine either of them would object to what she had done in the Chief Healer's cell. That did nothing to ease her discomfort, only serving to make it sit more uncomfortably within her, like a stone in her stomach.

"We always said that simply killing them was both politically imprudent and not the way we wanted to do things." Makkyd spoke carefully. "But leaving them alive may also present an issue."

"Surely not all of them are fanatics," Wren, the Chief Administrator, objected.

Lyssa spoke up. "They are still unlikely to appreciate the fact that we threw them out of power."

"Does that mean we should kill them?" Ashtyn was incredulous.

"It if means securing our position, shouldn't it at least be considered?" Makkyd said. Her eyes swept around the table, her expression daring anyone to question her further.

Nobody contradicted her and silence settled over the meeting. Makkyd was deliberately not filling it to prove her point. She knew how to manage her people, how to lead them to agree with the outcome she wanted.

Eventually Lyssa spoke again. "So what are we going to do?"

Bardan answered. "We'll leave them locked up for now. There's no need for us to do anything just yet. Grat, speak with the Ordained leader – she may be useful. Does anyone object?" Even though it was a general one, it was clear that his question was directed at Makkyd. It seemed Makkyd wasn't the only one who knew how to manage the people in the room. Nobody even breathed an objection.

Makkyd cleared her throat, the noise managing to sound both angry and authoritative. "There is one final matter that I wanted to discuss before we start talking about a plan for how we can co-ordinate more easily."

Everybody looked at her expectantly. The relief of moving away from the discomfort of the previous topic was a palpable thing, making the air in the room somehow easier to breathe.

"You are all likely to have heard the reports of violence on the streets between Kade and Pious. We have Kade groups attacking Pious in response to our uprising, and then Pious groups banding together in retaliation for the Kade actions and for the past six years. If we can't stop this, we're going to lose our legitimacy and risk the whole city breaking into open conflict between the two groups."

"Oh, so nothing major then," Ashtyn said with an acerbic levity.

He received titters of grim amusement, although Makkyd ignored both the comment and its response. "The reality may be less grave than the picture I just painted, but regardless this is a serious issue."

Freya had been fortunate thus far – she had avoided any contact with such violence, but she had certainly heard about the fights and she had seen their aftermath when she had been in the city's Healing Centres where there was always at least one patient who had been admitted due to the violence. Moreover, she had noticed the subtle tang of anger permeating the streets. It was impossible to miss.

"Nobody suggested it wasn't," Bardan interjected. "But we just changed the city completely. When the Kade did that six years ago, they secured their power with a great deal of violence. It wasn't easy for them, either."

Freya looked between Bardan and Makkyd, curious at this dynamic. If she didn't know any better, she would have sworn that Bardan was just short of being angry with Makkyd, despite the calmness in his voice.

"Is violence an option?" Ellan asked.

Freya wondered if he sounded slightly eager or if she was simply imagining it.

"Well, if we leave them to fight long enough, they'll certainly be glad if we step in," Makkyd said, almost carelessly.

"No. We are not Kade. The moment we start behaving like them, we lose everything for which we fought." Bardan's voice now held the distant rumblings of anger.

"Well, unless you have a suggestion, the only option we currently have is letting them fight it out until we can step in." Makkyd sounded like she also was on the verge of anger.

"Make good on our promise to bring Kade people into our administration," Bardan replied.

"No. It's too early," Makkyd objected. "We're still finding our feet."

"Exactly. Bring them in now rather than later. Let them have a voice in shaping society. Why do you think we rebelled in the first place?"

Makkyd glared at him across the table. "What does everybody else think?"

"I would certainly be willing to accept Kade input into how the city's administrators work," Wren said timidly. "They took good records but their methodology is complicated and we'd understand them faster with their help. And it is their city, too."

"Anybody else have thoughts on the matter?" Makkyd's tone indicated just how little she wanted someone else to speak.

"Many of the Guildsmiths' Masters are Kade – Pious were prevented from attaining that rank. There would be value in them being amenable to my leadership. That would be more likely if we consult with them," Ashtyn said.

Makkyd looked at the rest of the Council, naked challenge in her eyes. Freya shifted uncomfortably in her seat. Fortunately for her, the restructuring of the city's healers following the Kade takeover meant that it was organised far better than many of the other industries. The way healers were trained, assigned and promoted was excellent and she understood it well. That very system meant her competence and right to assume authority over the city's healers was unquestioned. She had the Chief Healer to thank for that.

When nobody else offered their opinion, Makkyd sighed. "And what do you plan to do if those people turn against us, Bardan?"

"Imprison them." Bardan had clearly thought about this. Freya had never realised he was so considered.

Makkyd held up her hands in resignation. "If there aren't any final objections, I suppose that's what we'll do, then. Feel free to consult with Kade individuals. But don't come crying to me when they try to work against you."

When the meeting finally drew to a close, the sun hung low in the sky. Freya stretched in her chair and stood, groaning as her muscles protested at the long time spent sitting down. Ashtyn hovered beside her, clearly waiting for her as she gathered her things. She was delighted by his desire to linger with her, even as she was at a loss for what she should say. She glanced at him as they left the room, headed for the staircase. A small frown creased his forehead. She didn't say anything, sure he would speak about whatever was troubling him when he was ready. The slowness to his pace was deliberate, a dragging out of each step, which meant everybody else overtook them on the way out. Once they were alone on the stairs he took a breath as though to speak, then seemed to think better of it.

"What is it?" she demanded, more sharply than she intended.

He paused, seeming to think more carefully. "Did you have anything to do with the death of the Chief Healer?"

"What?" She bought herself some time with the question, thrown that he would ask her so directly.

"You know what I mean."

"Spell it out for me." She matched his tone, irritation at his insinuation, however correct, flickering to life.

"You didn't react at all to the news. What do you know about her death?"

"Why does it matter?"

"Why won't you tell me?" He stopped walking. "Look at me, Freya," he said to her when she didn't turn to look at him.

Stubbornly, she refused to move. He grabbed her shoulders and turned her to face him. She had to tip her head back to meet his green gaze, his superior height and the fact that he was standing on the step above her making him tower over her.

"Let me go, Ashtyn," she snarled, anger unleashed at the way he had grabbed her.

"Freya, I'm serious," he begged. Anger had left his voice but that only served to incense her further.

"What does it matter?" she all but yelled.

"Because if you've done what I worry you may have done, it matters about how this affects you," he said. His fingers dug into her shoulders, stopping just shy of painful.

"What do you mean?"

"If you're running around killing people, it changes you, and not for the better."

"It's none of your business if I'm running around killing people, or if that affects me in any way." She hated that he did actually have a point. That fuelled her anger, too.

"Freya, I'll only ask you once more – did you do something to her?" Now his grip on her shoulders was painful.

"Anything I did or didn't do was for the good of the cause. You know all about that." She pulled herself free of his grip and stormed down the stairs.

"Makkyd isn't right about everything, you know." His voice echoed off the stone walls and seemed to chase her out of the building.

She didn't feel bad about killing the Chief Healer, but Ashtyn's reaction pricked at her. Of everybody, she would have thought he would have understood. His comment about Makkyd rang in her mind. She didn't necessarily agree with everything Makkyd proposed, but Makkyd had led them through the uprising well and she wanted to create a functioning and stable society. Freya could hardly blame her for that. Sometimes function and stability weren't easily created and required difficult decisions to be made in order to attain them. Freya couldn't understand why Ashtyn didn't see that.

She walked home quickly as the light faded. On her way, she passed a Kade worship square. She paused for a moment to watch the people gathered in prayer. Kade faith and the rituals that were the scaffold of that faith required collective worship. By contrast Pious rarely prayed together except during specific festivals and ceremonies. Habit almost had Freya's feet taking her to join the prayers, even though they weren't for her god or her way of life. For six long years she had attended those prayers as was required of her, fearing the consequences if she was not deemed devoted enough to the gods of the Kade. It felt good to know that she now had a choice about who and how she worshipped. To protect that, she would do anything

THREE

Breathing deeply, Freya sat cross-legged on the prayer mat in her work room at home and allowed her mind to clear. The words of prayer slipped from her lips easily, memory and habit guiding her to shape the words without even thinking about them. It was almost as though she hadn't been forced to worship the Kade gods over the past six years, hadn't been forced to abandon the Goddess even in thought. It was only when she considered all the ceremonies that had been lost that she realised how much had been taken from the Pious and how much they may never get back. Freya knew every personal prayer. She remembered the outline of the festivals, but the words that bound two people together in life eluded her in their totality, as did the words to welcome a new child into the world, or to bless the new harvest. Others may remember, or remember most of the words to the various prayers and rituals that formed the patchwork fabric of their religious and personal identity, but memory was an inconsistent friend. It was terrifying to realise how quickly and how effectively a culture could be erased. Anger and sorrow were her intermittent companions when she thought about how much of the Pious culture may be irretrievably lost.

Without realising, her lips formed a prayer for Zarech. Despite her best efforts, he never truly left her thoughts for long. She had been assigned to tend to the enigmatic and dangerous leader of the anarchic worshippers of the Dark Gods for several cycles. Their strange relationship, which even now she didn't quite understand, had changed her. Despite his occasional cruelty and the fact that he had ordered his people to commit acts of destruction, Freya had grown close to him. Perhaps that said something about her that was worrying. But it had been his needling questions that had made her join the Resistance. It had been he who revealed her ability born from her depth of faith. Now he was in her thoughts more than the question she most frequently asked herself about him: when he had blown up the Main Healing Centre, had he made sure to leave her alive? He claimed territory in her mind because he had been one of the Goddess' Children before he had worshipped the Dark Gods and their demand for anarchy. Perhaps he had been the last of the Goddess' Children.

Knowing that she had been with him for so long that he could have passed to her the knowledge of their people, and the opportunity had slipped through her fingers, was almost too much to bear following the Council's discussion of that day.

Freya opened her eyes, her prayers complete. Unusually, she was not left with the calm and tranquillity prayer normally gave her. While she had certainly felt that tangible connection to the other presence that reminded her she was part of a greater whole, it hadn't centred her in the way it often did. Too much was on her mind and the silence of the house didn't help.

After the Resistance won the city, she had been reluctant to return to the home she shared with Symon. The guilt at her deception hung too heavily on her. Symon had truly been the perfect collaborator; he had obediently worked and lived within the strict parameters outlined by the Kade, and while he had voiced occasional frustration with the Kade, he had never truly desired their departure. When she agreed to become joined to him, she had been a terrified girl. Her parents and sister had been killed for her sister's defiance of the Kade and she had been made to watch. She had believed that any resistance was futile, and Symon offered a way to live safely. She hadn't loved him but she had found a comfort and fondness in their life together. They succeeded where no other Pious had – they became exemplary Kade citizens, rewarded professionally and financially for their skills and loyalty. Symon wanted to prosper in Kade society and she had led him to believe that she wanted that, too. When she and Ashtyn had succumbed to the undeniable attraction between them over a year before, she felt guilt, but not much. At that time, she assumed that Symon would have been most angry about the social ruin to which she may have exposed both of them, given the Kade's severe laws against and punishment for adultery. It was only many cycles later that Symon had even hinted at the depths of how much he cared for her. Then, her guilt had fully woken. It was only fed by her leading him to believe she shared his desire for a child, for a family. She hated herself for the extent to which she had gone in maintaining the deception of their unity.

Symon preyed on her conscience, and planning an uprising while he planned a life and family with her hadn't helped ease her guilt. She had abandoned him, fearing he would turn her in if she even breathed a word to him of her life with the Resistance. And so the uprising commenced with him none the wiser that she was involved in it. Her guilt had been so strong that she had left to play her part without a word. That was the last she had heard of him. She had returned a few days after the final battle, readying herself for a different kind of battle – accusation, denouncement, anger. But the house had been empty. With each passing day, the likelihood that he would return seemed slimmer. Despite her surreptitious inquiries, nobody had heard of what had become of Symon Tuk, the finest tailor in Oranis. There were still a few among the dead who had yet to be identified. It was possible that he was among them. The dark part of her heart whispered that it would be easier for her if he had died in the uprising. There would be no messy confrontation, no need to see him staring at her with accusation. And of course, they were still technically joined under the law. That fact tethered her to him in a way that meant she could not simply walk away from him. Perhaps that was why she remained in the house where she had lied to him – some sense of obligation to be here and offer an explanation if he returned. Perhaps it was also stubbornness. She and Symon had moved into the Kade living district as a marker of their status. A part of her felt leaving would be an admission of guilt on her part, that she felt she had cause to run from the Kade.

She stood, easing the ache from her legs caused by kneeling in prayer for so long. The house was so very silent. It was the sort of silence that came when a space was inhabited by only one person. As she cleared away the arax root she had burned to give her even greater focus on her prayers, the noise seemed especially loud.

Hunger made itself known to her, grasping at her stomach insistently. It was enough to make her leave her workroom, even though it was the only place in the house where she felt truly comfortable. On an impulse, she detoured on her way the kitchen to Symon's workroom. In recent cycles he had worked more at home than in the tailor's store. She had hated his omnipresence and how it meant there was never a moment to herself in the house, but she had to admit the sound of rustling cloth or the quiet snip of his shears was something to which she had grown accustomed. Its absence was something she noticed acutely; the silence which pervaded the house in its wake had a tangible quality.

The workshop had been abandoned in a hurry. Symon was fastidious about putting everything away, yet there was a threaded needle pushed into a half-completed panel, a few scraps of cloth trailing along the surface of his worktable – a mess, according to Symon's exacting standards. A half-completed robe hung on the mannequin in the middle of the room. Like everything Symon made, the robe was exquisite. She lifted a hand to touch it but hesitated before her fingers met the cloth. She had never been allowed to touch an unfinished work, and even though he wasn't there to reprimand her, the years of his disapproval would not her permit her to do so now.

Cautious steps took Freya to the racks where Symon draped finished items so they wouldn't crease. Her breath hitched as she caught sight of the birthing robe he had made for the child he believed they would one day have. She picked it up carefully, the soft material sliding across her fingers. It had been a lovely gesture on his part. Her fingers traced the collar. Only Kade birthing robes had a collar.

The realisation slammed into her with abrupt force. Yet it did not stop her from putting the robe back down with gentle fingers. It reminded her too much of everything that Symon had wanted her to be and what she never could have been. A small part of her wanted to burn the robe and everything that it represented to expunge any reminder of the lies she had spun. The memory of her guilt would haunt her, regardless, but she could at least remove things which called forth those sentiments. But the work was too beautiful for her to bring herself to ruin it. She wasn't certain what she had been looking for in Symon's workshop, but she left more unsettled and threaded with guilt than ever.

She drifted through the empty house into the kitchen, trying to evade the guilt that pursued her. A meagre assortment of vegetables and grains were in the cupboards. Symon usually cooked, due initially to her underwhelming talent for the task and later because it was the comfortable routine of their life together. She hadn't bothered to replenish the kitchen's stocks, instead mostly purchasing meals from the street vendors who had returned only two days after the Resistance had taken control of the city. Given how early she left her home and how late she returned, she could easily rationalise the convenience of the vendors' meals. The act of cooking only for herself made her feel uncomfortably alone.

Tonight however, she had had no task that urgently needed completion, and no reason to be anywhere but in her own home. The prospect of attending one of the theatres did cross her mind – the classic plays were being staged in their original forms rather than the altered versions the Kade had required to suit the messages and way of life they espoused. It had been one of the reasons

Freya had avoided the theatres during the Kade's rule, claiming her long work hours. While the possibility of seeing the *Lament of Terisen* – her childhood favourite – had offered a vague temptation, she did not want to be out, reminded of her isolation by the people who would be going with their friends, families, or loved ones. So she took what ingredients she had and began to make herself dinner. The sound of her cooking clattered through the empty house.

She sat at the table in the living area as she ate. It wasn't the tastiest fare. Both her limited foodstuffs and limited culinary capabilities saw to that. But it was food and it gave her the sustenance that she required, so she ate it. She had nearly finished when she heard a commotion in the street outside. Under the Kade, the streets were almost always free of any kind of disturbance. Her senses humming, she put down her spoon and went to the door. She peered through the narrow windows on either side of the heavy wooden door but it was too dark outside for her to see anything clearly. The sound of raised voices persisted, so she opened the door a fraction and put her head through the gap. Reaching out to try to sense the lifesong of anybody nearby, she scanned the dark street, caution and anticipation swirling under her skin. She waited for the attack, readied herself to defend against whatever may be out there. The sound of raucous laughter had her readying that extra part of herself to find the source of the noise and clamp down on the lifesong of the perpetrator if they proved a threat.

Rather than the malignant aggressor she envisaged, two people stumbled into the range of her perception. In a manner distinctive to the very intoxicated, they leaned on each other as they stumbled along the street, uproariously singing a tune that bore a poor resemblance to a children's nursery rhyme; their rendition was spectacularly off-key and several words were missing or substituted with far less child-friendly alternatives.

Smiling, Freya closed the door and returned to her dinner.

Despite never fully prohibiting the sale or consumption of liquor, the Kade had punished anyone who drank it to excess. The citizens of Oranis had thus indulged in any fermented drink infrequently and even then with caution. Evidently there were some delighting in the opportunity to freely consume as much as they wished without fear of recrimination.

This small display of freedom reminded Freya why she had joined the Resistance and supported its rebellion. Living in a society that so harshly restricted even the smallest matters, such as the style of clothes people wore or how much people could drink, had been slowly suffocating her and the entire city. Even with the current threat of random violence, Freya would have sworn that Oranis was more vibrant, more alive, than it had been for any of the time the Kade had ruled it.

FOUR

The chanting of the Ordained dominated the memorial. Freya tried to quell the way it rankled her by reasoning that this was to be expected. The Pious did not have a religious authority to conduct their memorial prayers – they had all been killed by the Kade six years earlier. Yet their absence felt like the final triumph of the Kade. Freya stood in the crowd of Pious who had mumbled the Pious prayers for the dead, guided only by memory. After the Pious prayers had finished, the Kade's Ordained stepped to the top of the administrative district's square – one of the oldest in the city – and began their own prayers. In comparison to the efforts of the Pious, the Kade sounded strong and certain.

Similar memorials were being held throughout the city for both Pious and Kade who had been killed in the uprising. There had been some debate about Kade and Pious holding separate ceremonies, but there were enough firm voices on the Council who had pointed out that maintaining division between the groups at this occasion would only foment yet more violence. Freya saw the logic, even though she was dismayed and uncomfortable at being alongside Kade for something that felt private. Especially when the effect of the lack of Goddess' Children was so obvious. She wondered what thoughts and feelings nestled in the hearts of the gathered people. Did the Kade citizens feel pity for the Pious who so were valiantly trying to revive their religion? Or did they simply think the Pious efforts were evidence of their inferiority? Equally, did a feeling of pride swell within the Pious at their irrepressible faith, or were they more inclined to anger that so much had been lost at the hands of the Kade with whom they shared this ceremony?

The awkward peace between the two religious groups was noticeable in the clear divide in how they stood across the square from one another. Yet to Freya's eyes, it seemed the product of uncertainty rather than animosity. The two groups had been largely segregated during the time of Kade rule. Although everybody had been decreed nominally equal under the Kade, a thousand tiny reminders had been put into place to ensure everybody knew who was Kade and who was Pious. A long-standing habit, Freya reflexively ran her hand over the green band sewn into her sleeve. Her decision to continue wearing it had surprised her. On the first night she returned home, she had taken all of her clothes and prepared to rip the green band from each item, but her fingers betrayed her will. The band had been an ever-present reminder of her identity for so long that it had become a part of her. It was an unabashed announcement of her Pious heritage. For too long, being Pious had been something shameful, and Freya wanted the world to know not only that she was Pious but proud to be so. So instead of tearing the green band from every item of clothing she owned, she had laid aside the clothes most clearly in the Kade style with their high collars and embroidered hems – or indeed those which had any traces of the Kade colours of scarlet, purple or blue – and continued to wear the rest.

Makkyd was the only member of the Pious Council on the raised platform at the front of the square. In this, the Council had been unanimous – if they stood on the stage, they risked giving the impression of being overly authoritarian, reminding the citizens of Oranis of their power by standing in front of a crowd gathered in memorial of those who they had killed to gain that power. So the Council was spread throughout the crowd, mostly inconspicuous. That meant somewhere within the throng of people, Ashtyn also stood. They hadn't spoken for days. True, there had been no occasion when they would have been in the same place at the same time, but Freya couldn't help but feel he was avoiding her since they had argued about the Chief Healer's death.

Her gaze drifted to Makkyd. Despite her stocky stature, her leader looked tall and imposing on the elevated platform. Makkyd certainly had the ability to make everybody do as she asked. When she had told Freya that if she deemed it necessary, the Chief Healer was to die, Freya hadn't stopped to question it. Even on reflection, she didn't think Makkyd's instruction had been entirely wrong. Makkyd had a way of phrasing things as though she had already thought of every possible option – which in truth, she probably had. The question was whether she selected the best course of action after such reflection. Freya thought so, but Ashtyn's reaction had sowed doubt within her. She missed Astrom profoundly in the moments when she grappled with such questions. Astrom had possessed a clear-sighted way of looking at the world that Freya found cut through many of the turbulent thoughts massed in her head.

The memorial ended with flame solemnly touched to the symbolic pyres. There was a crush as most went to leave the square, but some remained behind to stare into the flames, lost in their own thoughts.

Freya slowly moved against the tide of people to reach the front of the square. As she squeezed between people with murmured apologies, she saw the flicker of recognition across many faces. Most shied away to avoid brushing against her. She pretended to ignore it.

Makkyd was still standing in front of the pyres, the red of her hair a mirror to the flames. Freya came to stand beside her. The other woman didn't immediately acknowledge Freya's presence. The two women stood in silence, their eyes lost in the flames for several minutes as people flowed around them.

"What did you think?" Makkyd asked eventually.

"I think it's a shame that we don't have any of the Goddess' Children left." The crackle of the fire ate up the pause. "How are Grat's efforts progressing?"

"To be honest, better than I expected," she said, leaving Freya to wonder exactly what that was supposed to mean.

"It was a good service," Freya said in eventual reply to Makkyd's opening question, lifting her eyes from the mass of flames consuming the huge pyre to glance around the nearly empty square. Her gaze came to rest on the old trees that lined one side of it, seemingly unaware of the dramas that had played out on the city's streets over the past six years. The square, while co-opted by the Kade for their prayers, had initially been a place for gatherings, prayers and proclamations. Hopefully now it would return to being a place not simply for one group's worship. The Pious Council had not yet discussed what would be done with the other squares the Kade had created in the immediate aftermath of their ascension to power to ensure everybody worshipped at the group prayers at least once, although preferably twice, per day. The wounds of the loss of the buildings they had torn down – most of them Pious owned – to create the squares ran deep, but to respond in kind seemed petty.

"What about the healers? Is everything all right there?" Makkyd asked after silence had stretched between them.

"As good as can be. I've put people I trust in charge of the three Centres – Mish is overseeing the Merchant District's, although she's not a trained healer, so I'll have to find someone else soon. No significant problems have come to my attention, although the Centres are struggling to cope with the number of patients. I noticed it when I was running the Market District's

Centre, but it's gotten worse since the uprising. Do you know if we can rebuild the Main Healing Centre?"

The Main Healing Centre had been blown up by Zarech over a year earlier. It had been a magnificent building, housing many injured and sick who were tended by the best healers the city had to offer. Its destruction had not only placed pressure on the city's other Centres as they struggled to keep up with the increased demand, but it had been a heavy blow against the authority of the Kade. It showed they hadn't been able to keep the city safe, despite their restrictions and heavy edicts.

Makkyd sighed. For her, an emotive gesture. "Certainly I'd like to. At the moment though, it's not so much a question of will we as can we. Our first priority must be to repair any buildings damaged during the uprising. Oltrem has a team of masons working on repairs to the city practically day and night."

"Surely there wasn't that much damage?"

"More than you'd expect. Little things here and there." Makkyd returned her gaze to the fire.

"What about the market?" Freya asked. The square which held the city's great food market had been the other location blown up by the Followers of the Dark Gods. She had been there at the time. It was where she had met Ashtyn. Only many cycles later had she learned that his presence there hadn't been coincidence; he had been following her in an effort to recruit her to the Resistance.

"It's not our foremost priority. There are other things to be rebuilt and we need to be careful about what we prioritise. Everybody's watching what we're doing, and many are waiting for something to use against us," Makkyd said. Her rationale was understandable, if not a little disappointing. The market square had been, in Freya's opinion, one of the most beautiful parts of the city.

Her disappointment must have shown. "After the repairs to the city's buildings have been completed, then we can look at rebuilding both the market and the Healing Centre," Makkyd said in a tone that made clear she was no longer willing to discuss this particular subject.

Minutes passed and Freya contemplated leaving. She didn't have anywhere to go other than an empty house, so she lingered, watching the fire burn down.

Makkyd spoke again. "You've done good work, you know."

Freya looked at her in surprise. "What do you mean?"

"You've made difficult decisions, you're organising your people well. You aren't giving in to sentiment when others may. I just wish others were more like you."

Freya shifted, not certain how she should feel at Makkyd's praise. She had always assumed she did allow emotion to guide her. Emotion was what had led her to return to the Resistance – outrage and hurt at realising that the Kade would always sacrifice Pious lives to serve their own purpose. Emotion was what had pushed her to learn how to kill – desperation to protect the cause in which she believed.

Despite her uncertainty over whether or not she agreed with Makkyd, she bowed her head in recognition that she had been given a compliment by someone who wasn't in the habit of giving them. "Thank you," she said.

Freya remained until nothing remained of the pyre but embers. She had lingered so long in the hope that Ashtyn would also remain and find his way to her side. Was he avoiding her? She was still vexed with him over their disagreement a few days earlier, but she had missed his humour more than she was angry with him. Resigned to the fact that he probably needed a few more days of space, she bade Makkyd goodbye and left the square.

Her pace as she walked through the streets was an uncharacteristic amble; she did not want to go back to her lonely home. The only reason she had left the square was an unwillingness to remain there with the weight of the dead which seemed to fill the air as the skies darkened. She toyed with the idea of going to the Merchant District's Healing Centre – the Centre she had once run. She would certainly find work there, either at an administrative level or in doing simple healing work, but she decided against it. Mish would certainly find something for Freya to do, but she may not appreciate her unexpected presence, especially given how competent she was. The uppermost reason for her decision to bypass the place she had once overseen was that unusually, the prospect of healing did not pull her – perhaps because of the way the dead so clung to her thoughts. So she meandered through the streets of Oranis without any real purpose.

As she passed a hana house, her stomach reminded her it had been a considerable amount of time since she had last eaten. Her feet made the decision before her mind, taking her inside for one of the grain loaves from which the establishments took their name. She sat at a wooden table in the dimly lit space, ruminating on the day.

The hana and the light broth accompanying it were quickly placed in front of her. She tore into the meal, only realising how hungry she was for having foregone breakfast that morning as she took her fifth bite of the freshly baked loaf. The food was good and filling. Better yet, she didn't have to scrounge through the meagre scraps in her own home to make it. On a whim after finishing her meal, she ordered a glass of mulled akash, the liquor for which the Third Country was famous. She had barely spoken the name aloud in public in the six years of Kade rule, so terrified had she been of being associated with customs and practices frowned upon by the Kade.

"Here you go, Healer Kuch," the server murmured as he exchanged a full mug for the empty bowl on her table.

She looked at him in surprise, not expecting to be recognised in the dull lighting of the hana house. She glanced at the man's sleeve to see if he bore a tell-tale green band, but there was no sign of it on his wrist. Of course, that no longer meant anything. Although, even if the man was Pious, it was no guarantee of amity. There was a substantial minority of Pious who had no thanks for the uprising – those who had lost someone during the battle for the city, those who had profited under the Kade rule, or even those who simply didn't want the threat and fear of violence to hang over Oranis, even if it liberated them from persecution.

She sipped the drink, enjoying the sting of the liquor as it hit her tongue and slipped down her throat.

"Can I offer you a sweetcake, Healer Kuch?" Another server appeared at her side, proffering a plate of sweets. After a moment's hesitation, she took one, smiling at the girl.

"Were you at the memorial service this morning?" Freya asked as she nibbled on the sweetcake. Slathered in honey and fruit glaze, it was absolutely delicious.

"I was at the service in the square near my home," the girl answered. "You were at the administrative district's square?"

Freya nodded. "How did you find the service?" She waved her hand to indicate the girl should sit down but received a shake of the head in a polite 'no'.

"I need to keep working," she explained. "I thought that it was nice that we were able to pray with the Pious, though."

Freya was surprised. "You are Kade?"

The girl nodded.

Freya found herself uncertain of what to say. She wondered what the girl thought of her, of the uprising. She didn't seem to bear any animosity, but looks could be deceiving, as Freya well knew.

"Was there anything else I could get you, my lady?" the girl asked.

Realising that she had simply been sitting there, lost in her own thoughts while the girl waited patiently, she forced herself to shake her head and smile. "No, thank you."

With a slight nod, the girl departed, leaving Freya alone with her thoughts once again. She finished her drink and the sweet, and took out coins to pay. The server who had brought her the akash rushed up. "Please, Healer Kuch, I cannot accept any payment from you."

Freya's expression of bemusement spurred him to continue.

"For what you did for our people, a meal is a small price to pay." His eyes caught the dancing light of the gas flames and seemed to shine with reverence.

"I insist on paying. Please," she demurred, putting the coins on the table.

The authority she could not dispel from her tone left him compliant. He took the money with meek hands. "Thank you for everything," he said, all but bowing as she stood.

Unsure how to respond to this sort of fervour, she nodded awkwardly and edged out of the hana house.

The streets were nearly empty. Even though law in the city had been relaxed since the uprising, people still remained wary of being outside in the evening, especially with the continuing sectarian violence. Freya walked at a brisk pace, taking the most direct route home through a narrow backstreet. After the behaviour of the man in the hana house, she wanted to avoid catching the eye of anyone she may pass lest she be recognised. She had experienced enough recognition for one day. She kept her gaze down, looking at the smoothness of the streets – one of the many beautiful things about Oranis. A footfall intruded into the cocoon of her thoughts. If it were possible, the sound had a certain menace to it. She looked up to find her way blocked by three men and two women. She came to a halt, feeling the kick in her chest as her pulse increased.

"Are you sure it's wise to wear that green band so openly?" one of the women called out. Her words were amicable enough, but Freya could hear an undertone of menace.

"The uprising fought for the freedom to wear whatever we choose," Freya called back, no tremor in her voice. In the waning light she couldn't quite see the faces of the people who had spread out to fully occupy the width of the street.

"Did you fight in it?" the other woman called out.

"Why do you want to know?" A thrill of nerves ran through Freya. She stepped forward, determined to push past them if she had to.

"Call it a casual interest," the woman who had first spoken replied. There was definitely menace in her tone now.

Freya took another step forward. "Well, if that's all then, I'll be on my way." She didn't let the tremor she felt in her limbs into her voice.

One of the men strode forward. Seven steps brought him to her side. The suddenness of his movement surprised her and rendered her paralysed as he grabbed her arm. He pulled her closer in a rough movement that brought her temper to the surface, and stared into her face.

His indrawn breath told her he had recognised her. "Well, well, I'm not certain I believe what I'm seeing." His coarse drawl sent her skin crawling. It was a tone that promised violence – was excited by it.

"Take your hand off me," she snarled, anger coursing through her to burn away the nerves.

"Why, Healer Kuch, wouldn't have thought you would walk in the street with the rest of us." He tightened his grip on her arm, fingers digging in hard enough to become painful.

"Did you say Healer Kuch?" one of the women called, her voice flickering with primal excitement.

"I certainly did." A cruel smile made its way across his face.

"We'll have some fun here," someone else said. Another laughed, an ugly sound.

"Let me be." Freya made one last effort to avoid a confrontation, although she didn't really want to just walk away anymore. Her fury was cooling into something hard and sharp and deadly.

"Let you be?" One of the women mimicked. Her face was made ugly by the way the sneer twisted her features.

"Like you let us be?" the man holding her demanded. His fingernails broke her skin. "You and yours have ruined us. I s'pose you don't care but, now that you've got power." His breath was hot on her face.

"You think we only wanted power?" she demanded. "You think we ruined you? You and yours ruined *us*." She tried to wrench her arm from his grasp but he was too strong. The pain was bright pricks against her skin.

"Feisty. I like it." His grin was animalistic.

She gave in to her rage. The anger which crashed against her skin, demanding it be released, gave her an eerie clarity of mind. Easily, she reached out with her ability. The hum of lifesong flooded her mind. She clamped down on it. Satisfaction flowed through her like soothing, cool water as she watched the life leave his eyes. It seemed as though an eternity passed between that moment and when his body finally dropped, pulling her slightly off-kilter as his hand dragged down on her arm. As his body hit the ground, the thump silenced the excited noises of his companions, who were nearly upon her.

The remaining four people stared at her. Silence reigned for several moments. Freya's movement as she straightened her tunic broke their stunned trance.

"What did you do to him, Pious scum?" one of the women screamed.

Her mind still overtaken by a rage-fuelled clarity, Freya reached out with her senses, feeling the four vibrant lifesongs. She focused, closing her eyes to better concentrate on four people concurrently. It was anticlimactic really, when they all simply crumpled to the ground. Freya looked around, wondering if anybody had heard the altercation. She was on the edge of the Merchant District, halfway down a narrow street between two warehouses. Presumably, that was why her would-be assailants had chosen that spot to ambush any Pious. Her lip curled in disgust as she looked at the bodies. There was an ugliness to that kind of thirst for violence that she had always despised. It felt good to be able to do something about it.

She glanced around one more time, casting out with her ability to see if there were any other people nearby. She heard no lifesong other than her own. Freya smoothed down her clothes again and took a moment to heal the wounds on her arm caused by the man's nails. Then she stepped around the bodies and continued on her way home.

FIVE

The many voices filling the hall took on a droning sound. Freya sat behind the wooden table, facing the petitioners who had come to her during the course of the morning. Every member of the Pious Council sat at identical tables spread around the large hall, listening to the requests put to them. Under the Dual Accord government the hall had served as a place for petitioners to directly address their leaders. People of the Third Country would come to voice their discontent, to ask questions, or to make direct requests to those in power. The Kade, not known for their consultative approach to leadership, had used the hall for their own gatherings. Dinner parties for the most elite members of Kade society had been held in a space once open to every member of society. Returning it to its original purpose had been a powerful statement and one that was well received judging by the number of people who filled the space.

Freya glanced around the room as she waited for the next petitioner to sit down. Because of the building's age, it was constructed from the beautiful pink mezite stone that was now almost impossible to obtain – the Followers of the Dark Gods had made their home in the mountains where it was found and nobody was willing to risk encountering the violent anarchists for construction materials. As the light came in, it gave the room a reddish hue that Freya couldn't decide if she liked or not. Columns interspersed throughout the hall prevented a clear view of the entire room. If you moved around, the perspective changed completely, revealing things the columns had previously hidden, and hiding things previously visible. In truth, Freya found she didn't really like the hall. She couldn't tell if the sentiment was because of the design itself or whether what she saw was overlaid by her knowledge of fact that the building had been appropriated by the Kade to affirm their own power. She found the columns lent the hall a slightly sinister air with the way they seemed to warp the reality of the room with every step taken. She could easily imagine the Kade's most powerful people in this space, dressed in beautiful, delicate clothes made for them by Symon, eating the finest food, laughing at jokes shared between themselves, all to a backdrop of musicians playing for their delight in one of the alcoves.

As her next petitioner began speaking, her gaze wandered over to the queue of people waiting to speak with Bardan. As the new head of the merchant guild, he was inundated. One of the crucial lynchpins in the Kade's power had been its stranglehold on any goods that entered or left the city. Anything deemed essential had been automatically bought by the Kade – at a price set by the Kade – and stored in their warehouses. They then sold those stocks on to merchants and traders, taking a profit for themselves. Nonessential items were taxed, often heavily. The measures had restricted the supply of a great many things for a long time, earning the ire of Pious and Kade traders alike. The merchants had been among the first groups to support the Resistance because of this. Their support had meant the Resistance had slowly but surely siphoned off materials until they had their own stockpile of weapons and supplies. However, now those people wanted their own contracts, leaving Bardan with a significant headache. Freya thought she could even hear the sound of foreign languages. It wouldn't have surprised her. While the Third Country's neighbours paid little care to who led it – as indeed the Third Country did to them – their merchants had seen their profits diminish as the Kade heavily taxed traders who tried to take the expedient land route through the God-skissed Continent that cut directly through the Third Country.

With an effort, Freya focused on the person in front of her. She was a young apothecarist – one of the people who mixed medicines for healers.

"Sorry, could you please repeat what you just said?" Freya asked, realising that her own musings had meant she'd not heard anything of what was being said to her.

"Of course, Councilwoman Kuch. I want to be assigned to the Healing Centre in the Merchant District," the woman said.

"Why?" Freya asked.

The woman blinked in surprise at the bluntness of Freya's question. "Because it's closer to where I live."

"Does your skill merit you being able to request such a transfer?" Freya asked.

The woman bristled. "I'm good at my job."

"If you are as skilled as you claim, then you can simply ask one of your superiors to transfer you," Freya replied. "I see nothing particularly unreasonable in where the Kade assigned you."

"But I wasn't allowed to be transferred because I was Pious," the woman spluttered.

Freya sighed imperceptibly. This was the eighth such matter she had been forced to deal with that day. People were seeking promotion or placement to more favourable locations, claiming they had been unfairly denied those positions because they were Pious. Undoubtedly, many people in the city had been barred from certain positions or promotions on the basis of their birth, but what had mostly occurred under the Kade was the denial of access to tutelage. The consequent lack of training and skill was why they were not awarded subsequent advancement. It was an effective system the Kade leadership had put into place, for while it undeniably barred Pious from gaining positions of advantage in the long term, anybody who was actually qualified and skilled at what they did was rewarded – Freya was living proof of that. The woman in front of Freya was older than her; she'd definitely had the benefit of unbiased training. If she hadn't been promoted, it was because she didn't deserve to be.

"I can promise, every person of any seniority in the healer's practice has been given instructions to promote or reassign those who deserve it. Now if you'll excuse me." Before the petitioner could say anything else, Freya stood and walked away.

Irritation pulled her features into a frown as she strode to the far wall, murmuring a word of thanks to the line of Guardians who parted to allow her through. She had initially thought the plan to place a bench laden with food and drink for the Councillors if they required a break preposterous. She had once worked for nearly two full days with only a few scattered minutes of rest – she had been sure she wouldn't need any reprieve in simply talking with people. Now she was grateful she had not voiced the protest. She hardly thought the presence of the Guardians necessary, though. A simple rope would have sufficed. But reports of intermittent violence had continued, and with them standing as though to keep a space clear for the Councillors, it didn't look as though they were there to act in case someone decided to try something. The complexities and subtleties required for leadership were beginning to unfurl themselves in Freya's comprehension and she found them increasingly stifling.

Ashtyn was standing at the table, sipping from a mug. He inclined his head in greeting. "How goes it?" he asked. He seemed amiable enough, although it had been over two fivedays since their argument – and the last time that they had seen each other.

"I hate people." She was still too irritated with her last petitioner to keep the acerbic response from slipping along her tongue.

He laughed. A part of her wondered if he harboured anger toward her after their last encounter, but he seemed to be reasonably without ire. She supposed she had never really known him to hold a grudge. "What happened?" He stayed by her side as she poured a drink for herself

"I just spoke with the eighth person who thought they could better their position for no good reason other than the fact that they're Pious." Her poorly contained outrage shone through each word. "You'd think we're no better than the Kade, seeking to take the best positions away from those who actually deserve it."

"Don't worry, I've been dealing with similar things, too," Ashtyn said.

"I think that makes it worse," she replied as she selected a piece of fruit and bit into it.

"Did you really think that the Pious are that much more morally upstanding than the Kade?" he asked.

She shrugged, her mouthful precluding a more articulate response.

Bardan reached past her and said, "If you think we are in any way superior to the Kade, then you court the danger of placing us above them. Then you invite thinking that it's justifiable to deny them access to training or apprenticeships in the way they did us."

Freya started at her friend's appearance. The hubbub of the hall had masked his approach.

"Are you sure you have the time to take a break?" Ashtyn's face broke into a smile that had mischief twined through it.

Their friend groaned. "Please don't remind me. I regret everything. I regret joining the Resistance, I regret the uprising. Please bring back the Kade so that I don't have to do this—" he paused to gesture to the room full of waiting petitioners "—ever again."

Ashtyn's eyes caught Freya's and she had to bite her lip to keep from laughing. "Did you see how short Freya's line is?" he asked Bardan.

The portly man glowered at them both. "I hate you," he told Freya vehemently.

"At least you have people with reasonable petitions," Freya said. "If one more person tells me that as a healer, they've been unfairly treated because they are Pious, I will flip my table over and walk out."

Bardan chortled. "Goddess, I'd love to see that. Well, I'd best get back to it. If I'm really efficient, maybe I'll be through this by the time the next cycle begins." He picked up a mug and ambled away.

"He's so cheerful," Freya marvelled.

"He's wonderful," Ashtyn said.

"How can he be so reasonable about everyone?"

"I think he just doesn't believe any one person is inherently better than another," Ashtyn replied. His face turned thoughtful. "Whereas I just think people are equally willing to exploit any opportunity."

"That's dark," she commented.

"Just look at what you've been dealing with today." He shrugged in emphasis. "People who see a chance to get advancement will more often than not take it. I mean, look at how the Kade behaved during their own rule. Most of them were more than willing to clamber over Pious to get luxury and comfort. Does it really surprise you that Pious would try to do the same thing?"

She looked down at her drink. He had a point, but the truth left her with a sense of lingering sadness.

"You're still so innocent, Freya." His voice was tender and it made her keenly aware of her heartbeat, the awkwardness of her hands, the distance between them. She wasn't sure if she was glad they were in public or resentful of it.

He cleared his throat and the moment dissolved. "Anyway, I'm sure someone has some thrilling matter for me to resolve." He put down his mug and took a piece of fruit. "I'll talk to you later," he promised before he left.

Freya stood for a few more moments, mulling over what Ashtyn and Bardan had said. She wondered what Astrom would have said. Loss gripped her as she felt anew the absence of her friend. With slow movements, she returned to her table.

Before she beckoned the next person forward, she wrote herself a note to investigate whether it was possible to offer some form of remedial training to the Pious who had been denied it.

It was a battle to believe the best in people and to not scratch out the note to herself. She wasn't sure whether her conversation with Ashtyn lingered in her mind, or mere coincidence had placed an abundance of self-serving individuals in her path, but the next five petitioners only just fell shy of blatantly requesting positions or assignations they clearly did not deserve for no reason other than the fact that they were Pious. Had she really fought, and killed, for these people? This was hardly the better world she'd envisaged. This small-minded pettiness seemed little better than the people who would have killed Freya on the night of the memorial. She'd thought little of them in the days since, trying to muster some sense other than satisfaction that they could no longer do harm to other people. This narrow focus on self-interest and their own sentiments was hardly going to forge anything better than what had come before. Freya kept her temper in check – barely – as she politely declined each request.

A reprieve came in the form of a timid merchant with a request to alter a delivery contract. She supplied food to the Healing Centre in the Weavers' District but had been forced to accept minimal remuneration for her work despite being asked for specific deliveries that cost more than she was paid.

"I'm surprised that the conditions of this were so severe," Freya commented as she idly rubbed her finger along the rough texture of the linen paper once she had read the contract.

The woman looked down at her lap as she replied. "The Kade governance did not even look after their own people. A great many of us supported your efforts because of that."

Freya supposed she shouldn't have been surprised. After all, she had been told a similar thing by Olek, another Kade merchant. She had been taken aback by the vulgar, hairy man and the fact that he was a member of the Resistance. Then again, he had been taken aback to learn *she* was a member of the Resistance; she had been infamous in Oranis for her perfect Kade citizenship.

Freya resolved the merchant's request, doubling what the woman was paid and affixing her signature to a revision of the contract between the woman and the Healing Centre.

Three more people after she heard the merchant's case, and she was ready to scream. She was trying not to glare at the latest petitioner asking to be promoted when Wren tapped her on the shoulder. She turned, ready to embrace him if he brought her respite from the banal grubbiness of people.

"Freya, someone has brought me a petition regarding a contract that includes you," he murmured.

Taken aback, she told the petitioner she would not grant his request and followed Wren, trying to think of what contract she may be party to.

"I think this matter may be better resolved away from prying eyes," he explained as he led her to one of the small rooms that had been used as chambers for members of the Accord to prepare themselves and later, for Kade revellers to slip away either to refresh themselves or for some illicit purpose.

Her confusion growing, Freya went through the door and found herself face to face with Symon

SIX

Shock rendered her speechless. Symon looked exactly the same. The same sand-coloured hair, immaculately styled. The same perfect clothes. The same unreadable expression. It was this familiarity as much as his unexpected presence that threw her.

"Hello, Freya." His calm demeanour, also so characteristic of him, gave nothing away.

She forced herself to reply. "Symon." His name came out a strangled gasp, half question, half greeting. It was wholly inadequate, and only through the strongest effort of will did she keep her arms by her sides rather than folding them across her abdomen as she desperately wanted.

Wren cleared his throat, an awkward sound in the otherwise silent room. "Freya, Symon has petitioned me to dissolve the relationship between the two of you. You were joined in a Kade ceremony, so it does technically count. I thought you two should perhaps talk about this." His discomfort was written into every word.

Freya's eyes widened in surprise. She turned to Wren and said quietly, "Perhaps you should give us a moment alone."

He nodded, looking far too grateful to leave the discomfort that remained in the room, and departed.

Symon broke the silence which descended heavily upon the room with the click of the closing door. "So."

Freya cringed. The single, quiet word was infused with so much rage.

"Symon—" she began, but he cut her off.

"I believe it's Councilwoman Kuch now?"

"I still prefer Healer Kuch." It was a pitiful response, really.

"Still trying to hide who you really are, Freya?" There was just enough scorn in his question to make her even more desperate to flee.

"I—" she began, but he cut her off again.

"How long?"

"How long?"

"How long were you a part of this? From the very beginning, when we joined?" Symon spoke quietly – he never raised his voice when he was angry. But the quality of dangerous softness to his voice made the hair on the back of her neck prickle, made her wish he would simply raise his voice in anger.

Her reply was in a whisper, but that whisper seemed to ricochet around the room, as though his fury had made the air cleaner, clearer, and allowed all sound to carry. It was amazing that the frantic beating of her heart, or the 'shick' of her sweat-slick hands as her fingers rubbed against each other wasn't audible. "I only joined the Resistance about a year before the uprising."

"A year," he repeated to himself.

"Symon, I'm sorry," she said, a helpless need to try to atone for her deceit driving her.

"What for, Freya?" His lip curled with contempt.

"For lying to you." She looked down at her feet. As much as she had hated her life with him, she had always felt uncomfortable deceiving Symon. He had loved her, wanted a life with her, and she had known that as she planned to destroy his whole world.

"Lying to me?" A note of incredulity crept into his voice. "You didn't lie to me, Freya. You made a fool of me." His voice rose now. The controlled fury was giving way to something else. Suddenly she wasn't so certain that she would rather he yelled.

"It wasn't about you," Freya protested. She wanted to return his anger with her own, but she couldn't. She had not done right by the man standing before her.

"We built a life together. We succeeded in the Kade's world together. You told me that was what you wanted, and then I find out you in fact wanted this. Councilwoman Kuch!" His final two words were delivered in an accusatory roar that filled the small chamber, seeming to bring the walls rushing in. He stared at her, his hands knotted fists by his side, a vein standing out in his neck. She couldn't tear her eyes from him, although she desperately wanted to look away from him and the anger and hurt in his eyes. Of all things, she noticed that he no longer wore the green band that denoted him as Pious.

"Do you really think that I did what I did for my own benefit? For power?" Anger came now, as much defence as outrage.

His eyes seemed to swallow light. "You certainly sought elevation by the Kade."

"I sought to *survive* in the Kade's world," Freya threw back. "Not everyone was so lucky. What I fought for was a world in which the lives of the Pious weren't valued below the lives of the Kade. Not my own advancement."

"So how do you explain your position?" Red was creeping up Symon's neck, blotching the skin on his face.

"I don't have to explain myself to you," Freya roared at him, sick of his insinuations. "You were so desperate to be favoured by the Kade that you would have been an informant."

Her own accusation rendered him momentarily speechless; his dark eyes burned with fury and shock.

"You really think I would have been an informant?" Suddenly he was no longer on the other side of the room but instead a hand's breadth from her. His face was contorted into a terrible rictus of anger. She wondered if he would strike her. She wondered if she would unleash the destructive side of her ability in defence if he did. Already, she had half reached out for his lifesong, instinct and rage readying her to fight. "Well?" he shouted.

But anger was unsustainable. Guilt weighed on her too heavily to allow her rage to truly take flight.

"I don't know what you were, Symon," she replied quietly.

"Gods above, Freya," he snarled. It was not lost on her that he did not invoke the Goddess but rather the multiple gods of the Kade.

He continued to stare at her for a moment longer, then his eyes snapped away from her. "I don't know what I thought I'd find here. I shouldn't have come."

He brushed past her, the only contact they shared. It was fleeting, but where his hand touched her arm felt as though she'd been seared. She didn't have time to react before he'd gone, the crash of the door filling the space left by his absence as it reverberated around the room.

Freya stood for a moment, a tremor engulfing her limbs. The explosion of Symon's rage had taken her by surprise. She had expected quiet fury, even disdain, but this outburst was unlike anything she could have anticipated.

Almost aimlessly, she moved further into the room, her legs quivering so badly with each small step that she feared she may tumble to the ground. She reached the window almost by accident. Both she and Symon had ignored the chairs, benches, and cushions strewn about the room, but now that the confrontation was over, she wanted to sink down and just sit for a little while.

Freya chose a seat right next to the window and folded herself into it, drawing her legs up so that her feet rested on the edge. Her arms circled her legs to hug her knees as if to push back the feeling that she was about to fall apart. She looked out the window to the garden. As with many of Oranis's larger buildings, this one was designed like a hollow square, leaving a garden in the middle. Someone was sweeping the path that ran through the middle of the garden with sure, regular strokes. It was oddly serene to watch and it gave her space to re-live the exchange with Symon. The uncharacteristic demonstration of the depth of the emotions he felt made what she had done to him all the more confronting. She had known her actions would hurt him, but to inspire such uncontrollable anger...the depths to Symon's heart were, it seemed, even more unfathomable than she had ever expected.

The worst thing was knowing that even if she never saw Symon again, he was somewhere in Oranis, harbouring a very justifiable hatred for her. Yes, him being dead would have been far easier for her – although that she thought as much was an unkind reflection on the qualities of her heart. There was an indissolvable bond between them, forged by their years together and her deceit, and it meant she could not move on with her life without remembering who she had been, and the life and lies she had lived. Her life with him and the hurt she had knowingly caused him could not be denied.

A rap on the door lifted her from the reverie into which she had fallen.

She looked up as Wren came in. "Is everything all right, Freya?"

"Well, in a more general sense, yes." She smiled with no humour.

"I saw him leave. When you didn't come out I was worried something may have happened."

Her smile grew knife-thin. "It wouldn't be inaccurate to say something happened, but he didn't try to hurt me."

"He certainly didn't seem particularly pleased as he left","" Wren noted.

"Well, if he didn't seem pleased with you, he definitely wasn't pleased with me at all." Freya was too resigned to even try to hide the bitterness from her voice.

"Is there anything I can do?"

She smiled, this time with genuine emotion. She didn't know Wren well, but she liked his warmth and courtesy. "If you could dissolve that contract, I'd appreciate it. I think that's what he wants, and what would be best for everybody."

"I can make it disappear entirely if you'd prefer," he offered.

Freya considered it for a moment. Certainly, it was tempting to think that the reminder of her connection to the man to whom she had done wrong may be undiscoverable. But that connection did exist and she couldn't simply pretend otherwise. "Thank you, Wren. That's most kind of you, but I'm afraid I'll have to say no."

"Just thought I'd offer. I'll find the record of your joining and get it sent to you to sign to affirm its dissolution."

Gratitude filled her for his efficiency and the absence of any prying questions. "Thank you, Wren. Without you, the city would crumble."

"Oh, I know," he said, his face completely serious. "Are you sure you're all right?" he added, a worried frown crossing his face.

"Yes, I think I'd just like to stay here for a little while," she told him.

He nodded and withdrew, closing the door behind him.

Freya returned her gaze to the garden. A breeze stirred the trees, blowing a few leaves down onto the path. Freya wondered if Symon was angry with her because he was hurt or because she had helped to ruin his perfect life. It would certainly be easier for her were it simply the latter, but she remembered the awkward sincerity with which he had declared to her that he loved her. She had known that he would be hurt, but he had never believed in the Goddess like she had, had never been forced to see the physical toll of the Kade on the Pious – his own people even if he wanted to pretend otherwise – like she had. She had to face the truth: Symon was not a bad person. It would have been far easier to lie to herself and claim that his actions, currying favour with the Kade while his people suffered, were that of the highest depravity. But Symon was just a person, like any of the petitioners who had come before her today. He was no monster. His actions during the Kade's rule were all too human.

The sound of the door opening made her turn, fearing Symon had returned to give yet more expression to his anger. But it was Lyssa. Freya tensed, wondering with what new hostility she would be confronted.

"Wren said you were in here."

Freya stared at her with mute suspicion.

"Is everything all right? There's quite a queue gathering for you," Lyssa asked, her customary sneer absent.

"I'm just gathering my thoughts. The person to whom I am – was – joined came in," Freya replied, begrudgingly giving the extra information in the hope that it would be enough to compel Lyssa to leave.

Contrary to her hope, Lyssa closed the door behind her. "I assume it wasn't a pleasant exchange?"

"You could say that." To her horror, her voice came out choked and tears invaded the clarity of her vision. That Lyssa was witnessing this made it so much worse. To try to conceal her unshed tears, she turned as if to look out the window, but she knew Lyssa had seen.

"I'm sorry." Genuine emotion laced the other woman's voice. Her steps as she came to sit in the chair opposite Freya had a hesitant quality.

Freya brushed away the tears escaping her eyes. "You did nothing wrong. Symon was understandably unhappy to learn I had deceived him. I suppose I just wasn't expecting him to be quite that...angry."

"Symon Tuk, the tailor, yes?"

Freya wondered just how many people knew various details of her personal life. She supposed she shouldn't be too surprised. She and Symon had garnered a certain infamy for their success. She nodded.

"Did you love him?"

There was frank curiosity in Lyssa's question that had Freya turning to look at her. Devoid of its usual contemptuous expression, the artist's face was even more beautiful than normal. Her green eyes were startlingly wide, framed by long lashes. Her mouth when not pursed in disapproval was full and sensuous.

Even though the question was quite personal, Freya found she wanted to talk, and Lyssa seemed willing to listen. "Do you have a man, Lyssa?"

Lyssa gave a small laugh and shook her head.

"Being joined – even though it's not the same as being bound – means sharing a life. Symon and I had a rhythm, a routine. Even though I didn't want what he wanted, he was still always there. It's odd to not have him in my home. I miss his presence in ways I never thought I would.

"But Symon always wanted me to be a particular person. He always wanted me to be a perfect Kade woman, successful in my work, and mother to his children. I don't know that he ever stopped to really consider that wasn't what I might have wanted. You know even Ashtyn wanted me to be..." She stopped, unwilling to talk about Ashtyn with anyone, especially not Lyssa, given her assumptions about Lyssa's interest in him. "Has anyone done that to you, Lyssa? Tried to make you something you weren't?"

To her surprise, the other woman laughed. It was a bitter sound. "You have no idea." An awkward pause settled between them.

Freya studied Lyssa with undisguised curiosity. Faint lines traced between her nose and the corners of her mouth – the telltale signs of anger and sorrow. But her skin otherwise bore no signs that would betray her as a nasty person. "Why do you dislike me so much?" Freya asked.

Lyssa raised an eyebrow. "I don't dislike you, Freya. But you have no idea how lucky you are. You seem to think your life is lived in the shadow of the Goddess' contempt."

Freya was incredulous. Her parents and younger sister had been killed by Kade officials in front of her. "Lucky?"

"Yes. You exist in comfort and success. When you came to the Resistance, everyone was so excited. You were placed in one of the highest positions immediately. Everybody loved you. You have someone who adores you, even after everything that's happened. And you're beautiful. You had so many choices before you joined the Resistance, unlike most of us."

"But everybody had a choice," Freya protested. She had come to that realisation a long time ago.

"Some more than others. You definitely had, and have, more." There was a bitterness in Lyssa's voice that made Freya uncomfortable. The artist's comment about "someone who adores you" anchored her reply.

"I'm not with Ashtyn. But there are other people out there," she said awkwardly.

Again, Lyssa threw back her head and laughed. "He really isn't the sort of person who catches my eye."

"I don't understand."

Lyssa's response was to lean forward and press her lips against Freya's. Her mouth was warm and soft, her breath sweet.

Freya's was paralysed by shock as Lyssa leaned back into her own seat. "You're definitely more interesting to me than Ashtyn." An amused smile played about the beautiful woman's face.

Suddenly, much of Lyssa's bitterness made sense. The Kade had treated those who bore love for their own gender with the same brutal efficiency as anybody caught as an adulterer, generally forcing them to undergo some form of public humiliation, if not execution. The Kade's priority was always on families that would produce more Kade citizens. Any act that may jeopardise that was immediately stopped. However, even the Pious did not treat people like Lyssa well. While she wouldn't be put to death, subtle – and overt – discrimination would permeate how everyone treated her.

Despite herself unease trickled through her at what Lyssa had just shared with her. "Do you..."

Lyssa smiled. There was a sorrowful twist to her mouth. "No, Freya, I'm not interested in you."

Freya blushed, ashamed of her own prejudice. "Lyssa, I'm sorry." She looked down, unable to meet her eye.

"It's hardly the worst thing that's happened to me." Lyssa shrugged.

"Do you... are you with someone?" Freya was curious, despite her discomfort. She had never met someone who she knew to be like Lyssa.

The other woman shook her head. "No. Although for a while, there was. But it was too dangerous."

"Well, at least now you can..." Freya's ability to construct coherent sentences had deserted her. She thought she must look like a rude fool. Her fingers began to pluck at the green band on her sleeve.

"She died."

"Oh." Freya blinked. She had no idea what she should say to that. She warred against her conditioned response to feel repelled by Lyssa. The prickliness with which the artist interacted with everyone now made sense, and Freya felt a stab of compassion for her. Nevertheless, her discomfort was born from a prejudice too deeply rooted for her to dismiss entirely.

Lyssa clearly noticed. "I would ask that you not tell anyone." She paused, the knowing look in her eyes making Freya want to squirm with embarrassment. "I'm sure you understand why. Even though I'd no longer be put to death, being treated with general revulsion isn't exactly something I'd relish."

Freya blushed a deeper shade of red. "Does anyone else know?"

"Makkyd and Bardan. A few others." Lyssa looked away. "Astrom knew."

Freya wondered if something beyond friendship had existed between Astrom and Lyssa – Astrom had never spoken to Freya of any male companion or demonstrated the slightest interest in a man. Indeed, Astrom and Lyssa had been close – she was the only person Freya had ever seen receive a genuine smile from the beautiful artist. She felt a roil of discomfort at the idea that

Astrom, too, may have preferred women, then asked herself why that should matter. Astrom had been her friend, had never given up on her as a fighter, had encouraged her to be kind to herself when she had no inclination to be so.

"Why did you tell me?" Freya couldn't fathom why Lyssa, who had disliked her from the first instant they met, had shared this dangerous and deeply personal secret with her.

Lyssa shrugged. "Because you act as though your life is the most difficult, most tortured of them all. And you have no idea how unbelievably lucky you are. I just wanted to give you a glimpse of that."

"And here I was thinking that you may not hate me after all," Freya said dryly.

"I don't hate you, Freya."

"You don't like me, though."

She received no response other than the slightest smirk.

Freya sighed. As much as she hated to admit it, Lyssa had given her a great deal to contemplate. She didn't like the prospect that she may not be the person she had thought herself to be. She liked even less the fact that it was Lyssa who had drawn her attention to that, petty though it was to feel that way.

"I should get back to those petitioners," she said. She didn't know what else she could say. The point that Lyssa had very successfully made, combined with Freya's discomfort at being around someone like Lyssa, instilled a fluttering desperation within Freya to be distracted from the knowledge of her shortcomings and prejudices.

The artist remained seated, going so far as to turn her gaze to the window and the garden below as Freya stood up and self-consciously smoothed down her robe.

"I am sorry, you know," Freya said hesitantly.

Lyssa turned back to regard Freya with a lazy motion. "Oh?"

"I'm sorry if I act in that way. I'm sorry that things are this difficult for you even now. It's not fair," she said.

"Hardly your doing." Lyssa's voice was cool, her eyes once more guarded.

"Even so."

There was a pause. Lyssa sighed, turning her head back to look out the window. "Go back to your work, Councilwoman Kuch."

As Freya re-entered the hall, the great hum of people washed back over her. She closed the door behind her, catching one final glimpse of Lyssa sitting with her back to the door, staring out the window in an echo of the pose Freya had been in when Lyssa had entered. Freya had never expected the truth behind Lyssa's dislike of her to be so unsettling, or indeed to provoke so many other uncomfortable truths. Freya wanted to believe that she was creating a world that was better for everybody – a world, yes, run by the Pious, but nevertheless allowing equal opportunity for all. Lyssa's confession had pointed out that this wasn't the case. People would always be stigmatised and ostracised, no matter who governed them.

She wondered what sort of world she was creating and how her biases were shaping it. Freya thought about the people she had killed in the street. The awful reality was that she hadn't paid their deaths any heed. She had put more energy into wondering by whom their bodies would be found than whether their deaths had been a reasonable response on her part.

As she re-took her seat, one thing was for certain: Lyssa had definitely given Freya more to think about than Symon.

SEVEN

Telling herself that she was simply moving for convenience, Freya took up residence within one of the living quarters of the administrative buildings. The truth from which she could not escape, its insidious incursions making their way into her mind late at night, was that she couldn't stand to be in the house she had shared with Symon. All she could see it as was a shrine to their perfect devotion to the Kade. Although he hadn't returned, she couldn't help but worry that he may walk in the door at any moment, and she didn't want to face another confrontation.

The apartments she occupied had been inhabited by a Kade official before the uprising. From what she could discern from the furniture and personal belongings that remained, this official had been one of the uppermost Kade members. None of the items gave much clue as to their position, though the first three days had been a curious game of picking through the detritus of another person's life and trying to piece it together.

In what constituted her first real use of her position as someone of power, Freya ordered that the quarters be redecorated, desperate to replace the rugs and curtains in the Kade colours of blue, purple and red. She also replaced the furniture; the idea of inheriting the furnishings of a Kade official unsettled her, especially as the overstated yet impersonal opulence of the quarters left her feeling somewhat queasy. She did not like the idea that someone with a position of power would live in such overt luxury. Something about it embodied the whole attitude of the old Kade regime. Yet she was keenly aware of the hypocrisy of her actions. Virtually all her possessions were new. The only things of her own that came with her to her new dwelling were the laastram – a series of metal bands placed on the arms used both in prayer and fighting – that Ashtyn had made for her, and her medical notes. Those notes were a legacy of the work to which she had devoted so much of herself, and the time she had spent trying to understand how the body was constructed and how it could be fixed when broken. To leave them behind because of her healing ability was more than she could bear, so now they sprawled across several shelves.

The clean, sparse lines she had created in the rooms she occupied as overseer of the Healing Centre in the Merchant District were recreated in her own space, minimising unnecessary furniture or objects. She kept the small kitchen stocked with snacks and drinks, but primarily began to ask for meals to be brought to her rooms. Given she was in them so early and stayed so late, it was easier to buy food when she was out. The efficiency of her lifestyle gave her the opportunity to do more work, which she gladly did. She gave her thoughts over to questions of healing, of creating new training programs to boost the skills of already qualified healers, of deciding to authorise use of the quarantine wings to ensure there was enough room for every patient. And in those moments in which the concerns raised by her exchanges with Ashtyn, her conversation with Lyssa, and her confrontation with Symon pushed their way through her mind, she looked to finish outfitting her new living arrangement. It successfully kept her from the more philosophical musings of who she was and the sort of society she was creating. And while her immediate worries about Symon had not vanished in the two fivedays since their altercation, they had subsided to the back of her mind in deference to more immediate matters.

Freya was one of few of the Pious Council members to use their allocated rooms in the administrative district. Those like Ashtyn who were leaders of guilds lived in their own workshops in their respective districts. Because the city's healers were spread out across Oranis, Freya worked from the administrative district. It was especially convenient given where she lived now – she was only a few streets from her primary workplace.

She was on her way there when Bardan came barrelling out of his rooms, nearly crashing into Freya and disrupting the thread of her musing over how to reduce the cost of voluntary medical procedures.

"Freya my love!" Bardan exclaimed, a grin breaking across his face.

A smile of her own appeared at seeing the big man. His obvious delight at seeing her was like a salve to a wound she hadn't even realised was there. "It's been so long since we talked properly," she complained.

"You haven't called on me. Now that we've taken power it seems you were just using me." His eyes twinkled with warm humour.

She laughed. "Just like a man to say that I used him!" she teased back. "How are your woman and daughter?"

His broad face softened into a gentle smile. "More and more beautiful every day. They keep a cynical man optimistic."

Freya couldn't help but be touched by his obvious love for his family.

"And what about you, Freya? From what I've heard, you've become a bit of a recluse."

"You know me, Bardan. I'm busy with work." She waved the sheaf of reports she was carrying to evidence her point.

A frown appeared on his face. "Freya, you do realise there is more to life than simply working."

"Of course." Freya gave a small laugh. "But there's so much for me to do. I'm running all over the city trying to ensure that the healers are behaving themselves. Surely you have a similar problem with the merchants?"

"It does occupy a lot of my time," he admitted. "But I do other things as well."

"You have a family!"

Bardan sighed. "I'm not attacking you, Freya. I'm just worried about you as my friend."

She gave him an impulsive hug around the stack of tablets and papers she carried. "You're a good man, Bardan."

"There's a celebration of dance on tonight in one of the squares. You should come," he replied. She raised her eyebrows. She hadn't realised that an event was being held today, let alone one of the old Pious celebrations. That she'd not heard of it spoke to how absorbed she'd become in the narrow world of her work.

"Now I really must be off," Bardan said as he hurried along the corridor. He turned midway down to yell back at her. "The dance celebration. I'm coming to take you."

Shaking her head at her friend's lack of regard as to whether or not she had actually agreed to go, Freya went to her rooms and began to work.

It was getting late in the afternoon when Freya put down one of the many reports she had been reading and rubbed her eyes. Random but persistent violence was still putting many people into the Healing Centres. The people she had assigned to lead the city's three Centres were trustworthy, both in their skill and loyalty. Nevertheless, she requested daily reports detailing even the smallest incidents. Freya knew all too well how important it was to firmly control the city's places of medicine. The Resistance had targeted the Healing Centre in the Merchant District as one of the key points to hold in the uprising precisely because whoever held it looked legitimate. She meticulously read through the reports each day, cross-referencing comments on individuals with the notes that she had on every single person who worked in the Centres. The healers were nothing if not thorough in recording the strengths and weaknesses of their own. What had caused Freya to pause, and what dug further into the lines of concern on her brow, was the mention of Flen. Her one-time assistant had once told her that he believed Pious were inferior to Kade. He had not been in the Centre when she had taken control of it for the Resistance and she had not seen him since. But it appeared that he had unobtrusively remained within the Healing Centre in the Merchant District. His quiet dogma had unnerved her then and she wondered now how it had been affected by the uprising. Was he waiting for his opportunity to sabotage the Pious? She looked back over the report. Nothing damning had been written about him, simply that he had been working in one of the wards. She hesitated, wondering whether she should send specific instructions to watch or even demote him. Undeniably, she wanted to. He could be a threat. But she wasn't sure how she could send orders for him to be placed under specific surveillance or moved without good reason. Her people had to feel that she trusted them. Sighing, she took out the ledger that she kept of people to watch and noted down Flen's name. That was the only action she could justify, although a voice that sounded distinctly like Makkyd whispered in her head that she was being foolish and should order him apprehended and interrogated. She remembered something Astrom had said to her once, that the challenge was not taking control of the city but of living in peace with the Kade afterward. She wished she could seek her friend's counsel on Flen. She wished she could just spend time with her friend and forget about these questions which seemed to be responsible for the new lines she saw on her face each time she saw her reflection. But Astrom was dead, and each time she remembered it was like a fresh blow to her heart. Wishing was not going to do anything than keep work from being finished. So with a sigh, Freya left Flen's name on the leger and moved on to the next task.

A few hours later, a knock at her door lifted her from the world of reports. By this time, she was reading through the Centres' inventories and comparing them against the lists of items being brought from merchants. Never one for numbers, she was glad for the interruption. "Yes," she called.

Bardan came in, needing only one large stride to cross her small office and tower over her. He put his hands on the desk and leaned down.

She put down the list of figures that was tangling up her thoughts and looked up at him, amused. "Can I help you?"

"That depends." He couldn't quite keep the mischief from his eyes.

"On?"

"Whether you'll come willingly."

She crossed her arms and pursed her lips. "And what if I won't?"

"Then anybody lucky enough to encounter us will witness Councilwoman Kuch being carried – perhaps kicking and yelling – by me to the celebration of dance," he informed her. "I personally hope you don't come quietly."

Freya considered it. Most people wouldn't follow through with such a threat, but Freya honestly believed that it wasn't beyond Bardan to do such a thing, and she had little desire for the whispers about her to include stories of her being carried along the streets of Oranis over Bardan's shoulder. "I'll come quietly."

"Excellent!" He clapped his hands, the sound nearly deafening in the small space.

Bardan led the way with cheerful steps to one of the squares in the Merchant District. Light was fading quickly – the days were still warm but noticeably becoming shorter. He told her about the concert he had attended the previous fiveday, speaking enthusiastically about the composition that had debuted. She was chuckling at his mock offence to the doubt she'd expressed at his musical knowledge when they rounded a corner and a scene straight from her memory greeted her. People hurried to prepare the bonfire on a bed of elevated slabs in the centre of the square. The smell of cooking food wafted tantalisingly in the air, coming from several street vendors who had set up their carts. Musicians were preparing, too. The only unfamiliar element of the scene was that the square was one the Kade had created following their takeover. Yet there was something nice about a square created in a takeover of prejudice being used in a celebration of dance, especially as that celebration hadn't been held in over six long years. Memory pricked at her – recollections she had not allowed herself to entertain, now refusing to be denied. The celebrations came at the quarter mark of every year, marking when the weather turned – not that Oranis felt much of that difference. People danced with family, loved ones, friends, possible lovers, in a way that was meant to remind participants how they were braided together, forming the community, the fabric of their society. She remembered her excitement as a child when her parents had taken her and her sister to the dances. They were allowed to eat food from the vendors and dance until their sore feet demanded they cease. Even as she had gotten older, she had never lost that childish enthusiasm for the dances, although the enthusiasm became increasingly less about the excitement of an adventure with her family and more about the excitement of seeing her friends or the possibility of dancing with a handsome stranger. It was a curious feeling to realise she could barely remember the faces of the friends with whom she had giggled and gossiped, rushing up to them as soon as they saw each other across the square. They had become mere acquaintances after the Kade take-over, divided by fear, especially once Freya's family had been killed for her sister's unwillingness to praise the Kade gods. And then, as Freya had suc-ceeded in the Kade's world when very few Pious had, she had been quietly shunned for her treachery.

"Have you eaten today?" Bardan's question interrupted her memories.

Without waiting for her to respond, he walked up to one of the vendors and asked for two skewers. He handed the steaming food to Freya who obedi-ently took it. One simply did not argue with Bardan over such matters, she was learning quickly. For a moment she simply inhaled the scent. The chunks of meat and vegetables, threaded onto a thin wooden skewer and cooked over the brazier in the vendor's cart, were a Pious dish that had been banned by the Kade. Gingerly, she bit into the hot meat, the childhood wariness of burning her mouth making her temporarily forget that she could easily heal such an injury. It was delicious. Exactly the same as she remembered it. Warm memory engulfed her, riding the flavour. She could clearly picture Rohana's face, re-splendent with delight as she tore the meat from a skewer. Her father's deep laughter was a phantom boom in her ears, long since passed from the night when his daughters took his challenge to eat a seventh skewer each.

"Daddy!" The cry of a young girl cut through the hubbub and the bitter-sweet nostalgia of Freya's recollection. Bardan turned, a grin nearly breaking his face in two as he bent down to scoop up the girl of ten or so years who came running across the square. A woman followed at a more reserved pace, pre-sumably the girl's mother. Bardan lifted the girl high in the air, eliciting a squeal of delight. Before he put her down, he cradled her close for a moment – almost too fleeting to see, but Freya, who was watching closely, saw it and the years of pain and worry etched into the gesture. The woman came into the arm he held open for her and for a moment, they formed a perfect trio, existing out of time and place with the rest of the world. Freya's loneliness enveloped her as her heart snatched at fragments of memory in which she had been held like that. Then, Bardan released the two most important people in his world and turned back to Freya.

"Freya, this is Chara," he said. The hard 'k' sound on the first syllable of his daughter's name sounded almost Kade to Freya's ear, but she wondered if she was simply imagining it. After all, Chara had been born before the Kade had taken power.

"I'm very pleased to meet you, Chara," Freya said, bending down to take the girl's hand and press her thumb into it in the Pious greeting. Solemnly, the girl offered Freya the Kade salute, bringing her clenched fist to her heart and drawing it down her abdomen. Uneasy, Freya looked to Bardan to see his reaction, but either he didn't notice or seemed accepting of it. After all, even if Chara had been born before the takeover, she was too young to remember anything of the Pious way of life. She had been all but raised a Kade.

"And this is Myrah."

"It's a delight," Freya smiled warmly, greeting Myrah in the Pious way. The woman returned the greeting.

Freya studied her. Myrah was small and delicate – a counterpoint to Bardan's largeness. It seemed their daughter took after her mother more than her father in looks, a fact for which she would one day be very grateful to the Goddess.

"Have you ever been to a celebration of dance before?" Freya asked Chara, who was staring at the transformation of the square around her with wide eyes.

The girl shook her head.

"You're in for quite a treat."

"Mama said there's going to be a fire!" Bardan's daughter looked up at her with the kind of unrestrained excitement unique to children.

"Have you taught her any of the songs?" Freya asked Bardan.

Myrah answered. "I've been trying, although she's so excited about the celebration that she's found it difficult to concentrate on anything else."

"I'm sure she'll pick it up. Anyway, there will be plenty of other opportunities for her." The realisation that there would be more to come seemed almost surreal.

"I can think of a different type of opportunity for Chara," Bardan said, his eyes twinkling.

At the mention of her name, Chara's head snapped up eagerly.

"The bonfire needs to be lit and it was suggested I should do it. But I think you'd be much better at it," he told his daughter.

Her mouth dropped open into an astonished perfect circle.

"But not until dark has fallen, so you'll have to be on your best behaviour until then," Bardan added, causing his daughter's face to transform into a picture of determined sincerity.

Freya smiled, buoyed by the child's enthusiasm. It seemed an eternity ago that she had ever been that young or that excited. The sadness that accompanied her memories was swept away in the face of Chara's enthusiasm, and the fact that Freya had been a part of bringing this experience back so children like Chara could delight in it once again.

Myrah was scolding Bardan. "How could you eat without us!" For a small woman she could clearly intimidate Bardan, who looked as though he was trying to diminish his bulk as much as possible.

"I was hungry," he said.

"You could have waited a few minutes!"

"But Freya needed some food."

"Don't use her as an excuse." Myrah lightly slapped his arm. Freya looked on in amusement. This was the man who had threatened to carry her over his shoulder to the celebration.

"Come on, we'll all get another one," Bardan said. Evidently the argument was over, Bardan having been sufficiently chastised.

Freya joined them as they walked back to the vendor who passed them four skewers. The bickering between Bardan and Myrah was so commonplace, so everyday. It shocked her to see the figure of authority, the man who she had known only through the prism of the Resistance, as someone with a family. He was suddenly so normal. It was reminiscent of her own parents, and it made her smile even if it made her miss them in ways she hadn't for a long time.

She ate her second skewer more slowly than the first, truly tasting the smoky flavour of the meat. Bardan appeared at her side, a mug of ale proffered in his hand. She took it with a word of thanks, thinking how surreal it was to be eating food that had been banned, and drinking ale, which had been restricted, only a few cycles ago. A part of her wanted to look over her shoulder to make sure nobody was watching her with judgment, but she held that impulse in check. Instead she looked around the square, which had filled over the past few minutes. People were gathered in small groups, eating and drinking. The excitement was palpable and outshone the memories from Freya's childhood.

Bardan looked up at the sky which had all but been drained of the day's light. "It's time," he said, handing his drink to Myrah. He wiped greasy fingers on his sleeve, earning him a glare. He laughed softly and pulled Myrah into a brief embrace, sealed with a swift kiss. She rolled her eyes at him but the smile tugging at her lips, despite her best efforts, gave away that she wasn't truly angry with him.

Bardan took his daughter's hand and walked with her to the middle of the square. Someone handed him a torch that he held high, catching the attention of every person. A hush fell as he knelt and offered the torch to Chara, who placed both of her small hands around it. Carefully, he let go and whispered something in her ear before he stood and took a step back. Very slowly, Chara lowered the torch to the intricate arrangement of wood. For a moment, nothing happened, then a solitary flame licked its way lazily around the base of the bonfire. A cheer went through the square and the musicians began to play a tune Freya remembered from her childhood. It started slow and sweet but would gradually speed up so that anyone dancing to it would struggle to keep time.

Freya's skin tingled at the magnitude of what had just happened. She couldn't help but give a little laugh as she wiped at tears she hadn't realised had fallen.

"You know, I don't think I actually realised that we'd won until just this moment," Freya told Bardan as he returned, his daughter's hand clutched firmly in his own.

He grinned and gestured to the square which was rapidly filling with people. "It's something, isn't it?"

"This is a celebration of dance," Myrah said, arms folded. "I expect dancing."

"Is that a request?" Bardan asked. Before she could reply, he gathered her in his arms. "Would you watch Chara?" he asked Freya.

She nodded and watched as the two ran into the clear space around the bonfire with the enthusiasm of children and began to dance. For a large man,

Bardan was surprisingly agile. As they whirled around the bonfire, people began to join in to cheers and whoops. Freya stood with Chara, who watched wide-eyed.

"Chara!" The call came from a girl of about Chara's age who ran up to them. The two began talking excitedly about the bonfire, Chara lighting it, and the various novelties the evening offered. Following at a more leisurely pace was a young man who looked to be slightly younger than Freya.

"Hello, Chara!" he said.

"Alyk!" She threw herself at him and wrapped her arms around his waist. He laughed good-naturedly and returned her hug with obvious affection.

It was easy to understand the girl's infatuation with him; something about him spoke of an easy charm. Coupled with his good looks, Freya suspected he was quite the heartbreaker.

"Alyk." He extended a hand to Freya once Chara had let him go.

"Freya." She accepted his hand, pressing her thumb into his palm. He returned the gesture. She saw the moment he recognised her in the way his eyes widened.

"Not Freyanna Kuch?" he asked, the shadow of a grin on his face.

"Guilty," she admitted, not certain to what exactly she was confessing.

The grin spread. "Would you believe I expected you to be taller?"

"I'll try to stand up straighter," she replied, amused.

"Definitely just as beautiful as I imagined, though."

She smiled at his brazen flirtation. "I aim to please."

"Would you dance with me?"

"I promised Bardan I'd watch Chara," she told him, the regret in her voice genuine.

"Well, I'll wait with you until they get back," he declared.

"That may be quite a wait," she said, casting a glance at Bardan and Myrah, who were still dancing with unflagging enthusiasm.

"I want to dance!" Chara announced.

"Well, that's settled, then. We'll all go together," Alyk said.

The two girls cheered and ran toward the growing crowd of dancers. Freya and Alyk followed at a more relaxed pace, still introducing themselves through an exchange of questions. She was surprised when he took her hand, but not unpleasantly so.

The sky was lightening by the time Freya headed back to her living quarters. Over the course of the evening, she had lost track of Bardan, Myrah, and Chara. Alyk had stuck fast to Freya's side, dancing with her at every opportunity. He was easy company and danced well. In his arms Freya was able to forget the violence that still prowled the city streets, and lose herself in the simple joy that thrived in the square. As the night drew to a close, he intimated that they should leave together. She was tempted but gently turned him down. Discomfort at the prospect of that kind of intimacy was distant enough that it did not intrude upon her good mood, but it kept her from taking him to her bed.

Alone, she walked back to her living quarters. The dancers had become more boisterous as the ale had flowed. It seemed they, too had discarded their worries and fears, for at least a time. While some parts of the Pious culture may have been lost, it was clear that others would survive. Filled with a pleasant fatigue and slightly intoxicated, she looked around the peaceful streets. Whatever pain and guilt the uprising may have etched onto her, it had definitely been worth it.

EIGHT

Freya didn't see Bardan until a couple of days later at the next Council meeting. He greeted her with his customary joviality. "Lost you at the celebration."

"Could say the same of you," she said, giving him a kiss on the cheek.

"Last I saw you were dancing with Alyk," he noted, a teasing edge in his voice.

"Yes, he was quite fun to dance with. How do you know him anyway?" she asked in an effort to steer him away from an awkward line of interrogation.

"He's the youngest uncle of Chara's best friend. You only danced?" He grinned wickedly, undeterred.

"Honestly," she scoffed at him, putting her nose in the air.

Unfortunately for her, Bardan didn't respond to such tactics. He instead leaned forward, his manner conspiratorial. "He seemed quite interested in you."

"He was." She shrugged.

He chortled.

"Don't be ridiculous," she snapped, amused despite herself.

"Well, I hope you at least had fun."

She softened. "I did. Thank you for dragging me out to it."

"That's what friends are for." He patted her shoulder affectionately.

"Where was my invite?" Ashtyn's tone was light.

Freya started, realising he had probably heard the bulk of her exchange with Bardan. She scrutinised his expression to see if there was any indication that he had heard about Alyk's interest in her, but his face was unusually unreadable.

"Decided we'd have more fun without you," Bardan responded with absolute solemnity.

"Well, if it was a festival of dance I would have put you all to shame," Ashtyn replied with equal gravitas.

"Exactly why I didn't invite you." Bardan nodded and sat down.

Freya looked at the notes in front of her as Ashtyn sat beside her.

"So who's Alyk?" Ashtyn asked in a low voice.

She felt a flush creeping up her neck. "A friend of Bardan's. I danced with him at the celebration."

"I gathered that," Ashtyn said.

Freya couldn't tell if there was jealousy or upset in his voice. If there was, it was too subtle for her to detect.

"That's all that happened," she said primly. "Not that it's any of your business."

Out of the corner of her eye she saw Ashtyn's eyebrows rise. "I suppose it isn't."

She opened her mouth to apologise but was prevented from saying anything as Makkyd entered the room, Lyssa immediately behind her. Before she could help herself, Freya's discomfort drove her gaze away from the artist. She forced herself to look back at Lyssa and found the woman staring at her, unblinking. A sardonic smile twisted her beautiful mouth. Freya fought to contain the blush seeking to claim her cheeks. She was still uncomfortable with the artist's sexuality – fighting the ingrained attitude imbued since childhood due to casual comments overheard from adults who used words such as "unnatural" or "deviant". The quiet pain in Lyssa's voice and the way she protected herself with an air of disdain and indifference was very human – hardly unnatural.

"How are we all?" Makkyd asked, her manner perfunctory. The question tore Freya's thoughts from Lyssa, and with no small amount of gratitude, she shifted her focus to Makkyd. The redheaded woman didn't wait for replies. "Let's get straight to it. I have reports of the attacks over the last fiveday." As she reeled off a list of attacks and skirmishes that had occurred throughout the city, the faces of the other people around the table grew more and more grave.

"Aren't the Guardians doing anything?" Oltrem asked.

Makkyd gave him a long, cold look. In addition to being the leader of the Pious Council, she was in charge of the Guardians. Her tactical genius had given the Resistance the upper hand in the uprising, especially against the deadly group of elite Guardians who surrounded the Kade leadership. Her knowledge of how to create and prevent trouble in the city's streets was unmatched. It made her the perfect and, really, only person to ensure those who kept the peace were well trained and disciplined; especially as so many of them had resigned – either voluntarily or otherwise – due to loyalty to the Kade.

"I'm doing the best that I can. Guardians can't be everywhere at once, and I'm not going to risk sending out Pious Guardians who aren't fully trained, or Kade Guardians who may take it upon themselves to enter into a fight in favour of one side over the other.

"It's not all bad news, though." Makkyd paused. "We've discovered the source of this discord."

Lyssa spoke, her voice filled with dry humour. "Well, don't keep us waiting."

Makkyd shot her a look of warning. "It appears that differences between Kade and Pious aren't the actual driving force behind the violence. The motivation, yes, but both sides are being stirred to action."

"Makkyd, I'm sorry, but you've lost me," Bardan said, his voice blunt.

"Agents of the Dark Gods' Followers are in the city, inciting the violence."

This time the silence had a tenor somewhere between surprise and shock.

Ashtyn was the first to speak. "How do we know this?"

"It seems one of them couldn't hold his liquor very well. Started talking about all manner of interesting things within earshot of one of our people."

"Have we questioned him further?" Ashtyn asked.

Makkyd pressed her lips together with so much force they turned white. "Unfortunately when Guardians went to apprehend him, he ended his own life."

Ashtyn cursed.

"Mm, I agree," Makkyd said. "Still, it means that we at least know what the problem is."

"Do we really?" Bardan spoke. His voice was clipped with something akin to anger. "We don't know how many of them are in the city, what they're doing, how they're getting in, if they have any abilities that could be dangerous, and if so what those abilities are. The list is endless."

"Well it's better than nothing," she said, her own anger clear in the bite her voice held.

"Do we at least know what their goal is?" Freya asked.

"The Dark Gods' Followers only want anarchy, as we know. Our newly dead friend was apparently saying how easy it is to sow chaos in Oranis because it is currently so disordered."

"Bringing order to the city is something we can fix, surely." There was a hint of desperation in Ashtyn's voice that echoed the feeling which had found purchase in the pit of Freya's stomach. Not for the first time, she wished Astrom were still alive. She missed the way the other woman seemed to balance Makkyd, offered comfort as well as a way forward, saw things that others missed.

"True, but we need to get these...vermin out," Lyssa said. "They'll pick at any bit of malcontent, inciting anger and violence. We can't fight against that. We know all too well how effective that can be."

"How can we do that when we don't know who they are?" Wren asked, raising his arm in a gesture of impatience.

Makkyd rapped her fist on the table. All eyes turned to her. "We may not know who they are, but they do."

"You've lost me again." Bardan was obviously unimpressed with the way Makkyd was making a show of revealing whatever she'd just thought up.

"One thing Freya learned from Zarech was just how much the Dark Gods' Followers plan everything," Makkyd explained in a voice that made clear she was ignoring Bardan's irritation. "Surely they've planned this, too. Perhaps for even longer than we realise. They must know who their people are."

"Yes, but they're in the mountain caves, killing anything or anyone who approaches them," Lyssa pointed out. "It's not as though we can go up and ask them nicely for the names of all the people they've planted in Oranis to cause dissent."

"Actually, you're only half-right," Freya said. Suddenly every face was pointed in her direction. She swallowed before continuing. "Zarech was originally Pious. He left Oranis after the takeover and was accepted by the Followers..." She trailed off, uncomfortable with how much she was revealing of her relationship with Zarech. Her fingers found the green band on her sleeve and traced along it. Even though the Council knew she had been assigned by the Kade to tend to him, nobody knew the closeness that had developed between them despite her best efforts to remain detached. She had told herself at the time that she shouldn't care for this man who was the architect of so much pain and chaos. Looking back now, having caused her own fair share of pain and chaos, she understood that he wasn't simply man or murderer. Her thoughts flew to the people whose lives she had exterminated with her ability. She still could find no real remorse for her actions. It was that lack of guilt more than anything that troubled her. Surely, she should have been revolted at the mere prospect of such an act. Perhaps Zarech had felt a similar way.

Makkyd was looking at her in a way Freya knew uncomfortably well. It was a similar expression to the one she had worn when she asked Freya to deal with the problem of the Chief Healer.

"If we could get someone to go to them, they may be able to bring us back enough information to deal with the threat that those Followers in the city pose," Makkyd said.

"There are a lot of 'ifs' in that," Ashtyn objected. "What if whoever we send isn't accepted? What if they aren't trusted enough to be told anything of worth? What if there isn't anything to be brought back? What if they can't get out?"

"It remains an option that we must consider if nothing else works," Makkyd replied, finally moving her eyes from Freya.

The silence that greeted her words indicated that she had made a point nobody could adequately refute. "Good. Can we move on?" Makkyd swung her gaze around the room to lock eyes with everybody. "Bardan, you indicated to me there was a matter you wished to discuss?"

"Yes." He sat a little straighter as the attention of the room went to him. "I've spoken with our merchants and they're generally very happy with us – we're now buying a small amount of the materials that enter the city for our own stockpiles, rather than everything. It gives the merchants greater freedom, which has made them considerably happier with us and our rule. Interestingly enough, it also frees up some of our own funds. I always thought that the Kade did it for profit, but it would seem not..." He shook his head to clear it from the tangent that he had started upon. "Anyway. The foreign merchants are somewhat less pleased. It seems that their own governments have heard of our...tiff over leadership and are worried that our instability may spread. Queen Latana of the Second Country was particularly worried – the Fourth Country less so, given their own penchant for violence. Those concerns won't necessarily stop their merchants from coming, but it may mean we need to be wary of our neighbours. Given we are the major land route for most goods, there is some concern that further instability may make those routes unsafe. That may be enough to justify some kind of action on their part."

"Is there anything we can do?" Oltrem asked.

Bardan shrugged. "Our cloths are the finest in any of the Four Countries, so there's definitely demand for that. I think at the moment, just try to stay on good terms with foreign merchants. And watch the borders of the Fourth Country. If there's going to be any kind of move, it'll be from some powerful family there looking to expand their land when they think we can't retaliate."

"How do you suggest we keep the merchants happy?" Lyssa asked with her customary coolness.

"Give them favourable conditions, be nice."

Lyssa shrugged, an elegant gesture that indicated her satisfaction with his response.

The meeting dragged on. Reports were given, various matters were exchanged and debated. Freya sat, listening with half an ear. Only when Grat started speaking about his efforts with the Ordained was her interest raised enough for her to pay proper attention.

"One or two are particularly resistant to the idea of giving any help to the Pious, but the others are quite helpful, directing me to texts that could be useful, even sharing their own knowledge. I think they may be very hopeful that we'll let them out," he said.

"And will we?" Ashtyn asked.

Grat shrugged, looking at Makkyd.

"For now, no," she said firmly.

"And what about those who haven't been co-operative at all?" Freya asked. She wondered if she would be sent by Makkyd to covertly remove the problem they presented. Discomfort curled within her at the prospect.

Makkyd stared at her for a moment as though trying to discern what Freya meant by the question. "I suppose we'll have to wait and see."

Nobody seemed to make anything significant of the exchange and the meeting moved on. Freya's attention wandered once again and, eventually, the meeting concluded.

"Freya?" Wren came up to her quietly as everybody gathered their belongings and the meeting notes provided by Lyssa.

She turned and gave him a tired smile. "What can I do for you, Wren?"

He kept his voice low. "Oh, nothing. Just...that paper is in your rooms when you're ready. Sorry it took so long, I wanted to find it myself."

Warmth didn't quite make it to her smile as the memory of her exchange with Symon encircled her, but she tried, appreciative of Wren's discretion. "You are a true treasure."

She gathered her things and was almost at the door when Makkyd called her back. Ashtyn, who had silently lingered next to her, following her exchange with Wren without comment or look, gave her a look of curiosity. She shrugged in reply.

She assumed she would be required to deal with the problematic Kade prisoners sooner than she had anticipated, although she'd hardly share the suspicion with him.

"If you're going to wait for her, Ashtyn, would you mind doing it outside?" Although Makkyd phrased it as a question, the order was clear.

"I'll be right outside, Freya," he said, shooting Makkyd an unimpressed look as he closed the door behind him.

"He certainly does adore you," Makkyd commented.

"So glad you held me back just to talk about my love life," Freya responded. She wondered when her relationship with Makkyd had evolved to the point where they spoke so frankly with each other. There was a time when she had been far too terrified of Makkyd to even hint at being blunt or sarcastic. Somewhere along the line that terror had disappeared.

"Hardly." Makkyd stretched her stocky frame and groaned as some ache made itself known. "Goddess, I hate meetings."

"Well we certainly had a lot of them before the uprising," Freya pointed out.

"Yes, but at least there was something vaguely fun about the sneaking around. Now it's all comfortable chairs and stairs. I hate stairs."

Amused by the change in Makkyd's demeanour from leader to person, as though she had shrugged off some cloak of authority, Freya leaned forward and rested her forearms on the back of one of the chairs. "So what would you like?"

"It's about the Dark Gods' Followers," Makkyd said.

Freya raised her eyebrows. This was not where she had expected the conversation would go. She would be far more comfortable with the prospect of playing assassin than whatever was about to be asked of her, she was sure. "What about them?"

"If we were to send someone there, it would be difficult. And it would have to be the right person."

"You like the idea that much?" Freya was surprised Makkyd was considering something that had only been raised at that very meeting.

"Like I said, only with the right person," Makkyd reiterated.

"Why do I feel as though I'm the right person?" Freya asked.

"Because you knew Zarech."

"That hardly makes me the right person."

"It gives you more insight into the Followers than anybody else."

"Makkyd, I healed him. It's not as though he gave me the keys to the front gate!"

"You and I both know you did more than simply heal him," Makkyd said.

Freya averted her gaze from Makkyd's. She sometimes forgot how incisive the other woman could be. It was one of the things that had made her such a good leader for the Resistance.

"I thought so," Makkyd said after Freya didn't reply. "Besides, you're also the person who can take care of themselves in a fight."

"I can barely defend myself!" Freya thought back to her time being forced to learn hand-to-hand combat. She had practised excessively but would be outclassed by any opponent with any serious skill.

"You can heal yourself and inflict damage on your opponents without lifting a single finger. That makes you deadly," Makkyd said.

"I haven't exactly tested that against an entire group of people," Freya objected. But her mind flickered to the four people she had killed in concert. That had been easy.

"If you really don't want to go, I won't force you." Makkyd held up her hands. "Just think about it."

Freya sighed. "Fine. Is that all?"

At Makkyd's nod, she left the room.

Ashtyn was leaning against the corridor wall.

"So are you going to do it?" he asked. She couldn't tell from his tone what he was thinking.

"Haven't you been told that eavesdropping is rude?" she demanded, amused, as he fell into step with her.

"It's an old habit, picked up from my days of subterfuge." She could hear the grin in his voice.

She shook her head at his irreverence.

"So are you going to do it?" he repeated.

"I'll think about it."

"Are you hungry?" he asked as they emerged into the street and the bustle of the city washed over them.

She shook her head. "I have work to do."

"I'll walk you to your building. You can get something to eat on the way."

Knowing that it was easier to simply go along with him than to argue, she offered her acquiescence in the form of silence. Besides, she enjoyed his presence. The excuse to remain within it wasn't something she was going to discard on the principle that she didn't need to be told when to eat like some child.

"I don't think you should do it," he said several minutes later as they were waiting for a street vendor to prepare wraps for them.

"Why?"

"A lot of risk for no certain outcome." He accepted his wrap and bit into it.

"You could have said that about the uprising," she replied as she took her own food.

"More certainty than with this." He took another bite, letting out a noise of appreciation as he chewed.

She evaded his point. "Well nothing's decided yet."

He did not pursue the matter and she was grateful for that. Instead, as they finished their food and walked, they discussed trivial matters. He had gone to see some of the plays that were now once again allowed to be shown, and he relayed with excellent description and gesture a costume disaster that exposed the backside of one of the actors in the otherwise very serious *Liamen's Tears*. Freya was wiping tears of her own – from mirth, not grief – when they arrived at her building.

"Thanks for walking with me. You always manage to make me laugh."

His own smile was lush green and bottomless sunshine. "Thank the fine actors, not me."

She chuckled again and he joined in, evidently finding her laughter infectious. Then he suddenly sobered and the green of his eyes became darker as concern filled them.

"Freya, please don't agree to go to the Followers if she actually asks you," Ashtyn said. Surprising her, he leaned forward and kissed her cheek. Then before she could say anything, he walked away. She stared after him, putting her hand to her cheek, as though she could capture the feeling of his lips and imprint it to her skin.

NINE

True to his word, when Freya entered her rooms, she discovered Wren had left the document that affirmed the fact that she and Symon were joined on her desk. In handwriting she could only assume was Wren's, a comment noted that the union would be dissolved upon receipt of both parties' signatures.

In the same script, an address was written on a wax tablet set on top of the document. Freya picked it up, idly flicking it as she mulled over the situation with Symon. With a sigh, she moved both paper and tablet to the side along with the thoughts they raised, and looked instead at the reports that had come in. They required her attention more than her personal affairs.

The afternoon bled into night and Freya read through the reports and wrote her own to keep herself busy. She didn't want to go to Symon, she didn't want to have to face him again. Yet when she returned to her rooms the next morning, the tablet and contract stared at her with accusation.

The address led to an unassuming dwelling in the weavers' district. The choice to live in neither the Kade nor Pious districts did not go unnoticed. As she walked along the streets – she had avoided taking a cart, private or public, to delay the moment as long as possible – she noticed that the area had a foreign quality. Most notably, it came from the stones of the buildings, which had a redder tinge than in other parts of the city. Some poorly remembered history lesson tickled the back of her mind with the suggestion that the district had been constructed when the cloths of the Third Country were gaining prominence around four hundred years ago. She seemed to recall that there had been a decree to ensure the quality could be standardised and overseen. A rather unsavoury district of brothels – legal and illegal – which were surrounded by criminals who made such establishments a fixed point in their lives had been torn down to make way for the weavers' district, much to the irritation of the previous occupants. They had refused to move and had been dragged out of the buildings by Guardians in a fearsome display of violence. The cheap wooden structures had been set on fire, although some residents had been hiding inside in a futile last stand. The Ire of Oranis, as the resultant fire was known, had set a precedent for all the buildings in Oranis to be constructed from stone... although that could have also been when a Councillor's husband set fire to his wife's bed after discovering her infidelity, not expecting the blaze to spread to the rest of the house and the buildings beyond. History had never been Freya's focus. It was strange to realise she had never noticed the subtle difference in architecture and stone before. She supposed she had rarely ventured into the district. Odd, considering it was where Symon had worked for as long as she had known him. Then again, she didn't think he'd ever set foot inside a Healing Centre.

Telling herself to stop procrastinating by trying to remember history, she made her way to the nondescript house and knocked on the door. For several moments there was no answer, then the door opened and Symon stood before her, pinning her with those dark eyes. "What do you want?"

She could hardly blame him for his rudeness.

She held up the paper. "I brought this."

He peered at it. "What is it?"

"What you asked for," she answered. "May I come in?"

"Do I have a choice? Surely if I refuse, a troop of Guardians will arrest me," he sneered. He stood aside for her.

Hurt, she edged past him.

His home was smaller than the one they had shared but larger than the apartments she currently occupied. He led her along a short corridor lined with closed doors. Freya wondered if he had a workshop behind one of those doors and if it looked like the one in their former house. She supposed she would never know.

"Upstairs," was all he said, leading her to the open living area at the top of a flight of stairs.

"Have you taken anything from our old..." She trailed off, unwilling to finish the sentence. Whatever she said would be a weapon for him to use for another nasty comment.

"Only my work things." His voice was brusque as he turned to face her. "I saw you did the same."

It wasn't quite an accusation but it left her with the same sting of shame an accusation would have.

"I'll organise for the things left to be sold, if you like. I think the administrators have already divided our funds. I can just instruct them to give you the money from the sale," she offered.

"Are you trying to buy me?"

"No, I just thought..." The silence into which she trailed off was awkward.

"Sell it, keep it, give it away. I don't really care what you do."

"I don't want you to be in any position of need," she said.

"Does it look like I am?" He gestured to the room. The furnishings were elegant, clean lines that displayed their fine workmanship. The rugs were plush and the space itself spoke of care and cleanliness. Freya also noticed that the colours of the furnishings were all neutral: soft, pale yellows, burnt oranges, and rich browns. There was no hint of green, or red, purple, and blue.

"Symon, I'm sorry." The need to apologise, to try to seek some kind of absolution, even if it was in vain, propelled the words from her mouth.

"Sorry for what, Freya?" he asked, leaning close to her.

"For lying to you."

"You broke my heart!" His yell took her by surprise. "I loved you. I wanted a family with you. Did you ever love me?" For an instant, his mask slipped and she saw all the pain and hurt that her actions had inflicted on him written across his face. It was a particular brutality to be so confronted with the consequences of her decisions so starkly. She wanted to cry, to rage, to accuse him of his own wrongdoing, but he had never done wrong by her, and the words to try to push away that truth would not come. This truth, at least, could not be denied. She opened her mouth but found voice robbed of her.

He spoke before she found words. "Never mind. What do I need to do to be free of you?"

The disgust in his voice was like a slap to the face.

"Just sign," she whispered, passing him the paper.

He strode over to a desk and, taking an ink pen, signed his name in quick strokes. "You haven't signed."

"Oh." She crossed the space between them and unthinkingly took the pen from his long fingers. She scrawled her signature next to his.

It was only when she put the pen down that she realised how close she was to him. The proximity was disconcerting. Symon and she had never been a physically intimate couple. This near, she could smell the scent that was unequivocally Symon, feel the heat radiating from his body, even feel his breath as he exhaled unevenly through his mouth. The moment, the closeness, paralysed her, and it seemed him, too.

"What didn't I do?" he asked softly, the words lanced with pain.

She shook her head as self-loathing coursed through her, leaving in its wake a greasy sense of shame. She felt contaminated, wrong. A monster.

He reached across the space between them and put a hand on her arm. "I wanted everything to be perfect..." His voice trailed off but his hand remained where it was.

Still, she said nothing, almost mesmerised by this insight into him when he had been so closed for so long.

He didn't look at her but instead at her arm where his hand rested. "I really loved you, you know."

She could see tears in his eyes. Shock at such naked emotion only served to make her feel worse.

"I'm so sorry. I promise you'll never see me again. I won't do you any more harm or cause any more hurt to you." Her words felt so breathtakingly inadequate.

The silence grew thick with anger and grief. Then he nodded and released his grip. He remained still, his eyes cast away from her as she picked up the document that now officially declared they were no longer joined, walked across the room and descended the stairs. As she reached the front door, she thought she heard a sob.

She stood outside, waiting for her own tears to fall. Yet while they pricked at her eyes, and her throat was dry and painful, true sobs deserted her, denying her even this release. The sunlight, so bright and warm, felt an insult given the misery that tugged at her from within. She felt pulled into a thousand different ways, a thousand parts of her dissolving, being changed, until the person remaining was unrecognisable.

The prospect of work gave her no comfort, for the work she now undertook was too different from the soothing work of healing injuries and sickness by which she had once defined herself. Instead, almost by instinct, she went to the one place she had at once lost and found herself.

Ashtyn still had nobody tending the storefront, instead letting the bell that rang as she opened the door serve as notice he was needed.

He came into the storefront, a salesman's smile on his face as he wiped dirty hands on his apron. There was something so familiar about the gesture; it took her right back to where they had started.

"Freya." The salesman's smile morphed into a genuine one that lit the green of his eyes from within. "This is an unexpected surprise."

"Are you busy?" she asked, her voice breaking on the last word.

The smile vanished, replaced with something serious, something concerned. "Nothing that can't wait." He took the apron off and laid it on a low table. "Come up."

She remained mute as he locked the door and led her upstairs. Stillness stole over her as she waited in the achingly familiar living area while he infused drinks for them both. "Now," he said, his voice gentle as he placed mugs on the table and sat next to – but not touching – her, "what's wrong?"

She made a valiant effort to refute his premise. "Who says anything's wrong?"

He laughed, but not unkindly. "Freya, if the expression on your face wasn't enough, you only come to me like this when something's really bothering you."

"I do not!"

He didn't reply, just fixed her with a level stare, one eyebrow quirked in soft amusement that for a moment lessened the concern settled across him.

Freya thought back to the last few times she had sought out Ashtyn. True enough, each instance was because she was seeking some sort of comfort or reassurance. "Goddess, I *am* a bad person," she whispered in growing horror.

"No you're not." The empathy in his voice called tears to her eyes.

She placed her head in her hands.

"Freya." His tone was still gentle, but firm too. He pulled her hands away and forced her to look up. "What happened?"

She took a deep breath both to steady herself as well as to collect her thoughts. The tears retreated, held tentatively at bay – for now. "I just came from seeing Symon."

Ashtyn's face betrayed no sign of surprise. His calm demeanour bore a passing resemblance to Symon's but was as far from Symon's as she could possibly imagine. Ashtyn allowed the intense passions he felt to show when and if he wanted. Symon kept everything locked away, only letting anything out, it seemed, when he was pushed very, very far.

"He...is not particularly pleased with me."

"I can imagine," Ashtyn murmured.

She squeezed her eyes shut as the tears threatened an advance.

"Maybe you should start from the beginning," he suggested.

Freya nodded. Breathing deeply, counting in and out as her healer's training had taught her many, many years ago, she brought her emotions under control and began to speak. She outlined her exchange with Symon on the day of petitions, sparing no detail. After a halting pause, she continued on to describe the events of the day. He said nothing as she spoke, merely listened as though he knew any interruption would give her tears the cue for release which they so demanded.

He was silent for a short while after she finished, evidently gathering his own thoughts.

"I certainly can see how that would be upsetting," he said finally.

She picked up her mug and took a sip. The ceramic vessel had taken on the heat of the water and was almost too hot to hold, but not quite. Ashtyn always left the water a little cooler so the fired clay mug didn't burn her hands.

"I'm not sure that I'm able to tell you what you want to hear, though," he cautioned.

"I don't think anyone can," she replied, one hand seeking the green band on her sleeve and tracing along it.

"I mean, we've talked about this before," he reminded her. "But that was before the uprising. Now you have to deal with the results of the choices."

"Do you know I hoped he had died in the uprising?" she confessed.

"It certainly would have been convenient," he agreed, no judgement in his voice or face.

"Does hoping that make me a bad person?" A part of her hoped that he would judge her, tell her she was the worst kind of person. It would be easier hearing it from someone else, rather than from herself.

Ashtyn chose his words with obvious care. "I think it makes you human. It would be far easier to mourn Symon than face his realisation of what you had done."

"I don't want to be like that." She looked back at her hands, unclenching them. They were smooth and unblemished. They didn't look like the hands of a person that would take lives, that wouldn't care about lives lost.

"How many of us really do?" he asked. "You did what you had to do for a greater cause. Sometimes to do the right thing, you have do a wrong thing."

He had a point. "I'm sorry for bothering you," she said.

"Don't be ridiculous. You're never a bother. Well...almost never."

"Thanks for that," she muttered.

He laughed and the sound eased a smile from her. Feeling at least as though she could face the rest of the world, she stood.

"You don't have to leave," he told her.

"I should go."

He reached for her hands, took them in his own. He ran his thumbs over her palms, his calloused fingers tender. She knew that look on his face, the one that made her tremble with fear at the depth of longing she saw. It was a raw, utterly bare, simple demonstration of how he felt. No, he really was nothing like Symon.

"I don't want you to go," he told her, tightening his hands. "Ever."

She couldn't bear to see that look any longer. Because she wanted to be exactly as wonderful as he thought she was and couldn't face herself if she failed to be that. Because a darkness had taken residence in her heart and she didn't believe that person belonged with him, wasn't even sure she wanted to scourge that part of herself. It had ushered her through so much bloodshed, so much conflict. Because what she felt for him was too powerful to face at this time.

"Ashtyn, I can't. Not now," she said, pulling herself free.

He made no move to retake her hand. "I know. I don't want you to feel compelled to do anything. Ever. But I'd like you to know how I feel. And one day, when...if you're able, I'll be here."

"I..." The words refused to be said aloud, too fragile to exist outside her mind.

"Freya, it's all right." Ashtyn said.

She walked back to her rooms, lost in thoughts of what it meant to do the right thing. Ashtyn had given her so much to think about, but the simple act of telling him what had happened with Symon had freed enough of the weight from her mind that she was ready to throw herself back into work. Questions of inventories and treatments and training were a seductive lure, offering distraction from thoughts that she was not yet ready to allow across her mind.

A new pile of reports was on her desk. It reminded her that whatever personal crisis wracked her, the world around gave little quarter for that, needing attention, management, direction. It was both a comforting and isolating thought as she picked up the first report and began to read.

The afternoon wore on as Freya made her way through page after page, the cheap pulp paper drying her fingers. Then she reached a report that she had to put down as shock and horror thundered through her. A vicious scuffle had broken out between Kade and Pious within the Merchant District Healing Centre – the Centre over which she had presided. No doubt this was another altercation fuelled by the Followers of the Dark Gods. Mish added at the end of the report the total of victims: five dead, seven gravely wounded, twenty with minor injuries. Freya put her head in her hands. Would this have happened had the uprising not occurred? She knew the answer. Of course not. Whatever the Kade may have been, they maintained order and ensured the safety of those who abided by their laws. In some small way, the blood of the people who had died in that Centre was on her hands. And there would be more to come if those Followers in the city who stoked the resentment between Pious and Kade were not removed. Lyssa's words had pierced her skin and stuck there. She had a choice – a choice to do something meaningful to stop the city from tearing itself apart. To not take it would make her worse than the Kade.

Her motions were deliberate as she stood and pulled on a cord running along the wall that connected to a bell in another part of the building. A runner appeared moments later.

"Please deliver this to Makkyd," Freya told her, handing over the note she had written while waiting.

On it, she had simply written, 'I'll do it'.

TEN

Makkyd's first response came quickly: 'Await next instructions. Be ready to leave.' And then Freya heard nothing. As the days wore on, ever-more worrying and numerous reports of violence across the city continued to be delivered. Each new report called a sick, swirling anxiety into the pit of Freya's stomach as she tallied the dead and injured. The need to take action made her feel like she was being slowly eaten away from the inside – strange, when she had once shied away from action. If she couldn't face herself, or the complex emotions that surged whenever thoughts of Ashtyn and Symon whispered through her mind, she could at least give herself to something where she could act and try to make a difference.

Finally, the message arrived, early one morning as Freya was dressing, telling her in Makkyd's economic prose that everything was ready for Freya to leave. She stood for a moment, looking around the space and trying to decide if there was anything she needed to take with her. When nothing came to mind, she strode to the door. But then she paused, went back into her bedroom and found the laastram Ashtyn had made for her. It had protected her in battle during the uprising and, despite her inability to confront how they felt for each other, she couldn't leave it behind.

Makkyd's rooms were far smaller than those of the Chief Healer's in the Main Healing Centre before its destruction by the Dark Gods' Followers. The connection her mind made as she stepped into the space sobered Freya, reminding her of the havoc and chaos that these people had caused for the people of Oranis. And of the need to do something to protect them. Yet while the Chief Healer had decorated her space of authority with ornaments and high-quality furnishings. Makkyd's space was without any aesthetic embellishment. Freya wondered if the woman had ordered her rugs and furnishings be salvaged from castoffs. Her eyes drifted down to the threadbare rug in what might have once been a shade of blood red. The thought of the Chief Healer made something squirm uncomfortably in her breastbone, sending her heart into an uneasy flutter.

Makkyd was waiting for her. "Ah good, you're here. Are you ready to leave immediately?"

Freya nodded, focus on the task causing those feelings of unease and discomfort to slink away.

"Excellent. I'll brief you before you change." The hint of a smile touched her face as she looked Freya's white healer's robe up and down.

Freya glanced down at herself. It made sense that she shouldn't be travelling to a band of outlaws in such garb – it was impractical for one thing, as were many of the clothes favoured by the citizens of Oranis. Even though she hadn't performed actual healing work since the uprising, Freya still wore the robe – and the green band sewn into her sleeve – as a reminder of who she was. To take off the robe made her feel she was slipping away from that person and what she stood for and believed.

"I have clothes for you here," Makkyd added, pulling Freya out of her moment of reflection.

"Ok. Tell me what I need to know."

Makkyd gestured for her to sit. "There's actually not that much that I can tell you that you don't already know," she began. "In fact, you probably know more than me. Most importantly, be careful, get information about their people who are in the city, and come back as soon as possible. And don't unnecessarily endanger yourself. I want you back in one piece."

"I'll do my best," Freya said.

"You know, you may be there for a few cycles," Makkyd warned.

"I wrote up instructions for the healers in my absence. It's on the desk in my rooms in a separate pile," Freya replied. It was the first thing she'd done after sending Makkyd the message that she was willing to go to the Followers. She was under no illusions about what she was about to undertake or the fact that she may not return, let alone be successful.

"You know, you're very different from the person who I first met," Makkyd commented.

"I suppose I am," Freya replied.

"You used to be afraid of nearly everything. Not anymore."

Freya looked down, uncertain of what she should say in reply. It was true. There had been a time when she trembled in fear at so much – being declared a traitor, not following the Kade's edicts perfectly, the truth of her own cowardice to fight for what she truly believed. Truthfully, she harboured fears far more multitudinous than her old ones. But she had learned that fear could not paralyse her in inaction. She was acting and pushing her fear to a place where it was muffled.

"A lot has happened since you first met me."

"I'm not sure I have anything else left to add." Makkyd's smile was hair-thin. "Except for the fact that you have the ability to defend yourself – don't be afraid to use it."

It was sage counsel. And another reason why she was the best suited person to go.

"All right, I'll be right back. Here are your clothes." Makkyd pushed at her a bundle of what Freya had initially assumed to be rags and left the room.

Hesitation stole movement for the briefest of moments, then the need to act, to not let doubt or fear have power over her, kicked in. In a single, deliberate motion, Freya took off her healer's robe. The light underclothes followed and she donned the trousers, shirt and jerkin, which she left unbuttoned. Despite her initial trepidation, the material was soft and comfortable, the brown of the pants and the sky-blue of the jerkin surprisingly nice once on. A pair of boots had also been provided – how Makkyd knew that they would fit her, Freya didn't know. The leather was soft and worn – sturdy. Boots weren't normally worn by the people of Oranis – sandals were generally all that was necessary. Freya had worn boots only twice. The feeling of them enclosing her feet was strange.

Finally, she plaited her hair, securing it with the strip of cloth – it seemed Makkyd really had thought of everything. The plait nestled against the back of her neck. That it was long enough to tie back, away and off her face, was quite a change from the short cut stopping just below her chin in the Kade's preferred style. She had maintained it for so many years out of desire to seem as loyal as possible. Regret for her cowardice curled around her, made her breaths bitter.

She pulled the laastram from the pocket of her healer's robe. The metal grew warm in her hand as she deliberated whether or not she should put it on. The impulse to slip it under the loose sleeves of her shirt warred with caution; would wearing it lessen her chances of being accepted by the Followers?

She was still locked in contemplation when the door was flung open and Ashtyn strode in, a look of pure fury on his face.

"What in the name of the Great Goddess is wrong with you," he hissed.

Startled, her fingers instinctively closed around the laastram. "What?"

"You're going on this fool's idea of an expedition to the Followers of the Dark Gods!"

"How do you even know that?" she asked, more surprised by the fact that he knew than his anger.

"I was in the Resistance for a great many years. I know how to find things out," he snapped.

Incredulity was quickly followed by rage. "So you're spying on me now?"

"No. I just know things that go on. Like Makkyd approving this insane plan."

"I happen to think it may work." She pulled herself tall, tried to match the advantage that his height gave him.

"I happen to think you may get yourself killed!"

"That's a risk we both knew we'd be accepting when we joined the Resistance."

"Well, I don't think that's an acceptable risk right now," he snarled.

"Since when did you decide what risks were acceptable and which risks weren't? What happened to not telling me what to do?" The hard rings of the laastram dug into her left hand as anger coursed through her.

"Since the mere thought of losing you tore me apart."

A pause hung between them as the words settled upon them.

"You and I both know that the cause comes before everything else," she snapped. "You've put it above everything for as long as I've known you."

His eyes seemed to glitter with agitation. "No, Freya, I haven't."

"What?"

"When I came to you in the Healing Centre to tell you about the final fight, I was supposed to ask you to come to the front. The thought that you may be injured or killed was more than I could bear. I asked to deliver the message because I didn't want you there, and I decided to not tell you. I put you before the cause."

The shocked silence from both of them that followed his confession filled the room as though it were a tangible thing.

Freya stared at him in disbelief. "What?"

"You heard me." His voice dropped low enough that she almost didn't catch his words.

"But...why?"

"Because when I joined the Resistance, I was fighting for a better life. And then I met you. And I was fighting for the chance of a life with you." He raised his hands as if to try and make a point, then dropped them by his side.

"What?" It seemed the only thing she could say.

"Goddess curse you, Freya. I don't know what I *am* without you anymore." His voice was almost a bellow, as though the truth of it left him in physical pain.

Anger and something far more powerful than anger crashed through Freya. It pushed her to a yell. "You can't just tell me things like this. I don't know who or what I am, and what I feel for you just makes things worse. I hate that I love you like this."

The kiss was rough. His teeth nipped at her lips, his tongue clashed against hers. His hands grasped her with a lack of temperance or restraint that set her alight down to her very core. She returned his kiss, pushing herself into him, her own hands digging into him. His hands slid around her waist, his lips found her neck, causing her breathing to come out in a jagged, shuddering exhalation. Her fingers fumbled with the waistband of his trousers, need and hot desire making her clumsy. He made his way back to her mouth, moaning against her tongue as her fingers slipped lower.

The knock at the door pushed them apart, hands smoothing tousled hair, patting down disarrayed clothes.

"Yes?" Freya called, her voice high and flustered.

Makkyd came in. "You're changed?"

"Yep," Freya placed a reflexive hand to her shirt, tugging to straighten it.

"Ashtyn." The barest hint of surprise crept into Makkyd's voice.

"Hello, Makkyd."

Freya was amazed by how composed he sounded, especially given the fact that had they been given a few more moments alone together, both of them would have been at the very least, half undressed.

"Are you ready?" Makkyd asked Freya as though Ashtyn were not even there.

Freya nodded, not trusting herself to speak.

"All right. I'll...let you say your goodbyes." Makkyd cast a knowing look between them, then left.

The ardour and arousal were still there, but the heedlessness had gone.

"So." Freya's voice trembled.

"You're going no matter what I say, aren't you."

"I have to."

"When you get back..." He lifted his hand, palm upward, but then stopped, uncertainty singing in his body, his eyes.

She completed the gesture for him, taking first the raised hand, then the one by his side. She pulled him close, placed his hands at the small of her back and then threaded her arms around his waist. He tightened his arms around her, engulfing her in an embrace that said more than his words ever could. Being held by him was so powerful. She wanted to melt into him, but there was still so much to say between them, much for them to face, and she could not bear to face such a discussion. So she pulled back.

"I need to go."

"Please come back safely," he begged, his hands finding hers once more. All pretence of hiding the extent of his feelings was cast aside, his care for her laid bare.

"I will," she promised.

She pulled her hands free and walked to the door, arrested by his call. "Wait."

She turned and found him bending to pick up the laastram she had dropped amid the furious force of their desire.

"Don't forget this."

She went back, holding out her hand for it, but instead of simply giving it to her, he slid the bands under the loose sleeve of her shirt, pushing the warm metal along her skin so that each band, linked by the delicate chain, rested firmly on her arm. His fingers traced a line of fire along her skin as they slipped under the collar of her shift to bring the final length of the chain out and clip it to the loop that he fastened around her neck.

His hand rested briefly on her arm before he let go. She walked to the door, opened it, and walked out.

ELEVEN

Freya was grateful when Olek pulled up in his battered wagon to accompany her for the start of her mission. Despite his crassness, the Kade merchant had proven himself a trustworthy member of the Resistance and she appreciated the hairy man's self-confidence. They followed one of the main roads and the travelling was easy. Sitting alongside Olek on the driver's bench, she watched the land outside the capital unfold as the hearat – the beasts of burden used by most traders – pulled them along at a gentle pace. Having only ever ventured a half-day's walk outside the great walls of Oranis, everything was a wonder. Seeing her interest in the surrounding world, Olek pointed out various land-marks and spoke about the trade routes that ran through the Third Country. It made her realise how much she didn't know of the world beyond healing and Oranis; she had not realised how important trade was to her country.

At intervals of an average day's travel, they came to roadhouses offering a warm meal and a comfortable evening's rest with a roof overhead for those with coin to spare. They also served as informal markets where traders of-floaded goods for onsale to nearby villages, which were often some distance from the main roads. Sometimes those deals were of a more illicit nature, skirt-ing the lines of legality – and morality, Olek said with a wink.

The man's friendly demeanour was a welcome change from the suspi-cion with which he had initially treated her due to the name she had made for herself as a Kade collaborator. In fairness, she had been equally mistrustful of him when they'd first met. By the end of the first day, she was surprised at how comfortable she was with him. Despite his crass language and the disconcert-ing carpet of hair which appeared to traverse the entirety of his body, not only was she glad of his company, but she enjoyed it – mostly. She had sidelined his subtle, and less subtle, propositions, but he was nothing if not persistent.

They spent the first night in separate rooms in a roadhouse and were away early the next morning, but the night apart had obviously given him food for thought, because they had barely reached the open road before he broached the subject again.

"You know, Kuch, you an' I could make sweet sounds together," he said conversationally. His accent had thickened as they'd travelled, as though he were shedding – or donning – a version of himself.

Once, she may have fought to suppress a shudder at the thought. Now, she repressed a laugh. "I'm not so sure, Olek."

"You dun' know what I can do," he replied sincerely. "I don't know if I could cope if I did know," she said.

"I would ruin ye for other men, it's true."

She laughed.

"That Ashtyn may end up being sorely disappointed," he added slyly as her laugher rose into the air.

She evaded his reply by sliding her gaze to the distant line of mountains on the horizon, rising up from the forest to which they were drawing ever-nearer. She couldn't deny that a not-insignificant part of her reason for having accepted this mission was to evade thoughts of Ashtyn, although he had been in her mind more often than not. She turned over and over in her mind the fact that he had tried to keep her from harm, even at the possible expense of the Resistance. She had once asked him to walk away from the cause of rebellion and he had refused. It had taken her a long time to get over the anger that refusal had planted inside her. She didn't know how to feel now it appeared that, in a way, he had done just that. It intensified the ache that shot through her whenever she tried to consider her feelings for him. So much heartache, betrayal, and deception steeped in the waters between them. And the person she had been when she had first been pulled into his world was a universe away from the woman who could kill with a thought and now rode out to glean the secrets of the Dark Gods' Followers. As strong as her feelings for him were, she had to face the possibility that maybe they were ill-fated, and both of them were holding on to the idea of being together when the prospect of them fitting well together away from rebellion and secrets and in the everyday was as insubstantial as smoke.

"Oh! There's hope fer me." Olek pressed a hand to his heart, maybe seeing some of what traversed her mind reflected on her face.

Freya stifled a snort, glad for the way his exuberance lessened her melancholy. "There's always hope for you, Olek."

"O' course there is."

The wagon rattled on, the two of them in quiet companionship. Toward nightfall, the grass plain gave way and forest loomed ahead. Olek laughed at the look of shock and wonder on her face as she stared at it. She had never seen so many trees grouped together, and it seemed a marvel that there was space enough between them for a road, let alone any wagon. That they had been felled to make room seemed almost impossible.

As they followed the road into the dimness of the forest, he said, "You know, I was wrong about you."

"Oh?"

"Aye. When I first met ye back in Oranis, I thought you likely a traitor or comin' to us because you saw some turnin' wind we'd not yet heard o'. But ye've risked yer neck time n' time 'gain with more likely death as thanks than success. 'S a brave thing ye're doin' now, too."

The tears stinging her eyes were hot against the crisp air of the trees' shadows.

"Thank you," she replied, touched by his sincerity.

"I mean, I don't think I was wrong about you bein' a mighty fine tumble," he continued, utterly ruining the moment.

Sometime near midmorning on the fifth day, Olek pulled up the wagon and gestured to the dark mass of the mountain that had steadily been looming through gaps in the trees over the past three days. The road they had been following continued on ahead, but a heavily overgrown trail speared off to her left.

"This is where ye leave," he said, pointing to the track.

Freya gathered her small pack of provisions. Her preparations felt entirely inadequate in the face of the dense, dark trees and the looming peak beyond. Her limbs still held the discomfort instilled by the previous night's sleep on the ground of the small camping site for traders outpacing roadhouses. It made her movements sluggish. She supposed she would hardly find anything more comfortable where she was going.

"Ye follow th' path for jus' under a day," Olek said. "Can' make a mess o' it, really."

"I'm sure some might," Freya replied, tightening the laces on her boots. She had gotten accustomed to their feel over the past few days but she still missed the freedom of her sandals.

"Kuch, you don' look like ye could survive off the road," Olek said bluntly.

She tugged on the coat Olek had procured for her when she complained of the chill in the forest on the third evening – after he had teased her about her delicate sensibilities. It certainly didn't seem to belie his assessment.

"I'm sure I'll make do," she said with a casualness she didn't feel. She held fast to the hope that too much preparation would make her appearance seem planned. She needed to look as though she had left Oranis in desperation.

Olek made a noise that indicated he clearly disagreed. "That'll be how ye die. Th' grea' Councilwoman Kuch, starvin' t' death in the forest."

"Thanks for your confidence," Freya muttered.

"Ye won' die o' thirst. But food? What if ye need food?"

The prospect of her starving seemed to greatly upset him. Perhaps because of his own hairy girth. "Time comes for ye t' return, come back to th' road here, then walk in tha' direction." He gestured in the direction he was going. "Walk a few hours, ye'll come to a roadhouse. From there, ye should be able t'organise transport back to Oranis. And food."

"Thank the Goddess for you, Olek," Freya said, only belatedly remembering he was Kade. But he didn't seem put out, as others may have been.

"Aha! Without me, yer arse would be done. An' we can' have that 'cause it's such a lovely arse." He gave her a frighteningly gap-toothed grin.

"Thank you, Olek. May you travel safely and return home swiftly," she said, unexpectedly filled with regret that she would no longer have his company.

"Take care, Kuch. I have high hopes of seeing ye naked one day," he told her, flicking the reins to get the hearat moving.

"What a parting," Freya muttered as she watched him go. Then she turned her attention to the forest which lay beyond the road.

The first few hours of walking were easier than she had expected. The trail followed a stream so slaking her thirst was not a challenge and she didn't have to worry about drinking from the waterskin she carried. , The path was not difficult to navigate which meant she thought she made good time. She stopped from time to time to marvel at the rich green of the land and the way the trees grew so closely together. It was so different from the clean, straight lines of Oranis, and yet the way the trees crowded together reminded her of the intimacy of the buildings all pressed up against one another. It was the difference in the light that she found the most off-putting. The light in Oranis was clear and brilliant, reflected off the smooth stone of the buildings. Here it was muted, coloured with the green of the leaves it filtered through.

What surprised her the most was how loud nature was. Bird calls, the wind winding through the leaves overhead, and the burbling stream dominated the soundscape, but underneath those noises, she could discern the whine of insects, the rustle of the leaves. She tried to identify the different sounds as she walked, but her knowledge of animals was too limited. Life within the city didn't require one to know of such matters. She realised yet again how narrow her perspective had been. For her whole life, the centre of the world had been Oranis. Walking through the forest, she was forced to realise that there was so much about which she knew so little. Her thoughts flitted briefly to the other three countries of the Godskissed Continent – the hermit First Country, the Queendom of the Seven Lakes, and the Fourth Country, ruled by women of power who constantly took land off one another. As far as she was concerned, they were merely ghosts on the fringes of the Third Country, but they had to be rich and varied in their own right, and as different to the Third Country as the forest through which she walked was to Oranis.

Finally, the path began to climb. Her legs started to ache. Since she had realised her ability to kill without having to engage in a physical altercation, she had allowed the combat training she had been required to undergo when she was in the Resistance to slip, especially as her time was taken up by managing the city's healers. As the climb became increasingly taxing, she regretted that decision.

The trees thinned and gave way to a clearer path, although she still had to pick her way through with care. It was wide enough for a wagon – given the mountains used to be mined for the beautiful mezite stone, she supposed she was walking on an old mining road that had been cut out of the mountain. It was badly maintained, uneven and crumbling in parts. She walked as close as possible to the mountainside that rose up steeply on one side. Fear of falling over the sheer edge seeped through her and she wondered what it would have been like to ride a wagon or cart along this road. Terrifying, probably.

Increasingly, she thought she could feel eyes watching her. It seemed impossible that someone could be hiding nearby – the rocky mountain cliffs looked far too sheer for someone to possibly traverse, even if there was some cover offered by stubborn bushes and the jagged rockscape. Yet although she caught no sight of anything and could sense no tell-tale lifesong nearby, the uneasiness refused to depart.

She rounded a bend and found the land laid out before her. The brilliance of the view held her feet in place, demanding that she look at it. The country unfolded itself below in shades of green that alternately warred and existing in harmony. The forest was a dark cloak immediately below, made somehow a deeper shade of green in the afternoon sun. On the horizon, she could see the beginnings of the yellow-green plain in whose heart Oranis was built. This was her country, the country she had fought for. The country she had wanted to make a better place. It was heartbreakingly beautiful.

She stiffened as a blade pricked her back. She hadn't even heard movement behind her, hadn't sensed the lifesong of the person until she was at their mercy.

"Don't move or I'll kill you," a voice behind her growled.

Freya obeyed, reaching out only with her mind to discern exactly how deep the trouble was.

As far as she could tell, she was surrounded by four people. The person behind her was a woman, and in good health. From where they had appeared, Freya had no idea. The mountain was as steep as anywhere else, and the road was flat with no obstructions or obstacles. She deliberated whether or not she should incapacitate them but she held the impulse in check. She was certain of her own success, but she didn't want her first impression on these people to be of her as a threat.

"Walk," snapped the woman with the knife in her back.

Freya complied.

The other three fell into step around her. Not wanting to give any reason to find the blade thrust into her, Freya didn't turn her head to examine her captors. She had to content herself with glimpses from the corner of her eye. They seemed hard worn. All looked muscled. All carried weapons with a comfort that suggested they would readily use them. The snatched looks she got of their faces showed seriousness and focus, but nothing like the incoherent rabidity of the people she had fought on the streets of Oranis during the uprising. But she knew these people were dangerous, and wherever they were taking her, there would be more like them.

It was only an hour later that they reached the encampment. The sun was beginning to kiss the horizon, lengthening the shadows, turning the light to mellow orange hues. The road threaded between two cliffs but was barred by walls made up of large logs lashed together. They angled outward, making any attempt to scale them difficult, especially given the sharp points into which the tops had been shaped. The mountain rose sharply on one side of the path. On the other, it fell away. A very small gate was the only way through. It was open, guarded by two people holding swords that looked old but sharp. Fear tapped a rhythm through Freya's heart, made her stomach lurch. This seemed more and more a fool's plan.

"Lynna, we found someone on the path," a member of her escort shouted.

Despite her fear, her curiosity raised its head at the organisation suggested by the hierarchy. She wondered what she would find beyond the wall – itself another marker of organisation, of something that most definitely was not a state of pure anarchy.

One of the guards in the gateway took a few steps toward them. "Who are you?"

Freya swallowed. "My name's Yalaen. I'm from Oranis."

"Why have you come here?" Suspicion imbued the woman's voice.

"It's chaos there, with Kade and Pious killing each other every day. I heard...I heard that you take in people who no longer wish to be there," Freya said, sending a plea that the Goddess would sweeten her words and make them ring true.

A low whistle escaped Lynna's lips. Within a second, ten more people appeared, armed with spears, swords, and bows with arrows nocked. All were aimed at Freya. It seemed the Goddess hadn't heard her prayer, or the Dark Gods had intercepted it. Freya tried to stay calm, to draw upon the healer's training that taught her to keep a level head amid a crisis. But in all her training, she had never been the one in danger.

She swept her gaze across the people. It would be impossible to incapacitate that many without at least one of them doing her serious harm. Even if she were then able to heal herself, there were simply too many others nearby for her to deal with and leave safely. It was the first time since she had realised the extent of her capabilities that her ability would not be enough to protect her. A line of sweat trickled between her shoulder blades despite the rapidly chilling air.

"You're lying," Lynna said with the calm of someone who had the advantage.

"What makes you think that?" Freya asked, trying not to panic. The taste of her saliva turned sour.

"How many of you are there?"

"There's only me." Desperation lay naked in her voice.

"Why are you really here?"

"I told you. I'm fleeing Oranis." Freya's voice rose as she saw her death approaching. She was under no illusion that it would be painless.

She had been foolish to think she could simply walk up to the Followers of the Dark Gods and tell them she wanted to join them. The only reason she'd thought it was at all possible was because Zarech claimed he'd done a similar thing, but she had no idea about the circumstances of his arrival or his acceptance. Her arrogance was breathtaking. Ashtyn had been right. That she would never be able to apologise to him was like a knife to her galloping heart.

"She's lying. Kill her." Lynna's eyes were merciless.

"Wait! I knew Zarech." What Freya had intended to come out as a confident call ended as a terrified squeak.

One of the archers lowered his bow with a chuckle.

"Hold that," he said, crossing the distance to stand in front of Freya.

Despite the fear engulfing her, she stood tall, finding herself almost exactly the same height as the man in front of her. With the last measure of defiance she could muster, she met his gaze.

He was disconcertingly good looking with eyes the colour of Kade blue and a sensuous mouth. "Well, well, well," he said softly. Something about his voice was reminiscent of Zarech's melodious way of speaking. Freya couldn't tell if she found it disconcerting or reassuring.

"Councilwoman Kuch." The man bowed sardonically.

His seeming inclination to not kill her emboldened her a measure. "I'm afraid you have the advantage here."

He stared at her a moment longer, then his eyes flicked to the fighters. A grin eased its way along his mouth. "My name is Alyk. I lead the people you see around you."

The coincidence of him sharing a name with the man from the celebration of dance seemed almost farcical. The fear that had claimed her yielded in the face of something as mundane as a shared name. Such things seemed uncharacteristic of terrifying anarchists.

"I'm honoured to be greeted by you personally." The faintest trace of sarcasm made its way into her voice as she pointedly looked at the weapon in his hands, and still with an arrow nocked.

He laughed properly. "Please, won't you come in?"

He took the arrow from his bow and returned it to a quiver slung over his shoulder, then waved at his people. They all melted away with much the same silent fluidity as the ones who had appeared on the mountain road leaving her abruptly alone with Alyk. She blinked in surprise, trying to discern where the people had gone, but had no time to further investigate as Alyk offered her his arm.

Freya looked at him suspiciously. Such gallantry seemed out of place for a rabid anarchist, but that too had been Zarech's way. She took his arm and allowed him to lead her inside the compound.

TWELVE

Contrary to her expectations of near-bestial standards of living, the Followers of the Dark Gods lived in what could only be described as a settlement that could even be considered a small village. Sheer mountain cliffs surrounded the valley which the Followers had made their home. Timber huts were arrayed across the rise which began a short distance from the gate. The road forked, one arm continuing around the curve of the mountain, the other, which Alyk took, made its way uphill past the huts. Children raced around Freya and Alyk, chasing each other and yelling with unselfconscious glee. Alyk chuckled as they ran past, heedless of the newest arrival in their home. Freya found it hard to reconcile this ordinary domesticity with the near-feral Followers against whom she had fought during the uprising when they had tried to use the chaos to cause yet more destruction in the city.

In front of one of the huts, a girl of maybe fourteen years was holding out her hand with a twig levitating above it. Before Freya had enough time to look more closely, Alyk strode on, pulling her gently yet firmly with him. Her delay caused his muscles to tense in reflex, and she noted the strength there.

The climb was deceptively steep and Freya's already-aching legs protested. The deepening shadows made the green of the grass a lush shade and the sounds of normality – of happiness – floated up and settled on the still dusk air. Whatever Freya had thought she would find here, it certainly wasn't this.

They stopped in front of the final hut along the path. Freya extricated her arm from Alyk's and turned to look back at the way they had come. She could see all the way down to the wall where she had nearly been killed. Over the top of the wall, she could glimpse a section of the road she'd come up before it was cut off from view by the curve of the mountain.

"Excuse me for one moment." Alyk went inside, leaving Freya to take in the surroundings before he returned with an armful of items.

"Please." He nodded to the simple seats by the fire pit in front of his house.

Not sure if it was an invitation or a command, Freya sat down, surprised by how comfortable the seat was.

Alyk arranged pieces of timber in a pyramid in the pit, his movements careful, considered. Once he was satisfied, he rocked back on his heels and extended his hand toward the wood. Flame bloomed in the curve of his hand, shockingly bright in the gathering gloom. It hung against his cupped hand, then jumped to the wood. For a moment, it looked as though it wouldn't catch, then flames seemed to come from nowhere and engulfed the structure.

"So carefully arranged, only to be burnt," he remarked. His voice had a reflective quality that called forth memories of Zarech.

Freya wondered if he had put on the display just for her. She hoped she had disappointed him by not reacting. If she had, he did not react as he set up a metal tripod over the flames and hung a pot of water from it.

"You know, you could get that girl back there to hold it over the flames for you rather than bother with the tripod," Freya suggested.

He laughed and said nothing, continuing with whatever it was he was preparing. The water boiled quickly and he poured it into two carved wooden mugs, straining it through a piece of cloth. He handed her one of the mugs. Dubious, she looked at the infusion. She presumed she would be able to heal herself if there were some sort of poison in it, but she really didn't want to find out. Unfortunately, she couldn't see a way to get out of drinking whatever he had given her. She sipped cautiously. If it was poison, it tasted refreshing. It struck her that they had exchanged only a handful of words and she wondered if he had been getting the measure of her or trying to throw her off-balance with that silence. Certainly, she was under no illusion that she was out of danger. Although the surroundings and semblance of normalcy had totally upended her expectations, she knew this was a place that spawned violence and danger, however well it may be concealed.

She caught Alyk's eye as she took another sip. The late afternoon sun made his eyes bottomless blue. A faint smile played about his lips as he took a sip.

"So, Councilwoman. What brings you here?"

Freya chose her words carefully. "You don't seem particularly surprised to see me."

He shrugged, his eyes never leaving hers. "I'm still curious to know what you have to say."

She wondered whether, if so required, she could kill him and slip away without anybody noticing. She concluded it unlikely. It seemed she was stuck, for now, and she would have to give him an answer that he would find believable.

"You know who I am. You know what role I played in the events of the last few cycles. I wanted to create a better world, a safer country. And I sit in meetings where I see the same mistakes being made while we receive reports of the same conflicts occurring in the streets. It's a cycle. A cycle of violence and killing and hatred, and no system is better than the rest. And I'm terribly, terribly tired of it all."

She looked into the depths of her mug rather than at him as she spoke, as though the liquid there held some truth. The funny thing was nothing she said was a falsehood. Even to her own ears, she sounded convincing.

"So why did you come here?"

She could feel his eyes on her, still. It was as intimate as if he had touched her.

"You know I knew Zarech?" She glanced at him long enough to see him nod before returning her gaze to her mug.

"He once said to me that he lost everything that made him who he was. He came here after that. I...I've lost so much. My family, my life, myself..." She fell silent, wondering if it would be enough, wondering if the truths tumbling from her lips had been given substance and power by the fact that she'd finally given them voice.

Alyk was silent for such a long time that Freya looked up from the depths of her drink. He was leafing through the pages of what she could only assume to be a journal. Few people kept journals – books were costly to produce and so were used almost exclusively for texts rather than as blank offerings for personal use. She caught a glimpse of handwriting on the pages as he turned them, clearly searching for something. Whether he found what he was looking for or not, Freya didn't know. He eventually closed the journal and sat in contemplation for a moment.

"How close did you become to him?"

"I don't know," she answered truthfully. "Some days I think very, others I think he was just toying with me, manipulating me for his own ends."

"That certainly sounds like him."

Something in his tone made her look more closely at him to try to read the nuances of his expression. "Were you close to him?"

The slight twist to his mouth gave away his answer before he spoke. "Your description is quite an apt one for my own relationship with him."

"He'd been through a lot," she said gently.

He lifted one shoulder in a shrug, an acknowledgment of her point but a clear disagreement with the broader sentiment. "Why did you lie about who you were?"

"Because Freyanna Kuch is liked by nobody. I walk through a crowd and people steer clear of me like I've got a contagious disease. I am...alone. I thought that perhaps by not being Freyanna Kuch, I might find a place here." Again, the truth gave her words a ring of sincerity that she couldn't have mimicked. But putting voice to the sentiment that had sat heavily with her for so long left her feeling exposed in a way she hated.

"Councilwoman." This time when he used her title there was only a gentle teasing edge rather than the previous biting sarcasm. "You would be welcome here any day."

The constriction in her throat took her by surprise, as did the prickling of tears in her eyes at the kindness of his words. Kindness, more so than rage or cruelty, had always been her undoing.

"Come." He drained his mug and set it aside in nearly the same motion that he stood and offered her his hand. She placed her empty mug aside and took his outstretched hand, letting him help her to her feet.

"Let's go and find you somewhere to sleep," he said. He gestured at the fire and the flames died out. "Can't have my home catching fire, can we?" he joked.

As they walked back down the hill, Freya saw more signs of people using the abilities of the faithful. A little boy was idly pulling a tiny raincloud together, releasing a very small deluge onto a patch of dirt. Cloth was rippling under the still hands of a man. A woman was surrounded by a variety of animals who all sat docilely staring at her. And the girl who they had first passed was now stacking a pile of twigs and logs without touching them.

"Do all your people know of the abilities of the faithful?" Freya asked.

"Of course," he replied.

"How is that possible?"

He seemed genuinely puzzled by her question. "Why would we keep such knowledge from them?"

She was silent, not certain how she could respond. Makkyd had been very clear about what she believed would happen if the abilities became public knowledge. The portrait she painted of mass panic and suspicion of some inhuman quality to those who claimed such power was compelling enough for Freya to keep her capacity to heal and harm with only her mind hidden. Besides, she was already infamous enough. She had no desire to give people even more reason to regard her with that awful combination of fear and resentment. But Alyk's confusion threw Makkyd's certainty into the shadowy realm of doubt.

He stopped in front of a hut about halfway down the hill. "Hm, if I remember correctly..." he said, mostly to himself as he pushed the door open. "Ah, perfect. This is vacant, if you're happy with it."

Freya stepped inside as he held the door wide for her. The hut was a single room with a mattress of dried grass pushed up against one wall. It was a far cry from the mattresses packed tightly with wool that most people in Oranis with any wealth had. Three blankets were folded neatly on top of the mattress. They looked worn but warm. The floor, rather than the tiles or wood to which she was accustomed, was packed dirt. There were no windows, but faint light seeped through the cracks in the wooden slats that formed the walls. A small chest was placed on the wall opposite the mattress, presumably for personal items.

"Did you want to put your things down? Maybe change?"

"Change into what? This is all I brought with me." Freya hefted her small pack and gestured to her clothes. "I had to sneak out of the city." The lie slipped easily off her tongue. In a way, it was the truth.

Alyk knelt beside the chest and opened it. "There are a few things here," he said, pulling out a pair of trousers and a tunic.

They looked a bit too large for her, but she accepted them nevertheless.

"Whose were they?" she asked.

"The previous occupant's."

"What happened to...them?" Freya couldn't discern from the clothes whether the previous occupant had been a male or female.

"An accident." His voice was casual, almost blithe.

"So you're telling me that I'm inheriting a dead person's home and clothes?" Freya asked, incredulous.

"And?" Even in the darkness of the hut's interior, she could make out the same surprised expression as when she'd asked about abilities.

"It's a bit morbid, don't you think?"

"This is a free house and clothes of perfectly good quality. Would you rather we burned them in tribute? We don't have an endless supply of luxuries, Councilwoman. I suppose you're accustomed to having new clothes as you desire, and sleeping on a pillow stuffed with feathers?"

"Yes," she admitted, abashed.

He threw back his head and laughed. "Life is different here. Simpler. It may take some getting used to."

"I didn't expect it to be like this," she confessed.

"Like what?" The amusement was back in his voice. It was playful, inviting.

"It's so normal. There are children, people sitting quietly. You're the Followers of the Dark Gods. All the ones I've met have been trying to kill me – or others."

"Did you expect a group of people sitting around chanting prayers while we sacrificed an animal?"

"Not quite, but I suppose that wouldn't have surprised me," she admitted, causing him to laugh again. He had a nice laugh, like he was enjoying the moment to its absolute fullest.

"Hardly. There are many true believers here. But a great many just want to live their lives in peace, away from the politics of two different groups of worshippers."

"And which one are you?" She was undeniably curious about him. He seemed so self-assured, so self-contained, and yet when he had spoken of Zarech, there had been a vulnerability and sadness that intrigued her.

"Join me for dinner and I'll tell you," he offered.

"Do I really have a choice?" she asked.

His teeth flashed in a grin. "I'll leave you in peace to change," he said.

He went to leave, her unanswered question hanging behind him as he opened the door of the hut. The laastram caught a ray of the setting sun as she rolled up her sleeve. Alyk turned back from the doorway and stepped close. He ran a finger along the fine chain that connected the bands, brushing the skin of her arm as he did. His brush was feather-light, but where his skin brushed hers left a line of intense sensation.

"Did you come expecting a fight?"

She bit her lip. "I came prepared for a fight."

"I thought you were a healer, not a fighter."

She blushed even though there was not even a hint of recrimination in his tone. But before she could answer he withdrew his hand.

"I'll come back to get you for dinner," he said, and left her alone in the tiny hut with a multitude of questions for company.

Freya took off the clothes she had been wearing since she left Oranis with some measure of gratitude. Although the roadhouses had offered bathing facilities, she had only the one set of clothes and they were in dire need of a wash. The ones Alyk had pulled from the chest were a loose fit but comfortable. She even found some undergarments. She hesitated at the prospect of wearing someone else's underwear, but a desire for clean clothes overrode that reluctance. She lay down on the straw mattress, putting a blanket under her head. It wasn't as comfortable as the bed back in Oranis, but it would certainly do. She closed her eyes, fatigue weighing down on her. She intended only to give some space for her raging thoughts, but sleep claimed her.

Alyk's knock on the door woke her. She called for him to come in as she sat up, shaking her head to clear it. "How long have I been asleep?"

"Not very. Maybe half an hour. Light's nearly gone."

"Time for dinner?" she asked, realising just how insistently hunger was gripping her stomach. She tugged her boots on.

"Absolutely. I should have asked if you wanted to bathe, before."

"Too cold," Freya replied, dragging on an extra tunic that she had found in the chest as well as the jacket she had been wearing that day. Seeing her, Alyk laughed. "I'm used to warmth," she told him, vaguely affronted.

It was true. The air on the mountains was far colder than the near-constant warmth of Oranis. Even though the nights in the city could be cool, this was downright chilly.

"You'll have to bathe some time," he pointed out.

Thinking of the clever contraptions in Oranis that heated the water for bathing, as well as the design that meant she could simply stand as the water ran over her, she drew the jacket tighter around her. "If you want to use your fire trick to heat the water, I'll consider it," she said.

He laughed again. "Doesn't that mean that I'd have to see you undressed?"

She blushed.

"Not that I'd necessarily complain," he added as he opened the door and stepped outside.

Her blush deepened as she followed him. The cold air pricked at her exposed face and hands. She gasped.

"You'll get used to it," Alyk advised, leading the way down the path. "Oh, the path to the stream, you can see it from here." He gestured.

"I can't see it," Freya said. In the near-total darkness, everything looked the same. She jumped as his hands alighted on her arms, but he only turned her so she had the correct sightline. Her blush, which had dissipated in the cold, returned. She was keenly aware of how close he was.

"Ah yes," she said, seeing the cleft now.

He released her. "Come on," he said, continuing down the path.

Freya slapped herself on the arm, telling herself to stay controlled. She may be physically attracted to him but that didn't mean she had to lose control of herself at every turn. She followed him down to the wall but hung back as he spoke with the person on watch there, not wanting to give the impression of eavesdropping. The exchange was concluded with Alyk giving the man a friendly slap on the arm and returning to her. Alyk led her along the other path, rounding away from the huts and coming to a large cleared area in a different part of the valley. A great many people were clustered around a large fire in the centre of the area, and more were arriving along the path they'd taken . A few people bustled around large pots suspended over larger versions of the tripod Alyk had used at his fire. An animal Freya couldn't identity was being slowly turned on a spit. Having only eaten a little that day, to Freya the smell promised the finest meal she'd ever had.

Alyk led her over to a seat near the fire. She edged as close to the warmth of the flames as she could get.

"Don't fall in," he cautioned.

"If I do, will you put me out?" she asked, playful flirtatiousness pushing past the voice telling her to be cautious around him.

"Maybe." He flashed a grin and sat on the seat next to hers.

Freya fell into silence as she became absorbed by watching the people around her. The hum of conversation was a backdrop to the scene. People moved about the fire, finding family, friends, exchanging the trivial banalities that comprised their day in a manner typical for any communal gathering. The faces she saw illuminated by the firelight were almost all smiling and open. A young boy flung his arms around an arriving man who shared his tightly curled locks. The normalcy, the way she could relate to what she saw, made the scene surreal. Where was the violence and anger she had fought in the streets of Oranis? Where was the anarchy and disarray for which Zarech had advocated?

A few people stopped to speak briefly with Alyk. Their eyes slid curiously over Freya, as did those of several others nearby, but nobody asked about her, and Alyk made no move to introduce her. She was glad for that; the fatigue of the day was settling on her once more, with her nap having done little to dispel it. The warmth of the fire didn't help, either.

Her thoughts drifted to Oranis and she wondered if the violence was escalating there. Certainly Makkyd's concerns about involving Guardians to maintain the peace was a fair one; many of the Guardians were Kade, many had been fanatically loyal to the old regime. She thought of Sord, the sweet-faced young man who had been assigned to the Merchant District Healing Centre. He was currently imprisoned on one of the prison farms that had been re-established outside the city, due to his fealty to the Kade and unwillingness to co-operate with the Pious Council. The look on his face when he had realised that she was a part of the Resistance still haunted her. Yet these cheerful people before her were apparently part of why the divisions and resentments between the Kade and Pious were being nurtured rather than let go. She had to remember that, remember why she was there. The irony that this fireside dinner gathering of Followers was far more harmonious than the city streets she had left was not lost on her.

Alyk disrupted her thoughts by handing her a bowl of food. It was simple but good, and Freya ate it quickly, content to listen to the chatter around her rather than speak with Alyk, or anyone else for that matter. She didn't feel alone, but she felt a sense of isolation that for the time being, she was happy to keep in place. It gave the perspective she would need if she was to find a way to discover anything about the Followers in Oranis.

As the bowls were emptied and put aside, the mealtime chatter died down and someone began to play an instrument. Lynna, who had so been so willing to see Freya killed that afternoon, began to sing in a heartbreakingly sweet voice. A few people joined in with instruments or their own voices. The song was one Freya hadn't heard before, but it seemed everybody knew the words, even if they weren't joining in. The melody was gentle, the music sweet, and Freya's eyes were compelled to close as she allowed the sound to enfold her.

The next thing she knew was the sensation of being carried. Strong arms held her firmly, cradling her against a broad, muscled chest to the sway of footsteps. She stirred, her sleep-clouded thoughts trying to unpick what had happened.

"Shh." Alyk's voice was a warm rumble in her ear, a counter to the cool mountain air. "You fell asleep."

"You never told me..." she mumbled, her mind still mired in sleep. She should be indignant at being carried but she felt too safe, too tired to move to outrage or the assertion of her independence.

"I can tell you tomorrow," he replied, his voice soft.

He reached the door of the hut and nudged it open with his foot, easily bringing her inside and laying her down on the mattress. She mumbled a vague protest, but sleep pulled too seductively at her, so she allowed him to cover her with all of the blankets. "Don't want you getting cold," he chuckled as he pulled off her boots with gentle hands.

"Thank you for carrying me back," she murmured, already falling back into sleep's waiting embrace.

"You're welcome, Councilwoman," he said as he stood and took the two strides required to cross the distance between her mattress and the door.

Through the gap in the open door, Freya glimpsed the shape of another figure standing outside her hut. As sleep claimed her, she could hear a murmured conversation between Alyk and the other person. It seemed that he wasn't as trusting as he appeared: he had put a guard on her door.

THIRTEEN

One of the body's more basic needs woke her. Sunlight crept through the cracks in the hut's walls, leading her to conclude she had slept well into the morning. She pulled on her boots with swift movements and exited the hut. Despite her certainty that a guard had been outside her door the previous evening, nobody was there now. She stood in the morning sun, looking at the surrounding hillside and the community it housed. The sounds of people going about their daily lives was everywhere in chatter, laughter, and hum of general activity. But her curiosity about this total inversion of her expectations could wait. Caution and urgency warring, she made her way to the discreet line of buildings that had been pointed out to her the day before. The facilities were certainly more basic than the running water of Oranis, and the smell of the open pits over which the structures had been erected was quite confronting. But they were adequate for the task at hand.

Having attained blissful relief, she washed her hands in the nearby stream. The iciness of the water had her biting back a yelp. How Alyk could have thought she'd submerge her whole body in something that cold, she had no idea.

She walked with slow steps back to her hut. Nobody seemed overly concerned by her presence, nobody seemed to be watching or guarding her. Indeed, nobody appeared to be paying her any heed at all. She glanced down at her clothes. The patched and worn clothes certainly meant that she looked like one of them. But in the capital she had looked like any other citizen of Oranis, and it was rare that she could walk down the street without collecting an assortment of stares.

For several minutes she stood outside her hut, wondering what she was supposed to do. The lack of any supervision or immediate task requiring her attention was unsettling. Finally, she accepted that nobody was going to come and find her, and that there did not appear to be a test of some sort being covertly applied. So she went in search of Alyk. The climb up the hill to his hut was just as punishing as she remembered, which made it all the more frustrating when she found it empty. She crouched and put her hand near the fire pit, but the ashes were quite cool. Her hand absentmindedly sought the green band on her sleeve as she wondered if that was any indication of how long ago he had left; his ability might take all the heat from the wood, not simply the flames. Finding neither the familiar strip of cloth nor any answer, she stood up and surveyed the area below her in the full light of day.

Certainly, nobody could accuse it of rivalling the beauty of Oranis, but there was nevertheless something charming about the Followers' home. Tufted grass covered the mountainside, interspersed by shrubs covered with delightful orange flowers. The huts were hardly great architectural feats, more four walls and a slightly sloping roof. However, personal touches that Freya hadn't noticed the previous day such as wind chimes, small statues, benches, even washing hung out to dry, or in the case of Alyk's, two chairs by the fire pit, lent them a homely and inviting feel. Of course, where Oranis could not compete was with regard to the beauty of the mountain itself, the way it seemed draped in folds that climbed ever higher. That this was born from the earth seemed magnificent, a testament to the existence of divinity.

A part of Freya wanted to explore the settlement, but even though nobody seemed to care much about what she was doing, she didn't think anything that looked like snooping would be kindly regarded. After a moment of contemplation, she decided that the best and easiest thing for her to do was to sit down in one of Alyk's chairs and wait, so that was what she did. Although Freya generally hated to be idle, there was something enjoyable about simply sitting in the sun and doing nothing, allowing her gaze to drink in the magnificence of the mountain on whose side she was nestled.

It wasn't long before Alyk appeared around the curve of the mountain. He looked quite relaxed, his hands casually thrust into his pockets. She silently watched the way he moved as he walked up to her, with the same lithe grace Freya had observed in the Resistance's best fighters.

"Did you sleep well?" he inquired as he came to stand before her.

"Yes. Thank you for last night...putting me to bed." She blushed at the memory of how she had nestled against him as he carried her.

"It was no trouble at all," he said pleasantly. He remained standing over her with his hands in his pockets. "Have you eaten?"

She shook her head. He disappeared into his hut and returned with a dried cake of some sort, which he handed to her. She bit into it warily. The previous evening's dinner had been delicious, but the experience of the privy had made her cautious. Discovering that the cake was quite pleasant, she swallowed the mouthful and took another. Alyk lit the fire with a gesture and put water on to boil.

"How long have you been awake?" she asked between mouthfuls.

"Oh, a few hours. The hide from the animal we ate last night was a good one, so I was helping to prepare it for tanning."

"Doesn't that need salt?" She vaguely remembered that fact from one of the Council meetings. Sek and Ellan had been arguing that the tanners should be separated from the weavers. Somewhere along the line, salt had been mentioned.

"It can. I'm impressed you know that."

She pulled a face at the condescension in his words, drawing a laugh and gesture of apology from him.

"Surely there's no salt here though," she said.

"Oh there isn't, we get it from traders," he replied.

"How?" She leaned forward to accept the infusion he passed her, wrapping her hands around the warm mug, grateful for the heat in the crisp morning air. Unlike the earthenware or more expensive fired clay mugs used in Oranis, the timber held the heat without making it uncomfortably hot.

"Oh, we kill them," he said casually.

At her shocked expression he burst out laughing. "I'm joking, I'm joking, I promise," he said, before relapsing into mirth.

"That wasn't funny," she told him, fixing him with a glare.

His only response was to laugh even harder. "You should have seen your face," he gasped.

She pursed her lips and turned her attention to the view and her infusion rather than the laughter beside her.

It took several minutes for Alyk to get himself under control. "We don't kill them, we trade with them," he said when he did, his deep blue eyes dancing with mirth.

Her eyebrows lifted in surprise. "What on earth do you have to trade with them?"

"You'd be surprised. But if we don't have anything they want, we offer our services – protection against bandits and the like."

"There are no bandits in the Third Country," Freya protested.

"That's a sweet view, Councilwoman. Although to be fair, there aren't many. There are in some of the other countries, though."

"You've been across the borders?"

"If you're with a trader, you can go practically anywhere." He leaned back, taking up his mug and sipping from it.

It was a throwaway comment, but it was valuable. That alone would tell the Council how the Followers were able to enter the city unnoticed. It possibly wasn't the only means they used, but it was at least a start. She wondered how Olek had known how to get to the Followers. At the time she had assumed the location of the Followers was circulated as a means of cautioning everyone against straying near them and risking harm. But perhaps it arose from a more personal knowledge. It was easy to reach for and find suspicion toward Olek. He was Kade, after all. Shame followed swiftly on the heels of mistrust. She needed to try to at least ease the death grip she held on her prejudice. That exact prejudice was what the Followers were stoking to cause bloodshed in Oranis.

"But surely not all traders would be so willing to hire you?" she asked.

"Most of them don't know who we really are. They just think that we're weapons for hire. Some probably suspect, but it's a different world out here to that in your city. Besides, we're careful who we approach." He closed his eyes and breathed out. "It's a lovely day, Councilwoman."

"You can call me Freya, you know."

"But Councilwoman has such a ring to it." His mouth curved into a smile, sharpening the lines of his already well-defined face.

As they drank, they sat in a silence that was strikingly companionable. Once both of their mugs were empty, Alyk stood. "I have something to show you."

Intrigued, Freya followed him as he led her behind his hut and up the hill toward the sheer stone cliffs that formed a hazy backdrop to the Followers' encampment. The mountain face looked deceptively close. As she followed Alyk through what was clearly the fringe of the settlement, Freya was again struck by the strangeness of the open space and absence of the straight, stone lines that she'd seen for her whole life. The randomness of the natural world refused to resolve itself into any kind of logic and she found her gaze sliding across the clusters of trees, the uneven ebb and flow of the hills, and the ever-rising peaks of stone and grass that encircled the steep valley on which the Followers lived.

"Keep up," Alyk teased, turning to wait for her to catch up to him.

"I'm not used to hills," Freya panted.

That quick-flash grin appeared. "It's a far cry from your city."

"That's an understatement," she gasped, putting her hand to a growing stitch in her side.

"You'll get used to it," he said as he resumed walking.

As her legs began to truly protest, Freya wondered what Alyk was doing in taking her here. The worry flashed through her mind that he might try to kill her – given how far from her expectation the reality of the Followers seemed to be, anything was possible. But while she knew she was not entirely trusted, she did not feel unsafe.

Finally, they reached the point where rock met grass. Freya looked up, dizzied by the way the cliff face stretched up and out of sight. She'd never thought anything could be so large.

"Here." Alyk's voice held unchecked amusement at her awe.

She tore her gaze from the mixture of sky and mountain and looked to him. She had been so transfixed by the steep rock walls that she had missed the cave entrance. The opening looked hewn rather than natural and stood wide enough to admit a cart.

"I was beginning to think that the mountain caves were a myth," she commented.

Alyk chuckled. "No, they're real enough. But few of us actually reside in them. We may follow the Dark Gods, but it doesn't mean we have to live in darkness. Come on." He walked through the opening. Battling hesitation, Freya followed.

Despite the daylight coming through the mouth of the cave, Freya found herself engulfed by darkness. Before she could say anything, a flame appeared in Alyk's hand.

"Useful," she noted.

As the flame danced in his cupped palm, glimpses of pink winked out at Freya from the cave walls. The mezite that had been used to make many of the buildings in Oranis came from these mountains. However, since the Followers had taken up residence a few generations ago and made it too bloody for anyone to try to mine more stone, it hadn't been used. There was something eerily beautiful about the way the flame picked up the pink of the cave's unpolished surface. Not much larger than the huts on the hillside, the cave contained very few items: a single mattress and three chests.

"Zarech lived here," Alyk said softly, forestalling her question.

Her breath deserted her. While she hadn't wanted to admit it, there had been some part of her hoping she'd find answers about Zarech in coming here. He had, in many ways, put her on the path of rebellion, and in so doing, made her into this darker, crueller, colder version of herself. Deep down, she hoped that if she found answers about Zarech, she may be able to untangle how he had seen her, and in so doing, help her see herself.

Her boots echoed in the space as she walked around the cave. It was so strange to be here, where he had lived. Now that she knew, she could easily picture him here. His secretive nature seemed written into the walls. She crouched in front of the largest of three chests lined up against one wall. Feeling as though she was invading his privacy, she hesitated.

"It's not as though he's here to be offended." Alyk's voice took on a sonorous quality against the rock walls.

Even though she wasn't sure she entirely agreed, Freya opened the lid. The moment felt entirely anticlimactic when she found it empty.

"Clothes," Alyk explained.

She nodded. It would make sense that what could be passed on would have been. It was the way of the Followers, after all. She opened the second chest. Papers filled it, all neatly bound in several piles. The handwriting covering the sheets of paper was tiny, filling nearly the whole page. Paper was hard to come by in Oranis – it would be near impossible in the mountains. It seemed Zarech used every scrap of what he had. Her fingers hovered over the pages, the tips brushing the dry surface. Curiosity over what the writing may reveal about Zarech warred with the desire to know what was in the final chest. She lifted the lid on the third chest, barely bigger than a jewellery box. Its contents were neatly organised but random: a comb, a small knife that didn't look like it would have been much use, a few sticks of charcoal wrapped in cloth. Realising that those items were on a shelf, she lifted it out. The shallow space underneath the assortment of everyday items held two things: a tattered strip of green cloth and a lock of hair.

"Must have been his woman's or his daughter's," she murmured, overcome by a wave of sadness. The sentiment hidden away in the bottom of the box made her fingers tremble as she replaced the shelf and closed the lid, careful to keep everything as it was, as though to remove all trace that she had seen the contents.

Alyk helped her to her feet.

"I wouldn't have thought him to keep anything from his old life." The rock walls made her voice unfamiliar to her own ears. "Why was he in the cave, anyway?"

"His choice," Alyk replied. "He preferred to be here. It's why nobody has taken the space – very few of us want to live in caves."

"Was he often alone?"

"He would join us for most meals, if that's what you mean. And he would wander around the settlement during the day. But he always kept a distance, if you understand."

"I do," she whispered.

"What did he tell you?" Alyk asked. The look on his face was hungry.

Freya looked at the flame in his hand. It was easier than looking at him. The desperation in his expression was echoed within her. At least she understood why Alyk had brought her here: he had questions of his own he hoped she could answer.

"About himself? That his family was killed by the Kade because of who he was. That he came here and became your leader. Is that the truth?"

"It's what he always told me," Alyk replied.

"How long did you know him?" she asked, looking up in time to catch the tail end of a bitter expression as it left his face.

"He wandered into the camp nearly six years ago. I had been here for close to three by then myself. I had twenty years at the time and I thought I was the king of the mountainside. He was quickly taken into the confidence of the woman who was our leader. I was curious about him, you know? He was so compelling. Even if he said nothing, you wanted to follow him around, wanted him to like you."

Freya nodded. She knew exactly what he was talking about.

"So I would often follow him around, asking if I could help with anything. He was either offhandedly cruel or warm and generous, asking questions about myself, showing me how to better stack a fire or teaching me some piece of history. When...when he became leader, he'd only been with us for a year, but there wasn't a person here who didn't trust him. He would speak with the most devout of those among us, surpassing their zeal, and then in the next hour he would be helping someone with their laundry. He never really spoke about his life before he came to us. Only once or twice when he and I were sitting by a fire late into the night, he'd mention something, but he never elaborated. He made me his second. I did everything he asked me, you know. I followed him everywhere.

"And then he told me one day that he would be going into Oranis with the next group we sent. He outlined the plan and then told me to take care of the Followers. And that was it. I begged him not to go. I begged him to send me instead, in his place. He was the one with the vision. I should have been the one sacrificing myself. I wasn't ready. But he just looked at me and left without a word."

The weight in his voice made her feel deeply sorry for him. Zarech had requested a lot of Alyk. Then again, he had demanded a lot of her, too.

"What else did he tell you?" Alyk asked.

"That I could be better than who I was. That I had a choice. That he was glad to have met me…" Tears began to run down her face. Regardless of his motives, Zarech had been instrumental in pushing her to reject the Kade. He had shaped her life so monumentally. The ambiguity over whether he had deliberately spared her life, and what he had really thought of her, didn't make her grieve his loss any less. In between the moments when he'd been needling her, tormenting her, there had been something calming about being with him. He had made her feel that everything may one day be all right. He'd been a confidante when there had been nobody else she could speak to about the deepest parts of her heart. Speaking with him had given her perspective, had helped her see that there was a world larger than her own petty concerns. For a while, Astrom had offered that, but she too had died. All guidance, all wisdom seemed robbed from the world.

The tears came harder and she started to sob. Alyk extinguished the flame so that he could put his arms around her. He held her in the darkness as she allowed herself to cry for the first time over Zarech's death.

FOURTEEN

Freya was surprised by how quickly she adjusted to life with the Followers. Without the days of rest every five days to delineate the passing of time, she stopped being certain of how long she had spent there. With each day, she felt she gained a little more trust – especially Alyk's, although not enough to remove the guard from her door each evening – and a little more insight into them.

She saw much use of various abilities. People conjured small rainclouds to assist in washing, or made logs twist when building so they could easily join the timbers. Her favourite ability was that of a young boy who could control plants. He would often make flowers bloom. It made the mountainside even more beautiful. The Resistance had never given her clear answers about these supernatural capabilities. In fact, Zarech had come closest to offering an explanation. He claimed they were the consequence of true piety, and that the act of prayer and devotion gave some part of the god's self back to the individual. It was an incomplete answer and Freya hoped to learn more.

She cheerfully took part in the various tasks required to maintain the small community– cooking, washing clothes, helping with repairs to buildings and equipment and making new ones. While she learned a great deal, she never heard any mention of the agents causing mayhem in Oranis. The only thing she could deduce was that they were likely people with no family, because there was no mention or signs of missing members from any of the families with which she had contact. And there were many small families in the settlement, far more than she would have expected. The Followers seemed the most harmonious and cheerful group of people she had ever met. Everything she had seen or heard about them seemed entirely untrue. The question niggled at her: where were the rabid, fanatical killers she had fought? So far, she had no answer, although she had chased her thoughts around and around trying to arrive at one.

She and Alyk met every morning to share an infusion before his campfire. They hadn't spoken explicitly about Zarech's cave except for when she asked for Alyk's permission to read Zarech's writings, to which he assented.

Perhaps taking her to the cave had been a test to see if she had truly known Zarech. Perhaps he had simply wanted a clean insight into a man with whom he had shared a complex bond. Most likely, it was a bit of both. Over the course of what she felt had to be at least a full cycle, an intimacy fuelled by their shared closeness to Zarech developed between them, an ease of being around each other that made her seek his company and enjoy it. Despite the fact that it was easy to make him laugh, there was a seriousness about him that she also liked. It helped that he was good looking. When he was engaged in some task or the other, she would find her gaze tracing the path formed by the contours of his face; brow to eyes to cheek to nose to lips. He was a different sort of handsome to Ashtyn, with a certain wildness, like the mountain that enclosed them. The way he moved, with wide-shouldered grace tapering to a hard waist, contrived to reveal his obvious fitness. Against his obvious athleticism, she felt self-conscious.

She even grew accustomed to bathing in the icy-cold stream water. Although she didn't like it, the choice was to bear it or smell, and she simply couldn't give up on regular bathing. But she took every opportunity to complain about the cold, much to his amusement.

Eventually, she felt comfortable enough to broach some of the questions that preyed upon her.

"Does everybody have abilities?" she asked one morning as he lit the fire.

"A lot of us do, yes."

"But not everyone?"

"Some people don't want anything to do with the Gods."

She leaned forward, intrigued. "But everyone knows of the abilities that those who pray can acquire?"

"It's not a simple transaction, Councilwoman. Surely you know that. You have to pray with all your being to truly touch the Gods. If you don't want to, if you can't really believe, then..." He threw his hands up.

She frowned. "But Zarech once told me that the Kade took over in part to empower their own Gods."

"It's true. But empowerment can come in many different forms."

"Was it Zarech who told you all this?"

He nodded, biting his lip and staring into the distance. She had quickly realised this was his usual response whenever she asked him a direct question about Zarech.

"You've read his writings?" he asked.

She nodded.

"What did you think?"

She mentally flicked through the pages she'd read. She had hoped she'd find information about the religious teachings and practices of the Pious. That alone would make coming to the Followers worthwhile. But it seemed he truly had forsaken the Goddess when his daughter and woman were killed by the Kade. It was curious to realise her own faith hadn't been extinguished by the murder of her family.

Zarech's writings were a curious mixture. Some of the papers contained poetic meditations on nature, human emotion, and violence. Others were speculations on the wants and nature of divinity in very abstract terms. He frequently referenced other texts or ideas, which made it difficult to follow what he was saying.

"I couldn't make much of his writings," she admitted. "Could you?"

"Some. He kept a great deal in his head, only writing down what needed working out."

Her disappointment that Alyk also couldn't unlock the mysteries of Zarech's mind was tempered by the way it offered some consolation to her own frustration.

"Is that what you do? Only write down a little?" she asked, gesturing to the tunic where he stowed his journal.

He shook his head. "I'm not so clever, I'm afraid. I have to put a lot down simply to remember it, let alone understand it."

She fought to keep her face neutral at the information. "Are you sure it's wise to tell everybody about their abilities?" she asked, trying to maintain the semblance of casual discussion.

He looked at her as though she'd just suggested he run around the settlement naked.

She grasped for an explanation. "Well...they can be hard to control. And surely telling people means that they won't necessarily believe, but they'll simply pray for ability."

"If they pray for an ability without belief, it's pointless – as I just said. Danger can always be managed. I don't understand why you think it should be kept a secret. That must mean you wouldn't have used your ability often in

Oranis." He idly turned the pot in his hands as he fixed her with a gaze of deep blue.

She nodded.

"What is it – the ability to heal?"

She nodded again.

"Isn't it tedious not using what you have? Doesn't it bother you to know you can help someone but aren't able to because of...whatever your logic is." He pulled his eyes from her and turned away to hang the pot from the tripod.

"It is," she admitted.

"So why bother trying to hide it? When was the last time you used your ability?"

"I last used it to kill people who were trying to kill me." Still she searched for guilt over her extrajudicial killings and still she found none. Of everyone, she knew Alyk would understand, which was why she was willing to speak of it so freely with him.

"Interesting that you can do that." His eyes hooded and his gaze turned faraway. "Have you often used it to kill?"

"What does it matter? It's not as though it's unconnected to healing. It's like fire. It can provide warmth, which in some cases can save a life, or it can burn to death."

He threw leaves into the simmering water then cast her a mild look. "Why do you feel compelled to justify yourself?"

"I don't," she protested.

"When was the last time you actually healed someone?"

Freya was rendered silent. She cast her memory back. Her hand sought the green band on her sleeve, and its absence threw her vaguely off-balance. "During the final battle in the uprising."

"That was quite some time ago," he commented.

"I..." Freya looked away, evading his steadfast gaze. "A friend came in. She was already dead. There was nothing I could do." The memory echoed back to her: Astrom's body brought in, the knife-cut sharp realisation that she was dead and nothing Freya could do would change that. It had seemed so preposterous that she could take life away with a mere thought but couldn't bring it back. It still did.

"I'm sorry," he murmured, reaching out to close the space between them and squeeze her hand.

She shrugged off the agonising sentiment as she swiped the tears from her eyes. "It's just what happens sometimes."

He handed her the mug in silence. She was grateful for that. Eventually, she found herself able to speak again.

"What was Zarech's ability?"

"The same as mine. Fire."

"I assume you had someone redirecting the gas vents in the Healing Centre?"

She settled back in her chair at his nod, a small stab of satisfaction running through her at the fact that she had been correct all along about how Zarech had blown up the Centre.

"Do you miss it?" he asked after another moment had passed. She liked the pauses in their conversations. It spoke to the fact that neither of them felt the need to fill the silences.

"Miss what?" she asked, closing her eyes and tilting her head to meet the sun that had just begun to hit the side of the mountain.

"Healing."

She exhaled deeply. "Yes. But the Kade's Chief Healer once said to me that in order to do good for a lot of people, you sometimes need to forego the work that you truly love."

"You were close to her?"

"I don't know that you could call it close." She shifted in her seat to get more comfortable. "But I did have some reasonably candid conversations with her, yes."

"Where is she now? Locked up with the rest of the Kade leadership?"

Eyes still closed, she arched an eyebrow, curious as to how he knew that although not particularly surprised that he did. "She's dead."

"How?"

"Does it matter?" Her tone was sharper than she intended. But this was one confession she would not volunteer. It wasn't exactly guilt that nagged at her – she agreed that the danger the Chief Healer had posed was too great for her to be safely imprisoned. But a certain discomfort over the act of killing a woman she had respected had come to descend over her of late.

"Ah."

She opened her eyes to see him writing in his journal.

"What do you mean 'ah'?"

"You killed her."

She wanted to lie, but she knew it was pointless.

"I'm not judging you," he added.

"Certainly sounded like you were." She drew her jacket closer around her and edged her seat closer to the fire.

"You did what you had to do for your cause. I understand that."

She knew he wouldn't pass judgement for the action, but that somehow made her less inclined to speak of it with him. She wondered what Ashtyn would say. While she saw similarities between the two men, they were outweighed by the differences. They both felt more deeply than they let show, but Alyk had a streak of wildness in him that he couldn't mask. She saw it in the way he held himself apart from his people – part of them but not quite one of them. In contrast, Ashtyn's loyalties ran deep – he pulled himself close to others rather than push them away. In truth, she thought of Ashtyn often, wondering what he would make of the Followers. But with thoughts of him came other feelings, ones she didn't – couldn't – face. So when the thoughts of him arose, as they often did, conjured by a myriad of things that reminded her of him, she pushed them aside.

She shuffled closer again to the fire, evading Alyk's eyes and the subject.

"Are you really that cold?" he asked.

She knew he was changing the subject because of her reaction but she couldn't bring herself to overly mind.

"I'm always cold here." Only a tiny whine entered her voice.

He laughed. "Come with me." He put his mug aside and stood.

Given the emotional intensity which characterised the last time he said that, Freya was cautious. Yet she followed him, anyway.

He led her to the stream but followed it higher up the mountain than she had gone before, hugging the cliff-face where Zarech's cave was and moving even farther away from the encampment than she thought possible. On her wanderings, she had discovered that the settlement extended much farther than it appeared from the gate. There were whole areas of the mountainside in which people lived. There was another stream, too from which the water used to drink and cook was drawn, but she had never bothered to explore it. As far as she was concerned, the stream was a place of frosty necessity, one was the same as the other.

"Where are you leading me?" she demanded as they entered a thicket and he paused to hold back a branch for her.

"You'll see," he replied.

She scowled, knowing he delighted in withholding the knowledge from her.

After a few more minutes of hard walking – another reason why she hadn't more thoroughly explored this part of the mountain – they reached a clearing where the stream widened out into a pool.

"Alyk, I've seen pools before," she said, panting from the exertion.

"Get undressed."

"Excuse me?" A flush crept up her neck – one that wasn't wholly derived from outraged.

"To bathe."

"I bathed the other day. I don't really need to bathe in front of you right now."

Humour glimmered in the depths of dark blue as he looked at her. "Why ever not?"

He held her gaze a beat longer than was necessary. Heat rushed to her face and he smirked. Then he knelt at the edge of the pool and lowered his hands so they just touched the top of the water. A ripple traversed the surface. "Don't worry, Councilwoman. I just thought you might like a warm bath."

She was undeniably tempted. The thought of hot water...But while she was comfortable being around him, she was not comfortable enough for him to see her naked, no matter how attracted she was to him. Especially because of how attracted she was to him.

"I'll close my eyes," he promised.

She deliberated, but only for a short while. The lure of bathing in warm water was too strong, especially after so many icy washes. She discarded her clothes quickly and stepped into the pool, shivering with delight rather than cold. She looked quickly over to Alyk but it appeared he was staying true to his word. His eyes were tightly shut.

"Is it too warm?" he asked.

"It's perfect," she sighed, sinking under the water and releasing her hair from the braid she had taken to keeping it in. She used the sand at the bottom of the stream to rub herself clean, luxuriating in the feel of the warmth. The pool was just deep enough for her to completely submerge herself and wide enough that she could splash a little. She didn't really know how to swim, so any deeper and she would have struggled. As it was, it was a delight.

"You know, if you wanted the company, I could always join you," Alyk suggested.

She blushed, hands reflexively covering herself, but his eyes remained steadfastly closed.

"I think I'm all right for now." She was glad that he couldn't see the blush staining her cheeks.

She would have stayed longer but she was conscious both of Alyk's presence and her nudity, and that he was likely growing uncomfortable from kneeling for so long. As she stepped out, she gasped as the cold air kissed her skin. She towelled herself off with her tunic then slipped on her clothes with a wriggle of glee at the sensation of being so clean.

"I'm done," she informed Alyk, who removed his hands from the water and opened his eyes.

"How do you feel?"

"Eternally grateful."

He stood and stretched. "You've barely complained about anything, I figured this was the least I could do for you."

"Barely complained?" she said in mock outrage. "I've been perfect."

"Perfectly pampered!"

"Well, forgive me my origins." She turned to leave, still smiling, but he grabbed her hand, tugging her gently back and turned her around to face him. Sincerity settled across his features, making his deep blue eyes still. "You've been a delight to have here."

Freya wondered if he was going to kiss her. Her breath caught as she imagined what his mouth would feel like against hers – if he would be tender or if that wild streak would drive his mouth to plunder hers. Her eyes fell to his lips, saw they were slightly parted, and as he moved fractionally closer, her heart felt as though it were rising into her throat. But he merely released her hand and started walking back down the hill.

A few days later, she was helping one of the women, Marma, to stretch and curry a piece of hide being turned into leather. Still nowhere had she seen any sign of the rabid fervour she had encountered in the streets of Oranis.

Nobody seemed particularly committed to creating a state of chaos. In fact, life with the Followers appeared ordered and calm. Uncomplicated.

Slowly, she was becoming a part of the community. It wasn't an altogether unpleasant feeling to be greeted by name and with a smile rather than with looks of uncomfortable recognition. The unacknowledged guard on her door in the evenings remained, but she couldn't blame Alyk for his mistrust. After all, she was there to gather information, despite her failure to do so with any success.

"One moment, hold this," Marma told Freya, passing her a length of cord as she pulled to stretch the hide in the frame as tightly as possible. While Freya pulled on the rope to the point that her fingers vociferously objected to the coarse fibre cutting into them, Marma tied a neat knot.

"Ok," she said, bending down with an ease that belied her advanced years to pick up a knife.

Suddenly she let out an oath and dropped the knife, clutching bloodied fingers.

"What happened?" Freya asked, gently but firmly taking Marma's hands in her own and turning it so she could see the damage. The discord of the woman's lifesong due to the injury sang in her mind before she even saw the cut.

"I wasn't watching," Marma answered, pain lacing her words.

The cut was deep, courtesy of the Followers' habit of keeping their tools very sharp, but it was as easy as breathing to heal Marma's finger.

"See, it's all ok." Freya smiled as she released the other woman's hand.

"That's much better. Thank you," Marma told Freya, giving her a brief embrace of thanks. Gratitude shone through the older woman's eyes, but no surprise.

It was nice, Freya reflected, to not fear using her ability to help people. It felt good to use it to heal someone, and she realised how thoughtlessly – how naturally she had righted the injury. A contentment stole across her. She hadn't realised how much she missed healing until the act itself had reminded her that, fashioned or guided by the Goddess, she was meant to help the sick and injured. She asked herself where or how she had forgotten that most basic truth of who she was, but found no satisfying answer.

It was a question that troubled her for the rest of the day, right up until Alyk found her at the fire that evening.

"I heard you did some healing work today," he said by way of greeting.

"Do you hear everything?" she demanded.

"Of course."

"Just for that, I'm not going to go and get you a bowl," she replied, marching off.

She heard his laughter as he followed her to the orderly queue of people chatting with one another as they waited to be served from the large pot. She accepted a bowl of food from him and moved to a bench. Alyk came to sit beside her with his own bowl.

"You know, for a bunch of anarchists, you certainly have a clear system of order," she commented before he could say anything.

Having just taken a mouthful, he motioned to her that he would reply. As she waited, she watched the neat procession of people around the fire with their food.

"Anarchy can mean a lot of things," he said after swallowing.

"Do enlighten me."

"Anarchy means that there is no order, no true governance. You may think us ordered, but is there a roster for what jobs people must do? Where is our advance planning, our systems which tell people who they must be and how they must live?" His eyes shone gold in the firelight. "Look at the people who cooked dinner tonight. Nobody told them to. They simply felt like cooking tonight. The same goes for the people who keep watch at the wall. They all choose to do so on the day and time that they wish. May someone occasionally ask another person to be on guard? Yes. But they are perfectly able to refuse. Anarchy is the ability of people to choose how and when they live their lives each day. It is a beautiful system that our Gods have brought us to."

Freya didn't quite agree with him about either his definition or his certainty that everyone would always perfectly choose to do the necessary task. Some level of hierarchy or order was necessary for the survival of the greater community. But there would be little worth in arguing with him about it.

"You still speak of us and you," he said.

She shifted uncomfortably. "I suppose I do."

"You still pray to your Goddess."

She wondered how he knew that. She'd always ensured her prayers were conducted when nobody else was near. "I do. I know you don't worship Her here, but I can't let go of Her just yet."

"Why is that?"

"I haven't been here long enough, I guess."

"Yet you spoke of feeling that you didn't belong in Oranis."

"Just because I didn't feel I belonged in Oranis, doesn't mean I instantly feel I belong here," she pointed out. "One day soon, I'm sure I will, though."

"I hope so," he said with a smile. The shadows of the fire played along the angles of his handsome face. "Tell me more about healing."

The eager interest in his voice surprised her. "My ability, you mean?"

He nodded.

"Once I started, I realised how natural it was. It's..." She thought back to the afternoon. "It's like breathing."

"You sound sad."

Her eyes flicked away from his, unwilling to let him see whatever her gaze may reveal. "I didn't realise how much a part of me healing is. Or how I'd let it slip out of my life." She didn't add "and let it be replaced with destruction and killing", but the unspoken thought hung heavily in her mind.

"Sometimes you have to let something go before you can realise how much it means to you."

Ashtyn's face came into her mind and the bittersweet ache that thinking about him brought followed almost instantly. She pushed him from her thoughts. He didn't belong here in this not-quite-wild world where Alyk sat beside her.

"How does your ability heal someone?" His voice was a gentle current pulling her out of her melancholy and self-recrimination.

"To me it's like a hum – someone's body. And I can hear all parts of it. When something's not wrong – say, a cut – it's like a note out of place."

"This is fascinating." Alyk put his bowl aside and pulled his journal from his tunic. He opened it and leafed through the pages, conjuring a tiny flame in one of his fingers so that he could read better. "Please, go on."

She went to run her hand along the green band on her sleeve and paused when she remembered it was not there. "Well, I guess different problems have different sounds. I haven't used my ability enough to be familiar with them all, but generally I can tell what's wrong. It's sort of intuitive, I suppose."

"And how do you actually heal?"

"I pick at it with my mind, think of how it should sound." Freya shrugged and kept eating.

He wrote something down carefully – calling to mind Zarech's cramped notes.

"What do you keep in that journal, anyway?" she asked, trying to sound as casual as possible. Enough time had passed since she'd last asked him about it that hopefully he wouldn't make a connection, even though it blazed in her mind.

"I write things I may find useful to know in it. Nothing particularly earth-shattering."

"What sort of things?" She watched his face carefully, trying to decipher if she was arousing suspicion.

"Anything. How your healing works, or a fact about Oranis that we may be able to use later. It's probably nonsense to anybody except me, really."

She caught the evasion in his demeanour. If pressed, she wouldn't be able to say exactly what it was, but she knew he was being deliberately vague and whatever was in that journal could be important. Feigning her own non-chalance, she returned her focus to her food.

FIFTEEN

The sounds of battle drew her. She rounded the corner, readying herself for conflict. Her breathing sped up, her skin felt it was constricting around her bones. But rather than a battle, she found Followers practising hand-to-hand combat. They sparred in every combination of styles and with a variety of weapons. Although she wasn't overly skilled when it came to such matters, Freya knew enough to observe the wide level of skill on display. What was unavoidably clear was the vigour and intensity with which they fought. Finally, here she was seeing traces of the savagery she had encountered in the streets of Oranis. And yet, she was reminded of the training sessions Astrom had run for trusted Resistance members. Astrom's workshop was where Freya had rediscovered the friendship and a certain happiness she'd lost when the Kade took power, along with the final vestiges of her childhood. It was curious that for someone who had been taught to heal, she had found a certain sense of belonging amid fighting.

Alyk was in the middle of the sparring people, a short sword in each hand. He fought shirtless and looked almost like a figure from legend as he danced around his opponent with fluid grace. As they scythed through the air, the blades looked like natural extensions of his arms. She was transfixed by the sight of him.

As he noticed her, Alyk said something to his partner and broke off the practice. As he walked to her, sweat and sunlight conspired to draw attention to the well-defined muscles on his arms and across his chest. She swallowed, her throat suddenly dry, as she noticed two cruel scars. One crossed his right shoulder, and she presumed trailed down his back. The other, which looked newer, curved up from his waist to stop at his sternum.

"I was wondering how long it would take before you found the fighting." He grinned, causing her stomach to flip.

"Do you train often?" She kept her attention steadfastly on his face, fighting the urge to run her eyes back down along his bare skin.

"Whenever enough of us want to." It was a reply typical of the Followers. Things happened when they happened. There was indeed no set schedule.

Clearly, on this day enough people had decided that they wished to train. Freya had given up trying to find a clear pattern to life in the Followers' camp. As much as she hated to admit it, Alyk did seem to be correct about an order of sorts arising from the lack of structure or hierarchy in the encampment. She had grown accustomed to it, even if she wasn't entirely comfortable with it. As someone who liked being busy, she often had to search for something to occupy her. There was always something to be done, but the tasks were eclectic. In the past few cycles, Freya had learned to do a number of new things.

"Did you learn how to fight in the Resistance?" That familiar mischievous glint was in his eye.

"I did," she admitted, uncomfortably remembering her fight against Followers in Oranis. For a moment, she was back in the desolate streets, surrounded by rubble, and the air made heavy by fear.

"What's your preference?"

"Staff." While she had been taught to use all manner of weapons, the staff was something that, to quote Astrom, "you're least likely to injure yourself with". It was what she had taken into battle with her.

Alyk went over to a pile of weapons and picked up a staff. "Let's see what you've got."

"I really don't think this is necessary," she protested.

"It's good to exercise," he retorted, tossing one of his blades onto the pile.

Knowing that it was easier to give in, Freya did a few stretches under his pointed gaze. Feeling self-conscious with his eyes on her body, she stripped off her jerkin in deference to the warmth spreading through her limbs. She was curious to know if she'd lost every skill Astrom had taught her, she realised, as she took up a guard position. She contemplated asking him to go easy on her but knew there was little point. It didn't escape her notice that the edge of his weapon was not blunted. Hopefully, he would pull any blows before they bit into her flesh, but she couldn't be certain. Alyk hadn't offered any evidence to suggest he was the type of man to be gentle.

He brought up his blade, eyes shining. She waited for him to make the first attack. They regarded each other for a moment, the air between them thick with anticipation. Then he stepped forward. The short blade flashed toward her. She deflected the attack easily enough and skipped back. He was stronger than her, and from what she had seen he was faster, too. But Astrom once told her she would always be able to defeat someone stronger and better than her if she was judicious in how she fought and waited for her opponent to make a mistake.

They exchanged blows, his fast, hers definite. Neither took the advantage, Freya because she wasn't certain she could, and Alyk, she suspected, not yet feeling it necessary.

"You're holding back, Councilwoman."

"I haven't fought in cycles," she gasped, circling him. He mirrored her movements, his eyes locked on hers.

"You aren't using everything at your disposal," he replied. "Just like I'm not." He opened the hand not holding the blade. Flame blossomed in it.

"That's cheating." The wood of her staff was now a liability.

"In an actual fight, do you think that something which gives you the advantage would be a problem?"

She watched him warily. She was now certain he would land any blow he could. Fear replaced mere unease. She'd thought he had been teasing her about combat, but it was possible he was really trying to kill her.

He came at her, blade from one direction, fire from the other. Her staff met blade. Freya ducked out of the way of the fire – just. However, the move put her off balance. He took advantage of that and came at her again with his blade. She barely brought her staff to meet it, but she knew his other hand was coming.

Desperate, she reached out with her ability and tore at the hum of his body. He backed away, clutching his left side. Blood seeped through his fingers.

His smile was fierce. Nearly feral. "And here I was thinking you weren't going to use what you've got."

She kept her guard up. "Do you want to stop?"

"I'm still standing, aren't I?" He stepped forward, raising his blade.

Freya was unsurprised. It was why she'd used the momentary reprieve to gather herself so that her attack wasn't one of blind panic but precision. A cut opened in the hand that held the fire. Gasping, he reflexively clenched it into a fist and extinguished the flame. She took the opportunity. Her staff came around to rap his right side. Smoothly, she stepped back to avoid his counterattack.

They circled each other again. Blood dripped from his wounds onto the dirt. He seemed not to notice. Suddenly, more quickly than she would have believed possible, he darted forward. The blade was coming toward her so quickly that she could only respond with another fierce pull at his lifesong. The internal damage sang out discordantly. Pressing the advantage, she stepped forward. Her staff smacked against his wrist. She heard the crack but didn't see him drop the sword because before she could even think about what she was doing, she dropped down and swept the staff around to knock his feet out from under him.

With him on his back, she straddled him, holding the staff to his throat.

"I yield," he croaked.

She released the pressure and stood up, holding out a hand to help him up.

"Not sure I can get up," he said in that casual way.

Her eyes widened as she realised the damage she had caused. Guilt flooded through her. "Oh, Alyk, I'm so sorry," she exclaimed. She dropped to her knees beside him and put her hands on him. The cacophony of his lifesong made her bite back an oath.

Like Zarech had once been, Alyk was remarkably calm considering the extent of his injuries. "Goddess. Forgive me," she pleaded, pouring all of her focus into fixing the injuries she had caused.

To her disbelief, he actually chuckled. "I told you to use everything you had. I just didn't realise how deadly you could be."

Finished, she rocked back on her heels, disconcerted to hear him refer to her as deadly. He sat up. "Or how spectacular a healer you are," he added, putting a hand to his left side. Blood was still smeared across it but the skin underneath was intact. He lifted his fingers and looked at them with interest.

Revulsion at herself – at what she had done, and the ruthless, dark part of herself that the injuries and his own words reflected back to her – was a physical presence crawling through her. She pushed herself from the ground, staggering back.

Twilight-blue eyes flicked to her, eyebrows raised. She took a stumbling step back, then another. Then she turned and walked away.

The thudding footsteps signalled his pursuit. "Wait."

She did not heed his request, instead increasing her own pace. But he caught up with her easily enough and grabbed her by the shoulder.

"Are you all right?" he asked. "Are you hurt?"

"Me?" Her voice was an incredulous shriek. "I'm fine. I could have killed you!"

"But you put me back together again." He seemed entirely unconcerned that she had walked away without even a scratch. Seeing the disagreement etched on her face, he led her to a seat.

"I'm sorry if I goaded you into fighting."

"I could have said no." She wondered if she'd wanted to fight. If some part of her had replied to the challenge in his eyes.

"You could have," he agreed. "But I didn't make it easy for you to walk away."

"I suppose you're correct." She looked down at her hands, flexed the fingers. Wondered if they were a healer's or a killer's fingers. "Using any tool at my disposal is important. But I enjoyed it." She was filled with disgust at the memory, the taste of her mouth going bitter as she voiced the admission.

"Well, you didn't kill me. So I'll take that as a positive."

She tucked her legs up so that her arms encircled them. The movement drew her eye to the dried blood on her sleeve. His blood.

"I'm a healer. I'm not supposed to enjoy killing. And I've killed people, Alyk." She buried her head in her knees, curled up into a little ball and wished she could just disappear. She didn't know how it was possible she'd become this. But it was inescapable.

"I think there are two types of people: those who have the ability, the desire I suppose, to make the killing blow, and those who don't. To finish off someone who's on the ground, or defenceless before you, it's not something everyone can do. Me, I've never had the thirst for it. I've killed in the heat of the moment, but that's when it's kill or be killed. In some ways it's a weakness. If I can't finish someone off when I've got them disarmed, then they may come back at me, might get the jump on me."

"Which one of those people do you think I am?"

"I think that you're not a natural fighter. That much is for sure. I mean yes, you can fend off blows, even get in a few good hits of your own, but at the heart of things, you're disadvantaged. And your ability? Yes, it's a powerful weapon. But it's entirely aggressive. It can't stop an arrow or a sword thrust to the heart. I think you have to be aggressive with it if you want to win a fight. If you need to win a fight."

Someone called from the training ground. "Alyk, Mal needs a partner. Are you free?"

"Will you be all right?" he asked.

She mustered a smile, even though she didn't feel even remotely all right. She wanted him to stay but she didn't want to keep him, either. "Yes, I think I'll just sit here for a while."

"I'll see you later?" He put a hand on her shoulder. He left it there until she nodded, then he squeezed it and walked away.

It was only after he had left that she realised he hadn't answered her question about what he thought of her capability to kill.

The nightmare woke her. Freya sat upright gasping for breath, the horror of her dream vivid in her mind. The cloying darkness of the hut pressed down on her. She needed to get out. Not bothering to put on shoes or jacket, she all but crawled outside. For once, she didn't begrudge the chill in the air as it sluiced away the final dregs of sleep. She breathed deeply, relishing the silence, the peace. The openness of the mountainside soothed her. She didn't want to go back inside the lonely darkness of her hut. A fire high on the hill caught her eye. It could only be Alyk.

The familiar climb took her only a few minutes thanks to the incentive offered by the cold.

He showed no surprise at her presence.

"Do you ever sleep?" she asked.

His gaze remained locked on the flames. "Sleep brings its own troubles, Councilwoman. I assume that's why you're awake now."

"I had a disturbing dream," she admitted.

His snort was soft but it held a world of derision. "A single dream. Lucky."

This was a side of him she hadn't seen before. Utterly withdrawn, solemn, clearly lost in some musing about his own demons. Night as it so often did, held a transformative power over people that burdened them with the thoughts daylight allowed to be pushed aside.

"I'm sorry I can't be more troubled," she snapped.

His eyes lifted from the fire and caught hers. The manner in which the shadows were arrayed across his face made his features seemed sinister, haunted. "Sorry. Sit. Tell me about your dream."

She did as he bade, fixing her gaze on the flames. The way they danced along the wood with no apparent method or purpose was hypnotic.

"I was in the room in which I used to tend Zarech. Except instead of healing him, I was pulling him apart with my ability. He was laughing, encouraging me. My hands were drenched in his blood. He said to me, 'you have the most beautiful dark heart'.

"I went to leave, but when I opened the door, the Chief Healer walked in. She told me I'd done good work. Then she told me I had to finish it. When I said I didn't want to, she replied that knew my dark heart and it was pointless to lie. I stepped back from her and she walked toward me. Then my back hit the wall and she nearly reached me. I was so scared, because if she reached me, I knew I'd turn into exactly what she claimed. She was about to touch me. I could feel the heat of her fingers – and then I woke up." She shivered, but it had nothing to do with the cold night air.

"I'll admit that's a disturbing dream," Alyk conceded.

"Do you think it was correct?" She hated the way weakness and desperation sung through every word.

"How should I know? It was your dream, not mine. What do you think?"

"I...don't know. I never wanted to kill, you know. I was so terrified of it. And then I did. It was so easy. And nothing changed. I didn't look different, I didn't feel different. And the next time, it was just as easy as the first. But then suddenly I looked back and the number of bodies I've left behind me is so high.

"I thought that having a cause would require me to sacrifice comfort or wealth, or my life. I didn't ever expect that I'd have to sacrifice who I was."

The fire's crackle filled the invading silence. She was grateful for the hiss and spit of the flames.

"Causes change people," he said eventually. "They use people."

"I just want to go back to being the person I was before all of this started." Tears stung her eyes, made her words quaver.

"What if you can't?"

She closed her eyes against the tears and swiped at the tingle on her nose tip. She couldn't bear that what his question suggested may actually be true. "All of these different people, they wanted me, they used me, they manipulated me. Zarech, I still don't know to what end, the Resistance, to aid their - our - rebellion, even the Kade. They all tried to make me something they could use."

"You are an agent of chaos. The scales are tipped in favour of whoever might call you their ally," he said.

"An agent of chaos? What is that supposed to mean?" She wrested her gaze from the flames to look at him. He was lost in the fire, speaking from a place beyond where they sat now. "Alyk?" she prompted.

His squeezed his eyes closed for a moment. "It means that you are quite a remarkable individual," he said softly.

She was silent, uncertain if indeed there was anything to say in response to that. She was uncomfortable at being the subject of their discussion so she turned to focus on him.

"What do you dream about?"

He inhaled deeply, letting his breath out in a long, deliberate exhalation. "I dream about a great many things, Councilwoman. Very few of them are sweet."

She said nothing, figuring he would be more likely to continue if she didn't prompt him.

"I assume you saw the two scars on my chest today?"

"Yes."

The firelight played across his face, making it hard to read his expression.

"I used to live in a village on the border of the Fourth Country. Did you know that those who live on the farthest edges of the Fourth Country are desperately poor? I didn't, until a band of raiders came across the border to take anything that we had. They were desperate people. They cut down any of the men who posed a threat, raped a few of the women. That...that I suppose I could understand.

"What I couldn't understand was that they then set fire to everything. It was such unnecessary cruelty. They were hungry. They were desperate for food. But to burn my village to the ground? It has never made sense to me in all the years since. My father was one of the first killed. I was cut down but survived – hence this scar." He gestured to his right shoulder. "My mother died trying to help some children trapped in a burning house. I had no family left and no home to stay in. My parents were good people. They had arranged for me to be joined to a nice young girl – I didn't love her, but I could have. And then it was all gone.

"I often dream about that day. It makes no more sense to me than it did all those years ago.

"So I came here. To a place where chaos was worshipped. It seemed to me that chaos was the only certainty. If I learned anything from that day, it's that order is as unstable and transient as everything else in this world. I didn't even know that the Kade had overthrown the Pious, or why they would want to, until Zarech came to us."

"Alyk, I'm so sorry." There seemed nothing else that she could say in the face of such a story. Even the horror she had endured of seeing her family murdered by the Kade because of her sister's defiance at least made sense, even if it was a horrible, twisted sort of sense.

"When Zarech arrived, something about him made me feel as though he knew what I had gone through, how I felt. I attached myself to him, followed him everywhere. He would either treat me kindly, talk with me, encourage me, or tell me to leave him alone in the most cruel of terms. I never knew which it would be. He gave me the other scar. It was in a fight three years ago. He said that I wasn't fighting hard enough. And to prove it, he struck me after he knocked me over. He said it was a lesson to always keep my guard up. Sometimes I dream of him staring at me as I try to run to him, harder and harder. I can never reach him, and he just has this look of such...disappointment on his face."

Perhaps it was because the scars of his family's murder wound through him, tainting any relationship he would have, but Freya only felt dull surprise that Zarech had treated Alyk so cruelly.

"You reminded me of Zarech's lesson today," he said.

"I thought you let me win," she replied, surprised.

"I wasn't careful enough with you at the start. By the time I realised how much trouble I was in, it was too late. You had me on the ground. Next time I won't be so careless."

"Is that why you took my guard away from my hut tonight?" She had noticed her door was unguarded as she desperately crawled out of her hut, but she had been too preoccupied with the clinging vestiges of her nightmare to wonder at it.

"Seemed a bit pointless," he admitted.

"Alyk, I'm sorry about today. I hate what I became in that fight. I'm just as bad as Zarech." She despised the glee that had overtaken her during the fight, for the delicious sense of triumph that had run through her at the realisation she could win. It wasn't a nice thing to know what nestled inside her.

He looked away from the flames and at her, his eyes the same as the night sky above them. "Yes, but the difference between you and Zarech is that you helped me after the fight was over. He left me in the dirt." He spat the last words out, as though they were bitter to the taste.

For the first time since her arrival, Freya felt she was intruding. This pain and anger were far too personal, far too deep-rooted. "I'm sorry for bothering you, Alyk. I should go." She stood. The motion brought the cool of the night rushing up to cradle her back. She wrapped her arms around herself in a futile effort to retain some warmth.

He stood, too, and took a step toward her. It might have been a trick of the light, but she thought his features were haunted, vulnerable. "Or you could stay."

SIXTEEN

His nightmares woke her. Freya reached across the dark and pulled Alyk close, murmuring words of comfort until he woke.

She had slept by his side for the past twenty nights and on all but one he had been plagued by dreams that ripped sobs and cries from him.

He came to consciousness, panting and wild, his whole body rigid with angst. Freya tightened her arms around him and rocked him gently until he relaxed and the Alyk she knew returned. By now, it was a practised routine.

"Thank you, Councilwoman," he rasped. A moment later, his arms encircled her.

"It's no trouble," she replied, bringing her lips to his.

A fiveday ago she had moved her things into his hut. She told herself that this intimacy with him was so she could find out more about the Followers' agents in Oranis. But every day Oranis seemed further and further away. Life on the mountain was peaceful, free from the machinations that had dominated the city, free from the sectarian vendettas. When Alyk suggested she stay with him that evening all those nights ago, she had said yes, giving in to the physical desire she had been nursing since the first time she laid eyes on him. But somewhere along the way the physical had given way to something more.

He asked little of her except for her company. He did not judge or even seem bothered by those parts of herself that troubled her. She enjoyed his company, too, as she had since her arrival, finding an ease at being with him similar to the early days of knowing Ashtyn. She tried not to draw such comparisons, though. Thinking of Ashtyn conjured guilt and sadness, and, yes, longing. But she wondered if perhaps she and Ashtyn were simply not meant to be. Maybe they had been yet another casualty of conflict and causes.

At Alyk's suggestion, Freya began to impart her medical knowledge to some of the Followers. Even though her ability meant most who were injured sought her out and were immediately healed, he reasoned – and she had agreed – it never hurt to ensure others knew how to set a broken limb or which herbs could heal and which could kill. Freya found a quiet satisfaction in both the tutelage she provided and the healing she performed. It had been longer than she remembered since she last undertook basic healing work and it felt good to return to it.

Alyk also goaded her to keep sparring against him. She couldn't decide if she hated or was amused that he knew the exact words to rile her into agreeing. There was a thrill to sparring against him – an intoxicating sense of danger that came from knowing he would allow the blade to connect with her if she didn't block or step aside in time. It left her skin tingling, and formed a sort of prelude to the wild passion that characterised their nights together.

"Why did you tell me to come back here if all that's ever going to happen is that I'm beaten?" she complained to Alyk the third time he had sent her flying one day. She willed the shallow cut along her arm closed as he held out a hand to help her up.

"Because losing is good for your ego," he informed her.

She accepted the hand but instead of levering herself up, she tugged sharply. Not expecting it, he came to join her on the ground. "That was for *your* ego," she said.

He laughed good-naturedly. "I can't argue with that." He leaned over to kiss her, unconcerned that anybody may see. There was a certain delight in showing affection without fear of others seeing, gossiping about it, using it against her.

Their repartee was interrupted by one of the Followers who had been fighting near them.

"Freya, I think I damaged my arm when I fell. Could you look at it?" he asked.

She got to her feet and dusted herself off. Even without putting her hand on his arm she could hear the break singing through his lifesong. From the distance of a few paces, she healed it. "That should be better," she said.

Alyk had watched the exchange from his vantage on the ground. "Are your abilities getting stronger?"

She turned her attention to him, offering him a hand to help him up. "I think so. Maybe I'm just becoming more confident."

"You're very attractive when you're confident, you know." He grinned as she helped him to his feet and made to take her in his arms.

She skipped away, her own grin unrepressed. "Don't be ridiculous."

"It's true."

"Well, I'm confident that you'll knock me down the next time we fight. Is that what you meant?"

He grinned at her again, rolling his shoulders back. The well-used muscles rippled with the movement. She liked that she could, and later would, run her fingers, lips, skin over them. He caught her stare and stepped forward. "Well, I do know you appreciate it when I put you on your back," he said in an undertone.

In a swift motion she picked up the dropped staff and struck him behind the knees. He crumpled to the ground.

"Still think you're clever?"

His appreciative laughter made her smile.

Later, Alyk accompanied her to the stream to rinse off the sweat and dirt that had accumulated during their exercise. While he cheerfully waded into the middle of the pool, Freya looked at him imploringly from the edge of the water, shivering in the cold breeze.

He laughed. "Really?"

"Please."

He relented with a roll of his eyes and placed his hands on the water's surface to heat it. This, too, had become a routine for them. She slipped gratefully into the water, shivering as his eyes devoured the sight of her naked body.

"You know, you'll have to get used to this sooner or later," he said.

"Why, when I have you?" She came up to him and slipped her arms around his waist. She was learning the way her body fit against his, each curve and ridge and nuance and form. The water was sleek between them. Desire coiled in his eyes, calling her own lust.

He leaned forward to kiss her but at the last moment she moved her head aside so his lips landed on her neck. She felt the curve of his smile against her skin and the intoxicating way it made sensation run along her body. She stilled as his teeth nipped the flesh and gasped as his hands left the water for just a moment to grasp her, turning the pool cold for a fraction of a moment. "You're lucky I have a soft spot for Pious Councilwomen." The vibration of his voice as he spoke against her skin was almost more than she could bear, need and want stoked by the caress of his hands.

The crack of thunder took them both by surprise. The warm water and the heat of their passion meant they hadn't noticed the way the air had so suddenly cooled. Alyk cursed and scrambled out of the pool. Freya shrieked as she was left in water one in calling icy. She followed his hasty exit, roughly drying herself and dressing quickly.

"We have hides drying," Alyk shouted as he ran back to the main encampment. She struggled to keep up with his pace, thinking it fortunate she could heal, as one of them was likely to trip on the uneven ground and break something at such a reckless speed.

They reached the hides which had been left stretched out to dry in the sun as the first fat drops of rain started to fall.

With fingers made clumsy by haste, they aided the people already trying to manoeuvre the bulky skins into a storage hut.

The rain fell harder as the chaos of their disorganised co-operation eventually saw the hides safely stowed.

"Good thing we bathed." Freya's shout to Alyk competed with the increasing roar of the rain.

He grinned and began the trudge up the hill. In the rain, the climb was particularly unpleasant. While they arrived at his hut, they were greeted by the sight of water pouring down from leaks in the roof. Alyk shook his head with a rueful smile and continued farther up the hill. Freya followed, increasingly miserable with each step, until they reached Zarech's cave.

He grabbed some branches lying near the entrance and set them in the hollow that had clearly been designated as a fireplace at the mouth of the cave. They began to smoulder under his furrowed gaze until finally, flames appeared.

"I don't suppose your ability can dry soaked clothes," she said hopefully, taking off her sodden tunic and wringing out a corner of her shirt, turning the dirt on the ground to mud.

"I've never tried. I could give it a go, but I may set you on fire. Or burn your clothes into nothing. Although that could be an advantage." He smirked at the thought, his eyes lascivious as he took his journal from the pocket in which he secreted it, and held it in front of the fire to dry.

"I'll be fine," she said, eliciting a chuckle from him. "I can't believe how suddenly that storm appeared," she commented, looking out at the air turned grey by the falling water.

"They come with nearly no warning and are always very violent."

To prove his words, a sheet of lightning streaked across the sky, turning grey to white. Almost immediately an ominous clap of thunder followed. She would never admit it to him, but she was glad that they were safely in the cave.

"How often do they happen?"

"Often enough," he said, idly turning a page of his journal. They lapsed into silence, broken only by the crackle of the fire or the occasional rustle as one of them shifted. The firelight caught the pink of the cave's walls. It was quite cosy.

"Do you want children, Freya?" His question seemed randomly drawn out of the idleness of the moment.

Caught off guard, she nodded.

"When?"

She edged her right side closer to the fire in an effort to dry it. "I hadn't really thought about it. I always figured not before the uprising. I..." She paused, remembering a similar conversation with Zarech. She had told him a truth she had been unwilling to admit to herself: that she would only bring children into a world where they would be free to choose their own path. "I want to raise children in a world that's safe for them."

"No world will ever be truly safe."

"But some are safer than others," she retorted. "Why do you ask?"

"Oh, it would be nice to know before I go into Oranis that some part of me lived on."

"Wait, when are you going into Oranis? And why?"

Silence stretched between them in the pause before he spoke. "Not immediately. But the city will sink into chaos soon enough. And that's our opportunity to strike."

"But you struck during the uprising," she pointed out.

"Plans within plans, Councilwoman," he told her, slowly turning the pages of his journal to ensure there were all dry. Finding one to be particularly damp, he let out a "tsk" of irritation.

"But I thought—"

"You yourself know that the city, that the whole Third Country, is perpetually teetering on the brink of instability and uncertainty. Chaos, even. That's why you came here."

"And you want chaos?" Freya's prickling skin had nothing to do with the cold. This was what she had come to discover, been waiting to see. It was what she had come to hope she didn't find.

He held up a hand, waggling his fingers at her. "I'm a true believer, aren't I?" He illustrated the point by sending sparks flying from his fingertips.

She couldn't really argue with that. "When will you go?"

He shrugged, turning another page in the journal. "The time is not quite right."

"But you will go?"

He nodded.

The depth of his commitment, of his genuine belief in the inevitability and desirability of anarchy, took her aback. It was something he kept hidden well, only letting it peek through here and there. For the most part, Alyk was an easygoing, affable person who seemed simply to be respected by the other Followers within the encampment. But sitting here in the cave, with the crash of the rain outside and the firelight highlighting the pink-toned stone, it was clear that this initial appearance was not all there was to him. It was becoming apparent to Freya how ardently committed he was to the Dark Gods and their cause, more so than he cared about having a family or being a father – his comment about some part of him living on was proof enough of that. Of course, there was a reason he had become the Followers' leader. That reason would have a lot to do with his commitment to the chaotic Dark Gods and what they would have him make the world into.

"And there are others who agree with you – with this?"

"Of course."

"Here?"

His smile held a touch of condescension.

"How many?"

"Enough."

"But everyone seems so content. Why would they want to leave here, to go and risk their lives to cause destruction and mayhem?" She fiddled with the way her tunic was lying on the ground so it was getting the most of the flames' heat. She hoped the nonchalance of the action might conceal her interest and concern.

"Why does anyone risk their life? Boredom or belief, really."

"Boredom or belief?" She couldn't hide her incredulity.

"Yes. boredom of the everyday, ordinary life can cause the desire to do something wild, something dangerous, to remind them that they're alive by evoking the rush that comes with courting death. That can give a story to push back the tediousness of an unexceptional life. Until that's not enough, of course.

"And belief? Well, you know better than anyone how powerful an incentive belief can be. If you believe that what you're risking your life for will lead to something better than what you have now, that's certainly difficult to resist."

She bit her lip, disliking the truth in his words. It was discomforting to think that everyday, ordinary people who had pulled her into their community, shown her how to plait sturdy rope or teased her about her cooking, could turn into rabid savages. But people who she'd joked with every day had become entirely unrecognisable, barely human, when pushed or given the opportunity.

"What will you do when you get to Oranis?"

Alyk seemed incongruous with Oranis. Her beloved city seemed to exist in a world apart from the one on the mountain.

"What any good anarchist does. Sow chaos." A grin spread across his face.

"And then?"

"You still don't think like us. There is no final plan, there is no 'and then'. There simply is the moment, what it offers, and what we take from it."

"But surely some form of order, of structure will re-assert itself," she protested.

"And that too will inevitably fall. Look at the Four Countries, Councilwoman. You know your myths. They broke apart to worship their own gods. You lived through what happened in the Third Country: the struggle for the dominance of one god over another. Do you really think that peace across the lands will last?" He flung his arm out as he spoke in a sweeping gesture.

"I hadn't thought about it," Freya admitted.

"Of course you hadn't. Because you're so caught up with the Third Country and the tiny struggle between the Pious and the Kade that you don't see where that fits into the bigger story." He stood and paced the small space as he spoke. "War is inevitable. Chaos is inevitable. These are the truths of human nature. You worry about your dark heart, Councilwoman? Worry about all our dark hearts."

"I don't know that I can believe such a bleak thing," she murmured.

"Hardly bleak. Just true." He paused his pacing to fix her with a meaningful look.

"I heard that true chaos will allow the Dark Gods to take on physical form, to enter our world," Freya said cautiously.

"Now wouldn't that be something to see!" His eyes shone in the firelight.

"Do you really think that it would be good?" she asked.

"Don't you? You believe in the Goddess, still worship her. Wouldn't you want her to take on a physical form, walk beside you?"

Freya's fingers sought the green band on her sleeve. Grasping only the drying fabric of her shirt, she pinched the material in thought. "Of course I still worship the Goddess," she said, her words slow and thoughtful. "But that doesn't mean I think Her place is alongside us. She has given me so much, has determined so much of who I am. And I'm grateful for that. But the realms of mortals and gods are separate for a reason. To have the gods among us would cause..."

"Chaos," he finished for her, a smirk playing about his lips.

Unease crawled about her now. She felt she'd walked right into a trap and somehow revealed herself. She tried to reach out to discern his lifesong and defend herself if necessary. But the sound of the rain and her own rising panic shattered the focus she needed.

He stepped toward her. Fear bloomed within her, but he cast his gaze outside and as he did, the fervour melted from his expression.

"Are you hungry?"

She blinked in surprise at the abruptness of the change. She followed his gaze to the mouth of the cave. Indeed, the grey had edged almost imperceptibly into darkness while they had spoken. "I am hungry, actually," she said.

"I'll go and get us something to eat." The zealot was tucked away again. The suddenness of the transformation was almost as frightening as the ideas he valorised. How many people, she wondered, had this rabid ferocity hidden inside them?

"You'll go out in the storm?"

"It's only a little rain, Councilwoman. I'll return shortly." With that, he strode from the cave and was almost immediately swallowed from sight.

Freya remained in the dry warmth of the cave, her mind in turmoil. Alyk's change in demeanour was unsettling on a profound level. More unsettling was how certain he had been. There seemed to be no limit to his zeal. She agreed to some extent that order and structure would always be tested, may even fail at times, but that didn't mean the success of chaos was guaranteed. At most, Freya thought, one could argue that chaos tested order, forced it to be better, punished anyone or anything that became too complacent. But its inevitable victory? She couldn't accept that idea. Standing and skirting the edge of the fire, she peered outside the cave's entrance and down the hillside. The torrent of rain made it difficult to see very far. She sighed. Yet again, she felt an enormous choice had been placed before her. Oranis had never seemed further away and she wasn't even certain that she missed it. There was something undeniably lovely about life with the Followers. It would be so easy to stay on the mountain forever. But as she looked at the fire, it tugged at the corner of a memory, and she recalled an entirely different fire – far larger, and surrounded by Pious celebrating something they'd not been permitted to for years.

An image of Bardan's daughter made its way into her memory, Chara shrieking with delight as her father lifted her high in the air. Freya couldn't forget the look on Bardan's face. His entire word was centred around his daughter. It was for her future that he had joined the Resistance, he had once told Freya. And seeing him with her, she understood why. It was her future that Freya had been entrusted with as a member of the Pious Council. Could she really live with herself if she didn't do everything possible to safeguard that future?

The returning figure of Alyk parted the rain. He handed her some fruit and a soggy piece of the hard biscuit that the Followers made in place of hana, then proceeded to shrug out of most of his clothes. She held the biscuit out to the fire in an attempt to dry it, but she swiftly gave up on the effort and just ate it. It reminded her of the stale hana she had eaten with Astrom while they had been trapped inside as the Followers wreaked havoc through the city during the uprising. Astrom, too, had been someone who was fighting for a better life, resisting the chaos in the world to make the structure of their lives better.

"You look sombre," Alyk commented from his seat by the fire.

She looked over to him and smiled reflexively. "The rain," she lied.

Her pulse quickened as his fingers found and traced the line of her collarbone. "Still cold?" he asked.

Her smile was wry. "Here? Always."

"There's an easy way to fix that," he said, slipping his hand under her shift as he claimed her mouth with his.

Alyk slept. The fire had died to embers. The soft pink of the cave's walls had returned to an unassuming dark grey. Freya lay beside Alyk, staring at the roof of the cave as her thoughts chased themselves. Eventually, she rose and quietly pulled on her clothes. She paused to look down on his sleeping face. She wondered if she could have truly loved him, if she could have built some kind of life with him. It was pointless to ponder such questions now. She would never know the answer.

His journal had been left by the fire so that the last vestiges of water would leave the pages. She closed it and wrapped it tightly in cloth to keep it as dry as possible. She didn't know whether or not the journal contained information about the agents in Oranis, but it was the most information she would get. She could no longer deny the sense that her presence was needed in Oranis, especially if Alyk and the Followers were planning on mounting another incursion into the city. However tempted she may be to start life afresh, she could not deny the part of her that had been forged in Oranis. The city called to her, and she knew she could never live with herself if she stood aside and allowed harm to befall it.

She didn't look back as she slipped from the warmth of the cave out into the rain.

When she reached Alyk's hut, she paused. It cost her time that she probably couldn't afford, but she retrieved her laastram, the prospect of leaving it behind created a dull ache in her chest. She slipped the rings up her arm and around her neck, then continued the journey down the rain-soaked hill.

The guards at the gate were easy enough to get past. With a mere thought, she sent them to sleep. Guilt prickled unpleasantly under her skin as she watched them crumple. She knew them both, liked them, had joked alongside and shared conversations with them. For agreeing to be out here in the rain, they would wake cold, wet, and covered with mud.

Despite the danger of the dark and rain, she broke into a run as she passed through the gate. She wanted as much distance between herself and the Followers' settlement before Alyk woke and found her gone.

It occurred to her that if she had really wanted to be safe, she should have killed Alyk. But even as the thought passed through her mind, she rejected it. She would never have been able to bring herself to do that, especially not while he slept.

Her muscles began to burn in protest – although before she'd come to the settlement, the ache would have started far earlier. Although her lungs burned and her body ached, she continued on through the rain and dark, allowing desperation and fear to drive her on.

The rain began to abate near dawn. By then, she was nearing the foot of the mountain. She took a moment to collect herself, then she pushed on through the forest, the sound of her hurried footfalls muffled by the thick carpet of leaves.

SEVENTEEN

It was midmorning when Freya stumbled into the roadhouse. She walked in still wet from the rain during the night, her legs covered with mud kicked up by her own steps. It seemed like another lifetime ago that she had bid Olek farewell, and her appearance certainly made her feel as far away from any kind of civilisation as it was possible to be.

The room was blissfully warm and had no leaks, which as far as she was concerned, made it palatial. Her eyes fluttered shut as she enjoyed the simplicity of a fully enclosed structure. Then she remembered why she was there, and what she was running from, and her eyes snapped open with purpose. A few patrons were looking at her with wary curiosity over their late breakfasts. Steeling herself, she walked up to the table reserved for the owner.

"Help you?" the man sitting there asked her. His clothes looked well-worn and practical – a far cry from the swishing robes that comprised the style of dress in Oranis. Something about him spoke of a man who was very capable of holding his own in a fight.

Freya stopped herself from taking a step back. "I was hoping you could help me secure passage to Oranis."

He looked her up and down in mercantile appraisal. "Got anything to pay for it?"

It was something she hadn't even considered. That fact must have shown on her face, for he let out a little huff. "Thought not."

"I could pay once we reach Oranis," she said hurriedly.

He gave a growl that might have been a laugh. "Not how it works."

Freya thought desperately. If she couldn't get transport back to Oranis, she would almost certainly be caught. This was the closest roadhouse to the Followers' settlement. Without question it was where they would come first. Panic threatened to overwhelm her. Nobody here would recognise her or care who she was or what position she held. In fact, revealing who she was may only hinder her further. She had no idea who surrounded her, whether they were Pious or Kade, if they supported the uprising or felt aggrieved by it. No, she couldn't draw on the authority of being Councilwoman Kuch. She fought down her panic and conducted a mental inventory of everything on her person. She pulled off her jacket and showed him the laastram on her arm. "This could be my security."

He held out his palm.

Conscious that every moment she stood there was time for the Followers to gain on her, she slipped the loop off her neck and slid the rest of it down her arm, placing the neatly stacked rings in his outstretched hand.

The laastram was subject to intense scrutiny for several moments. Then he stood.

"I'll need to go right away," she told him. Without responding, he strode across the room to a woman who was scowling into what looked like a very full mug of ale.

"Elyssa, if you want, I've got a passenger for you. Says she needs to get to Oranis. Quickly."

The woman glared first at the owner, then Freya. "She better be able to pay for it."

The laastram was dumped on the table with a carelessness that made Freya wince. The metal scraped against the wood as Elyssa picked it up and held it close to her eyes in a show of thorough inspection.

"That's my guarantee I'll pay you – double what it's worth," Freya said. No response was forthcoming. "Triple if you can get me there within two days."

Elyssa's gaze slid over from the laastram to assess Freya in the same appraising manner as the owner. Freya fidgeted as the seconds passed. Finally, the woman looked back to her mug, drained its contents in one draught, and stood, pocketing the laastram. Freya wondered if she would ever see it again.

She followed the merchant out to the rear of the roadhouse where the wagons were kept. Elyssa went to a smaller one tucked amongst six other, larger wagons, and checked that her goods were well secured, retying a section of the oiled cloth covering the wagon bed. Freya waited with poorly managed patience as the woman pulled back the cloth to better arrange it. She glimpsed a crate with "FARWAN" stamped into the timber. As she hitched her beasts, Elyssa told Freya to never under any circumstances touch the rest of her wagon. Her gruff manner was impersonal and Freya was glad, for it meant she wouldn't have to speak with the woman.

Elyssa's wagon was, unusually, drawn by two hearat, rather than the larger manaxas used by most traders. Freya was glad for it, though. While manaxas could haul a far greater burden, the hearat were much faster than their plodding cousins, a fact of which Elyssa took ruthless advantage. As soon as Freya climbed up on the seat beside her, she flicked her driver's whip and the animals set off, pulling onto the road at a quick pace.

Despite the rocking of the wagon as it clipped along the road, Freya must have fallen into a doze. The flight down the mountain and to the roadhouse all through the night had left her utterly exhausted. She only woke when Elyssa stopped the wagon abruptly, jolting Freya awake. Her heart thudded as she looked around for an ambush, but nobody appeared. Late afternoon sun glittered on the puddles on the road. The air was warm, far warmer than the mountainside's chill.

"Why have we stopped?"

"Have to give the hearat a few minutes' rest," Elyssa informed her, swinging off the driver's seat and deftly unhitching the beasts.

Freya cautiously dropped to the ground and stretched her legs. She bit down on the groan that wanted to be let out. Everything ached – her legs, her backside, even somehow, her arms. Elyssa wordlessly handed her a hana loaf. Freya ate it gratefully. It was the first thing she had eaten since the previous evening. She should have been far hungrier, but worry of both what lay behind and ahead of her was hard rocks in her stomach, pushing hunger aside.

True to Elyssa's word, they were off again a few minutes later at the same brisk pace as before.

The woman seemed dedicated to recouping her fee. They drove through most of the night, a fact for which Freya was grateful despite the discomfort of the wagon seat. She had taken to feeling for the journal that she had tied onto her side for safety with the spare cloth that she had taken, to reassure herself that it was still there. They only slept for a few hours, with Elyssa violently nudging her awake while darkness still clung to the land. Despite the fatigue seeping into her bones, Freya did not complain. She was glad that this woman was willing to go as quickly as possible.

The next day passed much like the first, broken only by short breaks for the animals. Freya did not doze, instead staring at the forest, warily expecting an attack. She could not forget how silently and invisibly she had been ambushed when she ascended the mountain. During her time with the Followers, she'd never learned how they had accomplished it. But with the multitude of trees surrounding them, there wasn't even the need for an ability that allowed them to conceal themselves. The trees thinned as dark began to fall, and they entered the grass plain that surrounded Oranis. Night fell but Elyssa did not pause. Eventually Freya thought she could glimpse a dark blot on the horizon that did not quite mesh with the rest of the night. As they continued, Oranis grew in size until Freya could clearly make out the city. The sight was at once familiar and strange. She had lived her life within the city but she'd rarely seen it from outside. It seemed a fitting metaphor to represent her own questions about her identity and future within Oranis.

"Go to the main gate," Freya instructed Elyssa as they approached.

The merchant looked at her with a frown of surprise. It was the first expression other than sullen resentment that she had shown.

"I won't be allowed in," she said. To preserve the city's sense of order, traders were required to enter the merchants' gate on the other side of the city.

"Then leave me there," Freya said impatiently. She couldn't afford to waste any time.

"What about my payment?" Elyssa demanded.

"I promised that you would get it, didn't I?" snapped Freya. Sleep-starved, hungry, and at the end of her temper, she fixed the trader with a glare.

"How?" The cart was stopped in the middle of the road. It was clear that without an explanation, no more movement would be made.

"When you get into Oranis, ask for Bardan Firston. Tell him that Freyanna Kuch owes you a debt. I will ensure that coin gets to you. But I need to get into the city *now*." Freya gritted her teeth, waiting for the woman to object.

"Freyanna Kuch. I know that name," Elyssa said slowly. "You're a member of the Pious Council?"

"Yes." Revealing her name was a gamble. She didn't know this woman's politics. Elyssa may be a Kade of the most devout order, hungry for revenge. While Freya was certain that she could protect herself against such an attack, she didn't know how to drive a cart and she needed Elyssa to get her to the city. Every moment counted.

"Bardan's a good man," Elyssa said. She cracked her whip and the wagon set off.

Freya sat, her skin tingling as the city became larger and larger. The gates would certainly be closed but, hopefully, she would be able to get the Guardians on duty to open them.

It only took an hour before they reached the gate. Elyssa stopped her wagon in front of the high walls. Gas flames flickered in their settings in the walls. The smooth stone and constant gas-fed flames were so very different to the wood fires and rough-cut huts of the Followers' settlement.

"No wagons are permitted to enter this gate," a voice called out from high on the wall. "Anyway, the gate is closed at night."

Freya alighted and strode forward until she was in the light. "I need to enter the city immediately. It's urgent." Her voice bounced off the stone, rendered nearly unrecognisable.

As the light shone on her face, the demeanour of the Guardians immediately changed.

"Councilwoman. What are you doing outside the city? And at this time of night."

"I'm afraid I can't answer that. But it is imperative that I get into the city."

"One moment."

The sound of low voices and shuffling footsteps echoed across the empty space for several moments before a rope ladder was thrown down the wall.

"I'm so sorry, but I can't open the gate while it's still dark. You'll have to climb up," the voice called apologetically.

"What's your name?" Freya asked.

"Glynd."

"Well, Glynd, there's no need to apologise for doing your duty. Might I ask if someone is spare that they give some food and shelter to the trader who brought me here?" She looked back at Elyssa who remained just out of the light of the gas flames, and shouted, "Thank you."

She didn't wait for a response before she started to climb the ladder. She wasn't certain that she would get one in any case.

The streets were strange. She had no real idea of how long she had been gone, but she knew it had been several cycles at least. The neat, paved streets of the city were so irregularly perfect after the haphazard chaos of the mountain. It was dizzying to be surrounded by so much, and for it to be so uniform. The streets were quiet and empty. Freya headed straight to the administrative district. She had declined the offer of an escort; she could deal with anyone who may try to accost her.

She passed buildings where the lights still burned inside, but the only sound in the city was the slap of her boots on the stones. The silence was unnerving. The Followers' camp had been suffused with sound: the susurration of leaves as the wind wove through them, the whisper of streams, the sighs and cries and murmurs of those nearby. But Oranis should have been filled with its own type of noise. Yet it was silent and empty. Freya felt as though she was walking through a world populated only by ghosts. Anxiety and worry curled around her. Had she stayed away too long? Was she too late?

Like her, Makkyd lived in the administrative district. The Guardian at the door of Makkyd's living quarters hesitated, but allowed her through. She supposed her attire raised questions, but her authority was too absolute to be questioned.

Makkyd answered her door only a few moments after Freya knocked on it. She was fully dressed and looked wholly awake.

"Freya." Her voice held no surprise.

"Sorry to bother you so late."

Makkyd waved away the apology and opened the door wider in invitation. Freya entered, feeling suddenly enclosed by the walls and roof. The way they shut out the night air and the nuances of the breeze carried upon it felt strange to her. She looked around the sparsely furnished room. It gave very little away about its occupant. Reports were strewn across a large table that dominated most of the space. Everything seemed impersonal, chosen for function and convenience rather than any aesthetic value; much like Makkyd's rooms.

"Did you get what we need?" Makkyd asked once she had closed the door.

"I'm not sure," Freya admitted. She brought out the journal. "I haven't had a chance to actually look through this."

"Take a seat," Makkyd said, sitting at the table and pulling a wax tablet toward her.

Freya put the journal down as she sat but kept her hand resting on top of it. Even sitting at a table felt odd. She looked at Makkyd and found the other woman regarding her in that manner that made her feel so appraised. Makkyd, Zarech, even Alyk, all had that quality. It was both powerful and disconcerting.

Freya glanced down at the journal. Especially surrounded by the smooth, carefully crafted furniture, it seemed so tattered and small to carry the hope of peace within their city.

"I think I should tell you everything," Freya said.

Makkyd nodded, her expression expectant.

The words danced along Freya's lips but she hesitated, wanting to keep her experiences, her thoughts, her life, really, for herself. But that was not the choice she had made. So she took a breath and began to speak.

Freya recounted her experience within the Followers' camp, sparing only the detail of her physical intimacy with Alyk. While she was certain that Makkyd would have approved of anything that got her closer to what she was seeking, she wanted at least something of her life to be unknown by Makkyd.

When Freya was finished, Makkyd let out a controlled sigh, looking down at the notes she'd made.

"Is it that bad?" Freya hardly dared to ask.

"It's not good," Makkyd said. "The attacks have continued, despite our best efforts. I had to implement a curfew at night."

Freya controlled herself enough not to let the shock show. The Kade's implementation of a curfew had begun the erosion of Oranis's confidence in their ability to lead. It explained why the streets were so empty, but the news still wrapped an ice-cold hand around her and squeezed. "Did things really get that severe while I was away?"

"No. And I didn't intend to allow that to happen. That's why I implemented the curfew. And so far it appears to be working. We haven't had anything blown up or set on fire. And only a few fights and murders happen every day. As far as I'm concerned, that's a success."

Freya said nothing, focusing all her energy on not letting the horror she was feeling show.

"Well, we'd better hope that there's something useful in that journal," Makkyd said, reclaiming Freya's focus.

"I fully expect them to come after me," Freya cautioned.

"I do, too. So you'd better start looking."

Freya nodded. The sooner they got the influence of the Followers from the city, the faster the curfew could be lifted. Nevertheless, she hesitated before opening the journal. This was an intrusion into Alyk's mind. But the time for such qualms was long since past. She turned the first page and began to read.

Many of the pages were filled with simple notes. A comment about a particular flower or herb and its possible properties, notes about tending animals and observations on the best way to cure various hides. Some pages were filled with reflections about dreams he'd had. There were many references to Zarech, several of them were questions about what Zarech might have been trying to tell him. In those pages, she could see the vulnerability she had glimpsed only on occasion. The damage that Zarech's cruelty had inflicted upon him was clear in every word. And yet, it was also painfully obvious how desperately Alyk had looked up to Zarech, how he was so intent on continuing whatever Zarech had set into motion. Those pages also revealed the side he had shown the night she left – the one far from rational and charming. He had also written notes about the Dark Gods: their purpose and ways in which he prayed to them. She'd never seen him pray, but from what he wrote, he did so often and with fervour. Here too was the zealot she'd only glimpsed. She wondered how he had become so skilled at hiding that part of himself, or whether everybody concealed a dark instability. She briefly wondered if she should show those pages to Grat – they might help his study of Pious beliefs in some way – but dismissed the idea. Even if they would have been useful, the violation of showing Alyk's journal to more people than was necessary seemed too cruel.

There were also detailed notes on all the members of the Followers. Even if there were only a few comments next to the name, the words were thoughtfully chosen, evoking a clear sense of the person. Alyk definitely was able to look at someone and assess them. Freya continued to read despite fatigue making her eyes ache. She was enthralled by the mind of the man laid out before her. His writing was like Zarech's, making economic use of the page. She had to lean forward to read it at times, the tip of her nose almost brushing the page.

At some stage, Makkyd placed a mug of something beside her, but Freya only sipped it once.

She paused when she came across his assessment of her: 'Asset – but to whom? Will never be a true believer. Exceptional.'

It was strange to read his description of her in such short, clear terms. Her eyes lingered on the last word. Its ambiguity gnawed at her. Guilt sought access to her heart. She had lied, stolen, and fled. For all her actions were done for a bigger purpose, Alyk had never with any word or action done wrong to her.

The sound of Makkyd closing a door made her jump. She wasn't reading this journal to discover what Alyk thought of her or to indulge in dislike of her own actions. She was trying to find out who of his people were in the city. She sternly pushed thoughts of him and what he may have thought of her from her mind.

The sun had well and truly risen when she closed the journal with a snap. Her tired eyes protested at the brightness of the morning light, made brilliant by the stone buildings. Makkyd, who had come to sit opposite her, looked up from whatever she was reading. "Well?"

"I think I have something," Freya said, hoping her uncertainty was well masked. She slid the wax tablet she'd been writing on across to Makkyd.

The redheaded woman looked at it. "Excellent. I'll assemble the others. Go and get changed, maybe get an hour of sleep. I'll send someone to fetch you."

Light-headedness momentarily stole Freya's balance and vision as she stood. She swayed, one hand going to the tabletop to steady herself.

"Life must have been very different there," Makkyd commented.

Freya nodded, the spots across her vision easily allowing her to picture the mountainside in the gentle morning light. A part of her wanted very much to be back there and mourned that she would never return. "I nearly didn't come back, you know," she said.

"I know," Makkyd replied.

EIGHTEEN

Freya's quarters were exactly as she had left them. As she walked in, she was struck by the same impersonality that she had found in Makkyd's. Sighing, she went into the washroom and turned on the flame to heat the water. That at least was one thing that she was excited about – a proper bathe in water that wasn't going to freeze her to death.

She discarded the dirty clothes, wrinkling her nose in disgust at the sheer amount of filth that had accumulated on them. Not certain of whether she wanted to keep them or not, she left them in a pile on the floor.

Freya sighed with delight. It felt almost obscenely luxurious to have the hot water sliding over her skin. That feeling was only intensified by the actual soap she used to clean herself. The perfume of the soap, the heat of the water – it was as welcome as it was strange after so long without it all.

Freya dried herself and walked to her bedroom, not bothering to pull on clothes. The still air of indoors had a stale quality she'd not noticed before. She wanted to open a window but the days of sleeplessness weighed heavily upon her. She pulled back the covers and slipped into the embrace of her bed. The soft warmth lulled her immediately into a deep sleep.

Rapping on the door pulled her from slumber. For a moment, she thought she must be in a cloud, so soft was the bed on which she was lying. Then she remembered that she was in her own bed rather than on heaped straw. She rose, hastily dressing before she answered the door to find a runner.

Makkyd had called a meeting, she was informed.

Freya stifled a yawn as she told the runner she'd be along presently. As she prepared, she glanced out the window, gauging it to be around the middle of the day. She had slept for only an hour, maybe two. Exhaustion clung to her more ardently than before. With no small effort, she reached for energy and focus in the way she'd been taught during her long shifts as a healer.

On her way, she bought a skewer from a street vendor, capitulating to the demands of her rumbling stomach. The street was almost as deserted as the previous evening.

"Where is everybody?" she asked the vendor between bites.

The woman looked at Freya as though she wasn't particularly clever. "Nobody's allowed to linger on the streets."

"What if they do?"

The woman shrugged. "I'm sure you'd know better than me."

The pointedness of the comment stung. It seemed she was once more recognisable as Councilwoman Freyanna Kuch.

The bitter melancholy that accompanied that realisation accompanied her through the rest of the journey. She was the last to arrive, finishing the final mouthfuls of the skewer as she entered the meeting room.

Heads turned as she walked in, placing the attention of the room entirely on her. There was very little doubt in her mind that Makkyd had deliberately ensured that she would come in late and announce her glorious return. Of their own volition, her eyes sought Ashtyn. His face was contorted into an emotion that she couldn't quite decipher but his eyes found hers and the expression in them seemed as though he never wanted to look anywhere else but at her. Her heart jumped and her breath flew from her chest. The rest of Oranis may have taken on an unfamiliar quality, but the sight of him was anything but unfamiliar. For the first time, she felt she'd returned home.

Bardan was the first to properly react, jumping up and engulfing her in a hug so great she feared he may collapse one if not both of her lungs. She nevertheless enthusiastically returned the embrace, more glad than she imagined she would have been of the warm welcome.

"We were starting to fear that you may have been converted by the Followers," he told her once he released her.

"Never," she replied, taking the empty seat at Makkyd's side.

Bardan opened his mouth to say something else, but Makkyd began to speak, her face an uncompromising mask.

"Freya came back last night with information that should hopefully help us put a stop to the unrest in the city. Freya, tell us what you found."

Freya wished she had been given the chance to ask how the situation in the city had worsened and what exactly was occurring. She knew she needed to update the Council, but she would have liked to do so with some context. What she had seen of the city inspired tightened her chest with concern. However, the order in Makkyd's voice gave her little space to disagree.

"As far as I can tell, there are twenty-five people in the city who are definitely Followers. Maybe one less, given how we found out about this. Obviously we don't know what they look like, but I have their names, their specialties, their abilities, and the names they are likely to go by within the city."

A smattering of applause broke out.

"Freya, you've outdone our wildest expectations," Makkyd said, her demeanour giving no hint that she'd already perused the findings.

True enough, what she had found in Alyk's notes was more than she had dared hope. "I would still imagine that finding them won't be easy. They won't be on the city's registers at all." She didn't add that there was also work to be done unpicking the knots of hatred woven between the Kade and Pious. If she had learned anything from her time with the Followers, it was that they exploited the underlying chaos that arose from the acrimony between the two communities.

"If we have all that information, we can certainly track them down," Wren said. "Ask people if they know of someone matching a particular description. That sort of thing."

"What will we do with them once we find them?" Lyssa's question cut across the table.

"Execute them, of course," Makkyd said. Her tone made clear she thought the answer an obvious one.

Freya turned her head in alarm. "What?"

"They're too much of a threat to remain alive. They know too much about the city," Makkyd replied.

"You can't just kill twenty-five people," Freya objected. "This was the exact issue we had with the Kade prisoners."

The sudden tension in the room was abrupt and uncomfortable.

"What?" Freya asked.

Ashtyn cleared his throat. "The problem was, ah, taken out of our hands."

"How?"

"An attempt was made to free them, but it was discovered. The Guardians were...very effective. There were no survivors, including all former Kade leaders."

"What, all of them?"

He only responded with a nod, his eyes burning green.

"So as you can see, there's no precedent to guide us," Makkyd sad briskly before anyone could say anything else. "And let's remember that these people we're talking about want to destroy us and our entire way of life. They're worse than the Kade."

In the ensuing silence, Freya looked at her leader. A feeling of unease slipped through her limbs. This seemed too convenient, too easy. Her hand fell to her wrist and she was surprised when her fingers felt the green band of cloth sewn into the sleeve. She glanced down and was rewarded with the jolt of unexpected familiarity at seeing herself in her own clothes. Her fingers began to worry at the material as she looked around the table. On some faces she saw indifference, on others, shock and on some, satisfaction; a few – like Bardan and Ashtyn – showed stony anger.

Makkyd spoke again, her voice hard. "I'll allow Wren to co-ordinate our efforts. He can also comb through city records to find anything that may be of use."

Lyssa suddenly spoke. "We shouldn't execute them."

"Excuse me?" Makkyd's voice held only the slightest note of a threat but it was unmissable.

"We shouldn't kill them," Lyssa repeated, this time more slowly, more defiantly.

"I'm with Lyssa on this one, I'm afraid," Bardan added.

Makkyd's lips pressed together. "And does anybody else share this view?"

Three other hands went up, Ashtyn's among them. When Makkyd turned to pointedly look at her, Freya swallowed. After a moment of hesitation, she raised her hand, too. Freya evaded Makkyd's glare, her eyes instead finding Lyssa. The artist found her gaze and gave her an almost imperceptible nod.

"It would seem that there is significant opposition to how I would like to proceed on the matter," Makkyd said evenly. Despite her calm response, everybody could hear the anger in her voice. "What would you have me do instead?"

"We have the prison farms for a reason," Ashtyn said.

"And if they escape?"

"Isn't that a risk we take with all prisoners?" Bardan didn't raise his voice, but the challenge underlying the question filled the room entirely.

"These ones are particularly dangerous. Especially given our own somewhat tenuous position of authority," Makkyd threw back, looking as though she wished she could shoot fire at him rather than just words.

"Is the situation really that bad?" Freya asked, her voice shaking with horror. She knew things were bad in Oranis, but an acknowledgement from Makkyd made clear that what they had fought for and won seemed terribly fragile, almost impossible to maintain. Freya wondered what Astrom would have said to this, how her level-headed friend might have offered a way to fix this that none of the Council seemed able to find.

There was a pause. It seemed nobody dared respond to Freya's question. Eventually, Makkyd answered. "Things here could be a lot better," she admitted. "Now. Does anybody have anything else to add?"

"Actually, yes," Freya said, wincing as Makkyd fixed her with a cold glare. "I suspect that the Followers may pursue me. The journal I took was quite a personal item. I don't think that the fact I took it would be let go lightly. We should be prepared for their response."

A ripple went around the table. The prospect of a group of Followers of the Dark Gods launching an attack on the city in retribution was not a pleasant one, especially given that Makkyd had just declared how tenuous the Pious Council's authority actually was. If that authority, given for the ability to keep the city safe, were called into question, the people who resented the Pious Council, and many who supported them, would have cause to rise against them. A band of the Followers assaulting the city was more than enough to do just that.

"I'll go and make preparations for that now," Makkyd said, rising as she spoke.

With that, the meeting was obviously concluded. Freya frowned. Makkyd had a way of anticipating things. She would surely have put measures in place to ward against the Followers. It seemed a convenient way to end the meeting and avoid further questions or challenges. Everybody stood, gathered their things, and moved toward the door.

Freya grabbed Bardan's arm as he passed. "There may be a trader by the name of Elyssa who asks for you. If that's the case, I owe her rather a great deal of money for bringing me back to Oranis very quickly. She has my laastram." Her eyes slid over to Ashtyn. He was lingering by the door, his eyes fixed on her. "I gave it to her as a down payment, but I'd really like it back."

"How much did you promise her?"

"Three times the worth of the laastram," she admitted.

He whistled. "You know, for a woman in your position of authority, you're a very poor negotiator."

"I'd like to see how you would have negotiated in the situation I was in," she retorted, amused nevertheless. It was good to see her large friend. His humour was like a physical pressure on the tension across her shoulders, easing it away.

"Don't worry, I'll take care of it," he promised. "Are you coming?" The slight jerk of his head indicated that he was asking not only on his behalf but on Ashtyn's too. She shook her head. She wanted to speak with Makkyd.

"All right. It's good to see you," he added, giving her another hug. He walked to the door, murmuring something in Ashtyn's ear. Clearly unhappy about whatever Bardan said, Ashtyn reluctantly exited the room.

Deliberately, Freya turned her back on the door and stood by Makkyd's side, waiting for her to acknowledge that Freya had remained. Freya realised a point was being made when Makkyd said nothing and continued to study a tablet in her hand.

"I still don't think you should kill them," Freya said.

There was a particular skill in the way that Makkyd conveyed the extent of her frustration with a single sigh. "I know what you think, thank you, Freya."

"What happened with the Kade leaders?" Freya persisted.

"I don't like what you're implying," Makkyd responded, still looking at the tablet.

"Don't play games with me, Makkyd. You've ordered me to do the same sort of thing. I know how you operate," Freya snapped.

At this, Makkyd put down the tablet and turned to regard Freya. "I ordered you? I didn't order you to do anything. I have never ordered you to do anything. I asked if you were willing to do as I requested, and you have always been more than willing."

"What if I'm not willing anymore?" Freya asked.

"Then you can do nothing."

"You still haven't answered my question. Did you have something to do with the death of all those Kade leaders?"

"Why does it matter?" Makkyd snapped, her dark eyes boring into Freya, as if trying to silence her.

Anger, hot and fast, coursed through Freya. "Stop avoiding the question!" She put a hand over her mouth, shocked that she would ever speak to Makkyd like that.

Makkyd however, looked unperturbed. "Why do you care now, Freya? You've had no problem about lives being taken for a greater good before. If you really think that I'm a problem, you could kill me right now."

"What?"

Makkyd returned Freya's stare. "You heard me. You could kill me right now. Nobody would ever know about it. If you really thought I was that much of a problem, that would be the end of it.

"But you won't," Makkyd continued. "Because you know that this city – this country – needs me to be where I am. Because I'm making decisions that are necessary, even if they're unpleasant. And any second now, the Followers of the Dark Gods are going to come looking for that journal that you took, and you need somebody who will make those difficult choices to keep everything together."

Freya stared at the woman she had followed unquestioningly through so much. Without doubt, Makkyd had a point. But Freya was no longer sure if having a point was enough.

"Well, Freya?" Makkyd prompted. From the hardness in her expression, it was clear she would say nothing more until Freya replied.

Freya swallowed, her throat dry. "I'll go and help Wren."

Makkyd's tone didn't change in the slightest. "I never doubted it."

Freya sought out the Chief Administrator. Time was of the essence and even the smallest delay was more than she was comfortable allowing. She could envisage the Followers approaching the city. Even though it was likely they would all be slaughtered by the city's superior numbers, if Freya had inferred correctly, their mere presence within the city's walls would upset the fragile stability. What she had seen and heard made clear that all it would take would be the tiniest spark and the city might end up burning itself to the ground. But that was always what the Followers had counted on – the Kade and Pious tearing themselves apart. Freya fervently hoped Makkyd had plans in place to keep the Followers as far from the city as possible if they did pursue Freya. But something about Makkyd's demeanour left Freya feeling that she actually wanted the Followers to enter the city.

Wren was in his rooms, the sleeves of his robes rolled up and a concerned expression on his face as he pored over a document. It seemed that in the short time since the conclusion of the Pious Council's meeting, he had got straight to work. The door was open, but she knocked on it anyway as a sense of uncertainty held her back from simply announcing herself as she once might have; she had been away longer than she thought, it seemed. He looked up.

"Here to brief me?"

She nodded and he waved her inside. She crossed the threshold with hesitant steps.

"When we detain them, do you really think we're going to kill them?" he asked. His had been one of the hands raised in opposition to Makkyd's proposal.

"I'm not sure. I wouldn't be surprised."

He ran his hands through his hair. "How did we get here?"

Even as she relaxed – it seemed he still viewed her as the same person she'd always been, she felt a fatigue that had nothing to do with the return journey enfold her. "I don't know."

"You know, I wouldn't even blame the people if they tried to remove us." He sounded tired. Defeated. Exactly how she felt.

"I thought Makkyd was exaggerating." Freya had been desperately hoping that Makkyd's comments had been simply intended to scare Freya into submission.

"I mean, the curfew has stopped much of the violence. But how long can we keep people living like this and expect them to support us?"

"Tell me, how bad is the violence?" Freya asked.

He was silent for a moment, choosing his words with obvious care. "The hatred between Kade and Pious is not abating. It's undeniable that the Dark Gods' Followers are picking away at it and exacerbating it. Getting them out is, I think, imperative to calming everything else down."

"Will it be enough?"

He sighed. "I wish I could say yes with certainty but I just don't know, Freya."

She pushed aside the sense of futility that threatened to overwhelm her and pulled out Alyk's journal. "Well, we can at least do this."

She recounted what she'd observed of the Followers' ways, how their behaviour might stand out or mark them as someone who was not accustomed to life in Oranis. According to Alyk's journal, some had been there for years, so Freya also outlined what she'd gleaned about where they may be within the city, their skills, and the habits they may have cultivated so as to work their way into people's minds and stoke the anger there. She'd spent a brief time with the Followers but she'd watched them closely. Poring over Alyk's journal had been the final key to understanding the logic that guided and organised them.

She felt guilty for so clinically dissecting the lives of those people. They were more complex, more personal, more human, than the amalgamation of words she used to describe them. They'd offered her a place in their lives and she'd recorded it for her own ends. Yet the new lines of worry on Wren's face pushed her on.

She came to an abrupt halt, her voice hoarse.

Wren stood and looking at the notes he'd taken. "This should be enough. I'll start the necessary investigations now."

"I should see if the healers have fallen apart." Freya rubbed a hand across her forehead as she contemplated where to start.

"You look exhausted. Go to sleep."

"Sleep? When I have work?" she joked.

The wrongness of the deserted the streets was inescapable. Even in the administrative district, she could sense the change that had spread across Oranis. This was even worse than the fear and repression of the days of the Kade's brutal crackdown, because now, Freya was a part of the group that caused this restriction and fear. She had only been gone a few cycles. How could so much have changed in so little time? She bought another skewer – at least the vendors were still out, although she couldn't imagine business was particularly good. The exchange was a hurried one both because of the woman's mistrustful brusqueness and Freya's lack of desire to linger in the streets made ugly by fear. Yes. Fear permeated the city, and that knowledge coated Freya's tongue with a bitter taste. Even if she hadn't been here when the curfew had been put into place, she had helped to put the Pious Council into power. She was on the

Pious Council. She held as much responsibility for what had happened and would happen to the city as did Makkyd.

The idea of work did not appeal to her at all. Even though she knew there would be many things for her to do, she couldn't bring herself to go to her work rooms. She contemplated going to see Ashtyn but ultimately decided to follow Wren's advice. Sleep was far less complicated than the prospect of seeing him, as much as she wanted to go to him, to see him in person rather than in her imagination's imperfect conjuration of him, uncertainty and a distant dread at the idea of being alone with him gripped her with bony fingers. She didn't feel guilty about her relationship with Alyk. She and Ashtyn weren't together and she'd made him no promises. But she felt awkward about it. Her time with the Followers had at once made her more accepting of the dark parts of herself and wanting to be better than them in the way Ashtyn seemed to think she was. Both ways of viewing herself were powerful and terrifying for different reasons. The more she considered it, the more she wanted to speak with Ashtyn, hear the way his perspective cut through her confusion and turmoil. But she was rendered inert by the enormity of taking that step to go to him, because if she did, she'd have to find the words to begin unravelling her heart before him, and she had no idea what they might be.

If the city did devolve into an anarchic mess as it seemed likely to, there would be so much that she had never said to him. With the end of everything that she knew looming, there was so much – perhaps too much – to say.

That was her thought as she fell into her bed where sleep claimed her almost immediately.

NINETEEN

The bells woke her. For a moment, Freya lay staring at the ceiling, feeling as though she was back in her old house with Symon, still living under the Kade's rule. She half expected to roll over and find him beside her. But then she realised that the low, continuous chimes bore very little resemblance to the ringing that used to delineate times to pray to the Kade gods. The constant ringing of the bells could only mean one thing: the city was under attack.

Freya rolled out of bed and dressed in the dirty clothes she had worn when she entered the city the previous evening. If there was going to be fighting, she didn't want to be encumbered by an awkward robe.

She had no way of knowing where the attack was occurring, but if she knew Alyk, he would want to cause as much pandemonium as possible to alert the whole city to the Pious Council's inability to keep the people of Oranis safe. The main gate was the only logical choice.

The resonant clanging of the bells gave the deserted streets a particularly desolate quality. Running through them felt like she was running through the end of the world. It felt similar to the uprising, but during the uprising, she hadn't been alone.

She reached the main thoroughfare in good time, continuing on despite the growing ache in her side and the way her lungs burned. Sure enough, as she approached the gate, she could hear the distinctive clash of metal and cries of fighting.

It appeared that Makkyd had taken precautions to prevent the Followers from being able to freely enter the city. A full troop of Guardians was engaged with about forty Followers. From her glance, Freya recognised many of the Followers, although the feral expressions on their faces were ones that rendered them akin to strangers. Makkyd's distinctive red locks swung into view. She had a blade in each hand and was fighting two people at once. She appeared to be maintaining the upper hand, too, unlike many of the Guardians around her.

Freya realised she didn't have a weapon. Of course she didn't. She was a healer. There was no reason for her to keep weapons in her home. She stood watching the fray, indecision paralysing her.

She wasn't certain if she was recognised or simply noticed, but a woman who had taught Freya how to cook ran at her, blade in hand. Freya reacted instinctively, her ability rising easily to her call, but she merely rendered her unconscious, unwilling to kill when she could incapacitate. The awareness that she had been well and truly spotted sent tingles along her skin. The sound of pounding footsteps behind her had her wheeling. She reached out to hear the person's lifesong, but relaxed as she saw it was a group of grim-faced citizens. Ashtyn and Bardan were among them. The reinforcements were armed with a wide array of weapons, from tools to actual swords. The reinforcements fought fiercely. Perhaps it was the knowledge that the Followers didn't just bring the end of the Pious Council, but of Oranis itself that gave them an added edge. Freya joined them, using her ability to drop anybody she could. With the fresh influx of fighters, the Followers would surely be overwhelmed in a matter of minutes.

A roar from the thick of the fighting sounded and resolved itself into a single syllable: "Hold!"

The primal authority in the sound had Freya freezing where she stood. So too did everybody around her.

Alyk's voice rang out clearly. "We surrender."

Freya pushed her way through the people surrounding her so she could see him. He held his weapon aloft, his chest rising and falling with heavy breaths. He looked every bit the leader he had appeared when she had first met him. He dropped his weapon. The single ringing clash of metal on stone was followed by the clatter of steel and wood as his people followed suit.

"Why?" Makkyd's voice from nearby held an understandably suspicious edge.

"I have a proposal," Alyk called back.

Everybody in the street remained inert, rendered still by the uncertainty of the moment. "Councilwoman," he called out, the single word a taunt. "Councilwoman," he called again.

Freya didn't even think about it, gave herself no room for doubt or overthinking. She slipped between the two people between them so that she stood before him. He looked at her, the familiar smile and wicked blue eyes fixed upon her. That he seemed amused rather than angry was yet more evidence of his fervour and it sent a chill through her.

"You took something that wasn't yours to take."

She fought the impulse to shrink under his gaze. Here, she was Councilwoman Kuch – even if only for a short while longer. She drew on that authority now and stood tall. "What is your proposal?" she asked calmly.

"You and I fight. If you win, we go, along with the agents in the city. If I win, we go, we take our agents, but you also give me back what you took from me. Either way, many lives are spared here and you will achieve the outcome your Council seeks."

Like that, she saw how he had won. He had put her in an impossible situation. No course of action was right: if she refused, the Followers would resume their attack and she, a sworn protector and defender of the City, would be known as the woman who let others die to save herself. The Council would be finished. She could only accept, and there was no way that she could beat him in combat without using her ability. If she used her ability, everybody gathered would see. And news of her ability – of the abilities of the faithful – would spread. Who knew what sort of chaos would be unleashed. The most brilliant part of his plan was that his offer of combat was heard by everybody. There was no way that news of the outcome would not spread. Chaos of some form or another was guaranteed, even if she simply fought him and died. There was a certain chaos born from making someone a martyr to save their city – especially if that martyr was a Councillor.

"I told you, Councilwoman, you're an instrument of chaos." He spoke softly enough that she would be the only person who heard, his tone intimate. He added more loudly, "take some time to think about it."

"I don't need time," Freya said, her voice loud and strong. "I accept."

His smile became a grin. "Excellent. Let us prepare." The crowd obediently stepped back, Followers and the inhabitants of Oranis on some instinct separating to different sides of the street. Freya retreated to her own people, her heart thudding sickly in her chest.

Ashtyn and Makkyd were immediately by her side. Freya forestalled their comments by holding up her hands. "Agreeing was the only thing I could do."

"I know," Makkyd said, at exactly the same time that Ashtyn said "No, it wasn't."

"I can't beat him without using my ability," Freya told Makkyd. Time was of the essence, and even though she desperately wanted to speak with Ashtyn, she couldn't afford to take those moments.

"Your death may suggest we can't hold our own," Makkyd said, calling over her shoulder for someone to find a staff.

"And I was so looking forward to being a martyr," Freya said dryly, amazed by her humour despite the possibility of her impending death.

"She can't allow herself to die," Ashtyn said.

Makkyd looked very much as though she wanted to hit Ashtyn. "Freya, the consequences of showing your ability may be more catastrophic than we could ever imagine. I don't think I need to tell you how important it is that you not reveal what you do." She spoke quietly and urgently, her eyes locked on Freya's.

"And let her die? You'd let her die for your cause? The city is crumbling around us. Why sacrifice her?" Ashtyn's voice wasn't much louder than Makkyd's, but his outrage was a counterpoint to Makkyd's controlled urgency.

"One life for an entire city? Are you really so blind, Ashtyn?" Makkyd turned her gaze onto him, scorn creeping into her voice. "If one of us dies protecting the city, who could really doubt that we're acting in the best interests of the Third Country?"

"I'd let the world burn for that life," he replied.

"And that's what he's counting on," Freya interjected, tired of being talked about rather than to. "Anyway, it's my life, and I'm doing what I want with it."

Makkyd's head snapped back to look at Freya. "Remember where your priorities lie," she cautioned, placing a hand on Freya's arm in emphasis.

"You're implying I could ever forget," Freya responded coldly, yanking her arm from Makkyd's grasp.

"Freya!" Bardan stepped around Makkyd. Freya was so glad he had made his way to her side that she even managed to muster a smile as he came to her side. He held out a hand, in it was her laastram.

"How did you..." She couldn't even complete the sentence as tears put a lump in her throat.

"Elyssa came to find me. I paid her and she returned this. It was in my pocket when the bells started ringing. It seems the Goddess smiled on us – it may help you."

Tears burned her eyes as she took it from her friend's outstretched hand. He wrapped her in one of his hugs. "We'll be looking out for you. Do what you have to," he whispered in her ear.

She looked at him, trying to decipher what he meant, but Makkyd held out a staff and claimed her attention. Freya removed her jerkin, remaining only in a sleeveless tunic. She took a deep breath to calm herself, then slipped the laastram up her arm. Ashtyn's fingers were suddenly at her neck, helping her to fasten the final loop. She looked up into his face. Unable to say anything, she simply put a hand to his cheek for a moment. Regret coursed through her at her earlier reluctance to see him. It seemed silly to have robbed herself of time with him. He tried to smile at her but he couldn't manage it. Worry and grief filled his eyes.

She took the staff Makkyd was holding out to her without so much as looking at the woman and walked into the middle of the street. She could feel the eyes of every person on her. It was unsettling, like a physical weight upon her. Yet she'd been stared at often enough in the streets for her to shrug off that weight and the nerves that accompanied being a spectacle.

Alyk walked out to meet her, the easy grace of each step a testament to the fact that she was woefully outmatched. One way or another, the fight surely couldn't last long, especially as he knew all her weaknesses from the many hours they had spent sparring. They said nothing, merely regarded each other for a moment. Freya moved her feet to balance better.

Alyk didn't even bother to drop into a fighter's crouch. He simply came at her. She reflexively blocked, her staff meeting his blade. He bore down. She feared that he may end it then and there, but she mustered a reserve of strength to push back so that he staggered away from her. He retreated, his guard still up. Those deep blue eyes were fixed on her. It was almost as though they were back on the mountainside sparring, but here there was no mischievous edge, no fun, and far too much rode on what happened.

She waited for his next attack. He stepped forward with that muscled grace, his short sword curving through the air. Once, twice, three times, she blocked. Then his blade came from a new direction. She raised her arm instinctively, then grit her teeth as the blade met the laastram on her left arm. Although she had warded off his blade, she didn't expect the knee he brought into her stomach. Pain shoved the breath from her. She doubled up and he swept her legs out with an insultingly careless kick. She crumpled to the ground.

Weak, winded, and helpless, she watched as he raised his blade. She wondered if it would hurt.

A gust of wind swept along the street. The dust on the ground swirled up toward Alyk. He took a reflexive step back, one hand going to his eye. Freya didn't pause to thank the Goddess for her outrageous luck. She scrambled to her feet and picked up her staff.

No sooner had she regained her footing then he attacked her. She tried to bring her staff up to block the blow, but she was too slow. It stung as his blade bit into her side. She gritted her teeth as she felt the metal scrape across her ribs. She fell to her knees, her right arm clutching the wound. Alyk stepped forward to press his advantage and finish her. She saw the intent in his eyes.

Instinct had her pulling frantically at his lifesong. He stumbled.

To truly use her ability Freya had to focus, clear her mind. The task of healing – or killing – required her to be able to place her whole attention into the one thing, even if it was only for a moment. When she'd lashed out, she hadn't been focused. The drive for self-preservation more than anything had seen her do exactly what Makkyd had told her not to. She had no idea exactly what damage she'd caused. From the way Alyk favoured his left leg, it appeared that her barely focused attack had inflicted damage there. Rather than being upset or angry at the injury, Alyk grinned. He shifted his stance and brought a ball of fire into his free hand. Then he waited as Freya painstakingly made her way to her feet. She could hear gasps and cries from the crowd around her at the sight of the fire he'd summoned. The flames danced with hypnotic grace. In those moments as she pushed herself to stand, ignoring the different kind of fire raging across her side, Freya's mind whirred. Revealing his ability would cause panic. If she died by his hand now, it wouldn't legitimise the Council at all. It would only secure their demise as fear borne on the story of the Councilwoman struck down by unnatural forces spread through the city and into the country beyond. It wouldn't just spell the end of the Council. It would mean the ensuing panic and chaos would see so many killed. There was only one thing to do.

She struck out at his lifesong. But she still had not honed her thoughts properly – she was too preoccupied by the wetness of her blood slipping across the fingers still pressed to her side. Alyk staggered again, but remained upright.

He gave her no opportunity to collect herself. Despite his injuries, he rushed toward her. The metal of his sword caught the sun, glinting with each step. She had dropped the staff when she had been cut down and her right hand still clutched her side. She was defenceless. All she could do was curve back in an attempt to dodge his blade. However, instead of swinging his blade into her, he brought the hand holding fire to her clothes. She registered shouts of horror coming from the crowd but her eyes were transfixed on the flames as they hungrily jumped onto her tunic. The flames against her skin felt curiously cold. His blade followed, sweeping toward her.

She ignored the fear and pain that tried to deny her focus and pulled again at his lifesong. It seemed miraculous that he dropped his weapon, a cry of surprise and pain escaping his lips. But it wasn't a miracle. It was her.

He gave her no time to focus, no time to gather herself. With his uninjured leg, he kicked her knee. The pain was spectacular. Once again, she went sprawling. The fall at least smothered the flames, a fact for which she would have been grateful had he not immediately stepped forward, hand aloft to pour fire down onto her.

And then he hesitated.

It was barely a moment but it was enough for Freya to pull herself together and truly focus. Ignoring the pain wracking her body, she sought out the broken refrain amid his lifesong that was his injured leg, and pulled. There was no outward sign of any damage, but he fell, his leg twisting underneath him. She turned her attention to the hand holding fire. To the outward observer it would have simply looked as though his hand suddenly curled up and extinguished the flames. But he had clenched the hand in reflex to the damage she had done. Freya moved on to his other leg, forcing him prone.

Bloodied, burnt, and battered, Freya used the last of her strength to crawl over to him. It took effort as she moved, her hand still pressed to her side, her knee screaming each time she moved, but she wasn't going to give in to the pain until she'd rendered damage severe enough that he was incapable of getting up. She broke bones and tore muscles as she pulled herself toward him, determined to finish this. She reached his side, readying herself to put a final end to the fight and kill him. She gathered the chords of his lifesong and prepared to silence them forever. Then his eyes found hers. Even now, damaged and defeated, the fire and triumph in his eyes burned clear.

Making the decision was easy. Getting to her feet was far less so. "It's done," she croaked to the watching crowds, one with stoic unreadable faces, one filled with faces of abject disbelief. It was nearly impossible to stagger back to the silent and shocked citizens of Oranis, but she managed. The citizens of Oranis cleared a path for her, whatever they'd seen, they knew Freya had performed something no normal person could. She was in too much pain to be able to care about the combination of fear and reverence in their faces. Bardan and Ashtyn each took one side of her, catching her with gentle hands as she stumbled. "Don't harm them," she ordered, her breath laborious. "Alyk gave his word and they'll keep it."

Makkyd stared at Freya, her expression hard. "Do you know what you've done?"

Freya accepted the water someone handed to her. With the last of her strength she lifted her chin. "I won," she said. "It's over, Makkyd."

Makkyd's cold fury remained on her for another moment before she snapped out orders to the nearby Guardians.

Freya closed her eyes, feeling the trembling in her body from the shock of her injuries. She focused on her many wounds and pulled them closed. Ashtyn's arm around her waist and Bardan's hands on her shoulders were no longer quite as necessary to hold her together. She was terribly tired, but she could stand by herself without blood pouring out of her and that was certainly an improvement.

She shook off their support and walked on unsteady but mostly stable feet back into the street. The Followers had surrendered to the Guardians. Alyk remained lying in the street. Two Guardians stood over him, the way they hung back, staring down at him made it obvious that they were unsure what they should do with him.

"I'll tend to him personally," she called. They wheeled at the sound of her voice, regarding her with open trepidation. She took a few more steps toward them, intending to issue further directives, but fatigue from the fight and the effort of healing herself had taken its toll and she stumbled. Ashtyn was by her side immediately.

"You need to rest."

"Nonsense, I'm fine," she mumbled.

He caught her easily as she fell in a faint.

TWENTY

She woke in her own bed wearing a clean shift. Gingerly, she sat up. Memories of the fight filtered through her mind. The peace and silence of the room were so strange. She had grown accustomed to the sounds of an entire group of people coming through the thin walls of a hut.

Ashtyn sat in a chair, an ignored book held loosely in his hands. "You need more-interesting reading material," he commented. "A discourse on human anatomy is hardly riveting stuff."

"Have you been here the whole time?" she asked.

He nodded.

"Were you watching me sleep?"

"Not really that much else to do." He hefted the book.

"You do realise that it's strange to watch someone sleep?"

He ignored her comment. "How are you feeling?"

"Did you undress me?"

"Nothing I haven't seen before."

When she gave a noise that indicated her lack of amusement, he laughed.

"What happened?" she asked.

"You fainted."

"I gathered that much. I meant with the Followers. And the city?"

"I've been here most of the time, with you. But from what I've gathered, the Followers are imprisoned and being very obedient about it, with the exception of their leader who is recovering in the Merchant District Healing Centre.

"The city is alight – sorry, poor choice of words – aflutter with news of the abilities you and he displayed. Last I heard, Makkyd was trying to come up with a way to explain it away."

"Not sure she's being realistic," Freya said. Even if a satisfactory explanation was found, rumours would almost certainly forever abound about what had transpired between her and Alyk. She had no idea what that would mean for the Council or her position on it.

Ashtyn made a noncommittal noise. "She wanted you to die out there, you know."

"I know," Freya said calmly. "I went out expecting to."

"What changed, then?" He came to sit on the edge of the bed beside her. His movements were careful, making sure he didn't touch her, even through the sheets.

"He showed his own ability." She looked down at the blanket, picking at it.

"I saw you use yours first."

"I didn't mean to. It was...instinctive." She kept her gaze on the blanket.

"Goddess above, Freya. I've nearly lost you so many times in so many ways." There was a world of anguish in his voice. She looked up to find him staring at her with those beautiful green eyes.

"I've hardly been in that much danger," she protested.

"I wasn't talking about just losing you like that." Tears sparkled in his eyes, intensifying the green. He didn't seem to be embarrassed, though. His hand found hers. "It doesn't matter what's happened – what happened in the camp, what happened when the Kade still held power. I adore you, Freya. I always will."

"I..." She didn't know how to face this truth. She'd never known how to face it. "We need to deal with what's happening in the city." She hated herself for once again avoiding what lay between them, but what had seemed foolish when destruction was imminent now seemed very real and very terrifying.

He nodded and released her hand. When he looked at her again, the tears were gone.

"I need to go to the Healing Centre to see Alyk," Freya said, sliding out of the bed. She was conscious of her bare legs, but didn't want to say anything lest she make things more uncomfortable. She crossed the room and selected clothes. Ashtyn said nothing as she dressed. The tenor to his silence was enough for her to know she'd hurt him. But, as always, there was something more pressing that stopped her from having to truly speak with him.

"How long have I been asleep?"

"Nearly a day."

"What!" She turned to look at him in surprise.

She could feel Ashtyn's eyes on her. She turned, straightening her robes. He was watching her with an expression that she couldn't read. She crossed the room to him, needing to give him some response.

"I can't do this. Not now, not with so much still unresolved."

He caught her wrists, one in each hand before she could flee to fulfil her next purpose. "Freya, I understand, I really do. I just need you to know. When I saw you out there, I was so sure he was going to kill you."

"But he didn't," she told him gently.

"Exactly. I swore to the Goddess I'd do things differently if you lived, and you did."

She smiled. "Ashtyn, I understand."

"I'm resigning from the Council," he blurted before she could say anything else.

"What?"

"After what Makkyd asked you to do...I can't."

"What if she weren't leading the Council anymore?" Freya asked.

"But she is." Bitter resignation hung in his voice.

"Ashtyn, I really need to go," Freya said.

With a sigh, he released her. "That life on the edge of the Third Country, away from all of this. Do you remember?"

Of course she did. There had been a time, more a moment really, when she wanted nothing more to live with him there. When she had found out that he had been sent to recruit her, she had begged him to prove he loved her by leaving the Resistance and going there with her, and he had refused. It had broken her heart. She nodded, her eyes finding his.

"Say the word," he said, his voice ragged, his eyes intense. "I'll go right now if you want."

She shook her head. "I can't."

Alyk had come from a village on the border of the Third Country. Even the safest parts of the world had hidden dangers. Nowhere was truly safe from instability and danger. There was no way to escape reality. And nowhere she would ever be able to escape herself.

His shoulders dropped. "Seems I'm the one begging you to leave the cause, now."

The irony had not escaped her, either. "Can we please discuss this later?"

His fingers uncurled from her wrists. Immediately, she missed the feel of his skin against hers. "I don't think I could stop you even if I wanted to."

She surprised herself by being brave enough to linger a moment, to drink in the sight of him. She crossed the space between them to kiss his cheek. His scent assailed. He smelled so familiar. He smelled like home. "I promise everything will work out, ok?"

"I trust you, Freya," he said.

Alyk was being contained in one of the quarantine cells of the Healing Centre. The parallels between his situation and Zarech's were unsettling. Freya mused on the curious circularity that seemed to define so much of her life as she walked down the corridor. Two Guardians stood on either side of the door to Alyk's cell. They stood to attention as she approached and opened the door without her even having to utter a command.

Alyk lay in restraints on the bed. His calm demeanour was so strongly reminiscent of the first time Freya had met Zarech. It was just another thread which pulled her back to the past.

His head turned at her entry and he smiled as she crossed the room. "I was wondering how long you would be."

"I was unavoidably detained," she replied.

"You mean you fainted."

She wryly inclined her head. She placed her hands on his restrained arm and closed her eyes, feeling the wounds she had inflicted on his body. There had been very little precision to her attacks and damage ran rampant throughout his body. She felt a twinge of guilt for the extent of the injury she had caused but told herself not to be silly. He would have killed her without hesitation. Except, he had hesitated.

After a moment, she opened her eyes and took her hands from him. "How do you feel?"

"Aside from the irons? Fine."

She thought for a moment, then undid the restraints. Someone – she presumed Makkyd – had ensured that they were metal rather than leather so he couldn't burn through them.

He sat up, circling his wrists to ease the stiffness then regarded her with that deep blue gaze. "Why did you unchain me?"

She was aware that he already knew the answer just as she was aware that he wanted to hear her say it. "Because you achieved your goal. You've sown chaos in the city."

He smiled again. He really was very good looking. "And?"

"And you aren't a threat. You yourself told me. You don't really have the taste for killing. Even though you would have killed me." She wasn't bitter for it. She had, after all, lied to him, stolen his journal, and fled in the night.

"Heat of the moment." He took one of her hands and lifted it to his lips. "I would have felt bad for killing you."

Amused, she let his lips graze her fingers. The physical thrill of his touch still flowed through her, but it was not as overwhelming as it had once been. She walked to the door. "Come on, you have a bargain to uphold."

He watched, his own amusement palpable, as she opened the door and the Guardians stared with shock at her and the very much healed and liberated prisoner. It would be just one more tale of the astounding abilities of Councilwoman Freyanna Kuch and she found nothing other than amused resignation at this.

"I'm taking the prisoner with me," she informed the Guardians. "You are dismissed."

"But..." The Master-ranked Guardian struggled to articulate her objection.

"Never fear. If he tries to do anything untoward, I'll kill him," Freya told her calmly.

Alyk let out a chuckle as they walked down the corridor. She glanced into some of the rooms they passed; patients were in many of them. "I think you've just made quite the reputation for yourself, Councilwoman," he told her.

She shrugged, a light-headedness settling on her. "I've always had quite the reputation."

He chuckled again.

They walked in silence through the Centre and out onto the street. Freya was most conscious of the robes that she wore in contrast to his own more practical trousers and shirt.

"I could have stopped you from doing all this, you know," she said. There was something surreal about the fact that they were both there, walking through Oranis together. She had been correct – he didn't belong in the city. Oranis had a certain distinct character, even when its inhabitants were reeling from the near-invasion by the Followers. That personality was at odds with Alyk. The wildness she'd always seen simmering beneath his veneer of calm amusement was more noticeable amid the order of the stone buildings and neatly laid out streets.

"Oh, of course you could have stopped me. But you would have had to kill every single one of us. Not one infant could have been left. I don't think you have that kind of darkness in your heart, Councilwoman."

She smiled. "You're right, I don't."

They reached the administrative district soon enough. Freya led the way to Makkyd's rooms. The door was closed, but Freya knew the head of the Pious Council and leader of the Third Country would be in there. Voices raised in argument came from the other side, confirming as much.

Freya knocked on the door. It was yanked open almost immediately by Makkyd. "Freya. And you." Her tone contained no surprise, only a faint hint of distaste. "I'm practically breathless with anticipation to hear your reasoning for releasing him."

"I defeated him. His life is mine to do with what I choose."

"And you serve the Council," Makkyd reminded her.

"The Council or you? Because you ordered me to die by his blade." Freya summoned all the authority that came with being Councilwoman Kuch and met Makkyd's hostile gaze, not quivering under it, not looking away.

"I've never ordered you to do anything." Makkyd's growing hostility was quite palpable.

A cough from inside the room arrested the increasingly heated exchange. Freya peered past Makkyd and saw Bardan standing in Makkyd's tiny rooms, his face the picture of someone who had overheard more than they wanted to. Freya turned back to Alyk. His expression was a mask of polite disinterest. The absurdity of it all was almost enough to make her laugh.

"Perhaps this is a conversation best not conducted in the corridor," Bardan suggested.

Makkyd's mouth thinned as Alyk and Freya entered her rooms. The space was suddenly crammed.

"So?" Makkyd demanded once the door was closed.

"Where are the rest of the Followers?" Freya asked.

"Safely imprisoned." Makkyd emphasised the word 'safely', her glare fixed on Alyk.

Alyk's soft snort of amusement did not escape Freya's notice. She had no doubt his people had abilities that would make escape a very manageable feat if they so chose.

"You need to let them out," Freya told Makkyd.

Makkyd's eyes widened. "Have you gone insane?"

"A deal's a deal." Freya's voice was uncompromising.

"You won," Makkyd objected.

"Really, Makkyd. How do you think the city will cope knowing we've got upward of forty anarchists locked up?" Freya asked.

"How do you think they'll cope knowing we let them go?" Makkyd's voice came out a hiss, her expression demented.

"If I may," Bardan interjected. "I think we may have quite a lot to deal with already. Do we really want to add the complication of the Followers?"

Makkyd turned to fix him with the most spectacular glare yet. After a moment, she threw up her hands. "Fine. Shall we offer them a tour of the city, too?" Disgustedly, she summoned a runner and scrawled a note.

"Tell them to meet me at the main gate," Alyk said. "We'll gather our agents and be gone." He offered Makkyd his most genial smile.

Makkyd looked as though she would have stabbed him then and there if had she a weapon to hand. "You want me to let your people loose in the city?"

"I may be an anarchist but I'm not a liar. No harm will be done by my people," Alyk promised.

Bardan made a subtle gesture of query to Freya. She confirmed Alyk's claim with a nod.

"Makkyd." Bardan put a hand on her shoulder.

She slumped as though his hand was the final weight she could not bear. "Just go," she said tiredly to Alyk and Freya.

Freya accompanied Alyk to the main gate. She trusted him to keep his word and do no mischief, but anyone who recognised him wouldn't feel similarly. Besides, she wanted to enjoy his company for a last few moments.

"You know, she really did want you to die rather than win," he said.

"I know." She knew she should feel much more angry about it, but she couldn't muster the energy to feel anything other than a calm the likes of which she hadn't felt for years.

The change in the city was almost jarring. People had returned to the streets. Even though most people weren't lingering in the customary manner for the citizens of Oranis, signalling a lingering wariness, the city felt a lot more like the home that Freya knew.

"It seems you may be becoming a legend," Alyk commented as yet another person stopped to stare at her. "Like Illonia walking among the sick during the height of the white fear, or Jeann battling the raiding clans."

Freya snorted.

He turned eyes the colour of twilight sky on the precipice of toppling into dark upon her. "The legend of how you protected the city from the man who held fire? You know it's already being told."

She had seen the truth of his words in the eyes of the people she'd passed on the streets. She was still the subject of stares, but the contempt had been replaced by awe. Perhaps her victory had offered more than a mere reprieve for the Council.

"You'll go back to the mountain?" She didn't need to converse further about her status as a legend.

"Of course. You could come with me, you know."

Her eyebrows lifted in surprise. "You'd have me?"

"I know what I'd be having. It's worth having." She smiled. It was pointless to deny a part of her was tempted, but the fight had clarified much for her. He did not want a family, nor did he want to truly bind his life to another person and find happiness. Besides, she could never leave her city.

She slowed as they neared the thoroughfare leading to the main gate. The street was busy with people hawking wares, talking, keeping street vendors busy with food orders.

"You knew I'd leave," she accused him, not sure if she was angry or impressed.

"I suspected," he admitted.

"Plans within plans," she said, repeating his words back to him.

"What can I say?" His grin was roguish.

She shook her head. "You're a zealot. You know that Alyk, don't you?"

"So are you, Councilwoman. Why do you think I knew you'd come back here?" He sounded smug but she couldn't blame him for it.

She didn't reply.

They reached the gate where the Followers were already gathered. They no longer looked like the fearsome, violent people who had been fighting in nearly that very space the previous day. They just looked like ordinary people. Only their garb gave them away as different to the other people on the streets of Oranis. Several nodded a greeting to Freya. None appeared to hold any grudge for the fact that she had defeated their leader or that she had fought against them. She returned their smiles, concealing her hesitance and her discomfort with their apparent return to normalcy.

"So you'll continue to sow anarchy and chaos and I'll continue to try and stop you?" Freya asked.

"Revealing your abilities sowed enough chaos for now. I think I'll have a rest," he said. She knew he was lying, and he knew it.

"Well, I'm sure you'll need this regardless." She pulled his journal from the pocket of her robe.

He seemed genuinely surprised. His eyes flashed deep blue as he regarded the battered item in her hand. "But you won."

She took the fact that she had managed to do something he didn't expect as a small victory.

"It was never mine to take." She pressed it into his hands. She couldn't take back the most personal parts of him that she had read but she could make sure nobody else read them.

"See, I didn't predict that." He smiled. "You know, Councilwoman, if you ever get tired of fighting disorder—"

"I know where to find you," she finished the sentence for him, smiling.

Freya found Makkyd sitting on the roof of one of the administrative district's buildings. The sunset that evening was spectacular, the silent, still clouds were illuminated with the pinks and gold of the sun as it slipped closer to the horizon. The noise of the city drifted up to them.

"You know, this would have happened regardless of yesterday's events," Makkyd commented, her eyes fixed on the dazzling stillness.

Freya said nothing. She sat beside the woman who she had followed into battle, who had wanted her to die the day before. The still, silent sky hung above them, indifferent to the world below.

The gold turned orange.

"It makes you wonder if there's any point to anything, really," Makkyd said as she tilted her head back. "The sun rises and sets and the world doesn't really care who wins or who loses."

The oranges melded into pinks as the depth of the clouds flattened out in the diminishing light. Neither of the women shifted their gazes from the sky.

"Makkyd, this has to stop," Freya said.

"I know," the other woman replied quietly. "It was never supposed to be like this, you know. Astrom was supposed to lead once we took over. I was the fighter, not the leader of a country. But she died."

"I didn't know." Freya tore her eyes from the sunset and looked at her leader.

"I didn't tell anyone. I was worried that everyone may think I wasn't up to the task."

Pity and sorrow met within Freya. Many times since Astrom's death, she had missed her friend's wisdom and guidance. She could only imagine how Makkyd must have felt trying to do what had come so easily to Astrom. She couldn't agree with how Makkyd had weathered this burden, but she understood why she had forged on in such a manner.

"No more lies. No more secrets. We can't keep on like this. Not to each other, or to the people," Freya said.

Makkyd's life as leader of the Resistance had been steeped in secrets. But she wasn't leading the Resistance any more.

"I know," the other woman said.

The outermost edges of the sky were turning purple-blue. The clouds looked like rippled cloth.

"Do you know how magnificent the sunsets are in this city? And how rarely I ever stop to look at one?" Makkyd asked.

"Me neither," Freya admitted.

"I need to step down, don't I?"

"You do."

"I'm better at just training fighters, anyway." Makkyd sounded somehow younger.

Now, only the farthest corner of the sky held palest yellow.

"Not even Lyssa could capture this," Makkyd said softly. "How could anybody recreate something so perfect?"

Somewhere in the city, a bird called out.

The sky was turning purple-grey. The clouds showed only the merest hint of pink at their very tips.

In the half light, it was still possible to make out Makkyd's expression. She looked as though a weight had been lifted from her shoulders. By unspoken agreement, they stood and walked across the rooftop to the door.

"Who will replace you, do you think?" Freya asked.

"Oh, I think there's been an obvious choice for quite some time, don't you?"

TWENTY ONE

The swearing-in ceremony was celebrated by every citizen in Oranis. Freya stood on the stage at the front of the square with the rest of the Council. Although, it could no longer be called the Pious Council. Olek's appointment to aid the overseeing of the city's merchants had ensured that. But in Freya's opinion, the change was a good one, even if Olek's repeated winks in her direction did give her some reticence at the prospect of working with him.

Freya fidgeted as she looked out at the mass of people. The formal robes that she wore were undeniably beautiful. They bore no Pious green, nor the purple, blue and crimson tricolour of the Kade. Instead, they were sun-yellow, edged in silver. Despite their finery, she longed for the simple comfort of her healer's robe. She was separated from Ashtyn by three other members of the Council, but her glimpse of him had shown he looked resplendent in his own formal robes.

It had been a few days since Makkyd had announced her resignation, and Freya had been too busy to spare time to see him. Their unfinished conversation hung over her, had given her extra reason to not find time to see him. She kept her eyes forward, focused on the ceremony, although conscious of him so close to her.

Two Pious and two Kade citizens had been chosen for the induction ceremony, each reciting their own people's prayers. While Grat was training a group of Pious to create a new order of Goddess' Children, they weren't yet confident enough in their knowledge of prayers and rituals to officiate at any ceremony. But the decision to keep the Ordained and Goddess' Children out of it seemed fitting. Too much division had lain alongside the lines of faith.

Nevertheless, it was encouraging to hear that people were turning to Grat's fledgling Goddess' Children to seek guidance. That number had increased significantly following Freya's fight with Alyk. It seemed people's faith and commitment to their faith had been renewed. How that would change when people began discovering their own abilities was anybody's guess, but hopefully the guidance of the Goddess' Children would help maintain order. Freya doubted most would have the diligence of prayer or strength of belief to truly gain abilities. That kind of faith was deep-rooted and rare, as she'd learned. But if people who held that kind of faith did awaken to any abilities that proved destructive, she was sure they could manage. Defeating Alyk had made the world-ending scenario Makkyd outlined seem far less likely.

Those who remained of the Kade Ordained were proving to be far more reasonable than their predecessors. Whether it was out of fear was unclear, but the offer that had been extended to them of a seat for the Ordained at the Council had almost certainly helped. With the announcements that the Council would have Kade members on it and that Makkyd would step down, and the lifting of the curfew, the city had awakened overnight. The vibrancy, the sense of delight that had been absent, reappeared. It seemed much of Makkyd's worst fears seemed to be unrealised.

The prayers finished and Bardan spoke his oath of fealty to the Third Country as its leader. As soon as he had finished speaking, Chara rushed up to her father from the side of the stage. Bardan swooped down to pick her up and hold his daughter in a tight embrace. The crowd – Pious and Kade alike – roared in approval of the very human display from their new leader.

It had been Freya's suggestion to have the foods of both Kade and Pious brought to the square. Freya found a spot of relative seclusion on the edge of the square and watched from it as Kade ate Pious food, some of them for the first time. She chuckled as a young boy dragged his father back to a Pious vendor for another skewer.

The festivities sprawled into several of the streets surrounding the square, too. Practically the whole city had come to see Bardan sworn in and now it was celebrating together. The music from Kade and Pious musicians set up throughout the area blended in a curious harmony despite the differences in songs and instruments. Tomorrow the acrimony and tension may remain, but perhaps a little less than it had been.

Bardan appeared at her side, a skewer in one hand and Kade wrap in the other. "I'm demonstrating co-existence is possible," he explained at her look.

She laughed. "Everything seems to be going very well."

"I must say, I'm a bit of a hit." He raised his eyebrows.

Freya laughed again. "I don't think I've met anyone who dislikes you."

"I could introduce some traders to you, I'm sure," he replied. "You know I did refuse when Makkyd asked if I'd take her place."

"I expected you would."

"I'm still not sure that I really want this."

"But we threw a party for you."

He shook his head sorrowfully. "That's all it is for you, isn't it, Freya? One big party after another."

She was laughing once again, more than she'd laughed in the longest time. Her cheeks ached but it felt good.

"But honestly, Freya. What will you do aside from being a Councilwoman? There's more to life than service to a cause." His eyes found his daughter, dancing with Myrah. "And I'd say you've more than served your cause."

"I didn't die at Alyk's hand like Makkyd wanted me to," Freya noted.

"You would have, though."

"How do you know that?"

"Because had that dust not gotten in his eyes he would have killed you. I saw, you were expecting it."

Realisation came slowly first, then all at once. "Hang on. The wind."

He forestalled a response by putting the rest of the wrap in his mouth and holding up his hand in an 'I-didn't-do-anything' gesture. But he had said enough. Bardan's ability was to call and direct wind. Freya had always simply thought it providence that the gust of wind had blown dust up into Alyk's eyes at the right time during their fight, but now she considered it, nobody had fortune that spectacular. "Why?" she asked.

He swallowed his mouthful. "Because you are my friend."

Tears blurred her vision. It was one thing to be saved by someone like Ashtyn. It was another to be saved out of friendship. Before she had joined the Resistance, she wasn't certain that anybody would have risked themselves to help her. "Thank you," she whispered.

"Of course," he told her. "Now. My original question: what will Councilwoman Kuch do with herself when she isn't being a Councilwoman?"

"I don't know," Freya admitted.

"You fought so hard for this." He gestured to the square. "It's time to start enjoying it – living it."

They said nothing for a while, watching the people laughing and dancing, Kade and Pious indistinguishable from one another.

"Anyway. I must be off. I'm owed a dance. Maybe a drink, too." His kissed her on the cheek and went over to Chara. He took her in his arms and spun her around, leading her with that unexpected agility.

Freya watched them together. She wanted a family, a life. She always had. But first she had been afraid to bring children into a world where there was no choice for who they could be. Then she had been too busy fighting for that world. Now, she had nobody to start a family with – to build a life with. Her living quarters were functional but not a home, not a place where anyone who wanted a family would live. Even where she'd lived with Symon had been more welcoming. Her rationale for choosing to live in the administrative district was that it was a practical decision, a temporary locale. But she had also isolated herself from the idea of being loved. Perhaps it was because she thought nobody could love what she had become.

She found Ashtyn on the sidelines, like she had been, watching everybody else.

"No dancing?" she asked.

His smile was open and sweet. "Haven't been asked to dance by the right person."

"Can you even dance?"

"Can I dance! Well, actually, not very well."

She laughed. "Didn't you go to the celebrations of dance when you were younger?"

"I was too busy trying to sneak ale or glimpses of pretty women."

"You're shocking," she told him, still laughing.

"Haven't seen much of you in the last few days," he commented.

"Bardan and Makkyd had me doing things practically nonstop."

"Ah, that would do it," he said, turning his gaze back to the people in the square.

"Ashtyn..." There was so much to say. So much lay between them that there didn't seem to be any right place to start.

"Yes?" A smile touched his face. It seemed so unreal that she was standing here with him, not afraid of who may see them together, not afraid of being arrested for dissidence or treachery. Not running to the next crisis, but standing still to watch as Kade and Pious celebrated together the appointment of their friend, a good and fair man, as leader of their country. Perhaps she did not have to heave her heart into her mouth. Perhaps all she needed to do was to take a tiny, tremulous step.

"What are you grinning at?" he asked.

She hadn't realised that a grin had indeed crept across her face. She hesitated, trying to find the words for everything that swept through her. But perhaps they could wait. "Will you dance with me, Ashtyn?" she asked.

His own smile grew. "I'd like that."

ACKNOWLEDGEMENTS

Whenever I reach this stage of a book, it brings me to reflect upon the sheer number of people who support and encourage me and without whom I simply would not be able to produce these works.

As always, the first thank you goes to my family. My wonderful parents – you two have supported me so ardently in such a variety of ways. Thank you for encouraging and helping me in such extensive ways, be it formatting, or a sympathetic ear over lunch. I would not be the person I am today without you two, nor would I be writing like this without you. To the rest of my family, thank you for always being excited for what I'm doing and writing. It means the world.

I must extend again my thanks to Jason whose editing is just the best (and remains scarily fast). Additionally, Sarena and Jess are the best writers group girls I could ask for. Although they have not had much of a look-in at this book, their influence as readers and fabulous writer-friends has made such a difference. Marcus has again delivered an international cover – especial props to him for diving the exact shade I wanted from this sentence: "like, red but burnt red, sort of pinky, dusky, not too red, but not pink, either". You guys all rock.

And then there is everybody else.

My bookstagrammers – there is a clear reason why this book is dedicated to you. You guys have in many ways been the people I go to when I'm feeling insecure, when I need to remember why I write (so that I tell a story which resonates with people), and when I just feel like a bit of a chat. I have been blown away by surprise giveaways, by people quite literally wearing my words, by being (at times, aggressively) recommended to other readers, and by the beautiful beautiful captions. Madi (from Spar + Sparrow, a brand you *must* buy from) has produced my launch products for three books now, and she is always so excited to read the ARC, and she knocks it out of the park every time. You are a hero.

Also, my thanks to my wonderful not-internet friends who buy and read my books – I love you all so much for reading and liking and telling me you like it, and telling other people that you like it, and for being willing to analyse my own work with me. I can be a bit of a wanker when it comes to books, so bless you all for indulging me.

And finally, thank you to Mitch. You already know what I would say, so I'll leave it at this: I adore you most profoundly.

My bookstagrammers – you guys are so supportive and lovely. Thank you to the stars and back, because that's what you guys are; stars. Jayse, Blue, Jess, Jess (all the Jesses, really), Mel, Nat, Madi (who also made the launch products and whose store Spark+Sparrow produces amazing stuff), Jem, Tay, Nil, Sam, Kat, Angie, Abi, Julie...I know I'm missing people, and I'm so sorry to those who I have forgotten.

All my wonderful real life friends who buy and read my books – I love you all so much for reading and liking and telling me you like it, and telling other people that you like it. I don't deserve such fabulous people as you.

And finally, thank you to Mitch. With every day that passes I come to appreciate that really, there are no words.

ABOUT THE AUTHOR

Alice Jane Boér-Endacott was born and raised in Melbourne, Australia.

In true alignment to the cliché, she started writing at the age of six, although thankfully she has tried to avoid other clichés both in life and in writing since then.

In the intervening twenty-one years since she began writing, she has acquired degrees in the very practical fields of Anthropology and Executive Management, eaten a significant quantity of chocolate, been stung by a jellyfish in Malaysia (and still has the scars to prove it), and bitten by a redback spider in Melbourne.

She hopes to spend her next years writing, eating more chocolate, using esoteric concepts from her degrees to confuse other people, and avoiding all wildlife.

You can find her on Instagram @alicejaneboere

And on twitter @ajendacott

And on her website at **www.abendacott.com**

COMING 2020

Get ready to enter the final country in the Godskissed Continent, The First Country, coming in the second half of 2020.

Like all Blessed in the First Country, Kaylene is kept behind the stone walls of the Sanctuary to ensure the protection of others. Life has not been unbearable, though. She has found friends – and in Luka, even love. Then Luka dies in a terrible accident and Kaylene's entire world falls apart.

Life itself seems devoid of any hope until a chance encounter with a stranger gives Kaylene a purpose that sets her on a path that challenges everything she's ever believed: To reach beyond death itself and bring him back.

Read on to dip your toes in...

Sunlight cascaded down from the high windows. It seemed to coat the room in an ethereal haze. Kaylene walked with careful steps through the hall of mysteries, her path taking her through shadow, then light, then shadow again. It should have been far warmer, but the thick stone of the Sanctuary walls kept out the sun's heat. She passed by innumerable rows filled with artifacts and items deemed worth sequestering away from the world. What she was looking for was near. She could feel it. Leshan walked on her left, her gaze straight ahead. Merika and Callam were right behind them. Their presence quelled her fluttering nerves.

The Senior Blessed of Mysteries, a title that Kaylene had always thought a little pompous if not impressive upon first hearing it, stepped out from the shadows. The crimson of her tightly-fitted garment seemed traitorously soft in the warm afternoon light.

"What are you four doing here?" Her voice was thick with suspicion.

Kaylene stepped forward. "Good afternoon," she said with what she judged to be the appropriate amount of deference. She carefully kept her fear and nerves from her face and far in the back of her mind. She didn't think the Guardian of Mysteries was a mindsmith – Callam's Blessing was rare – but this was not a time to discover her error.

"And to you, child," the Senior Blessed of Mysteries replied. A frown creased the woman's face as she looked at Kaylene and her three friends. "What brings you all to the hall of mysteries?" Disapproval was definitely in her voice, as was the heavy irony in her emphasis on the word 'child'. Kaylene and her friends were all clearly into their adulthood. Their presence in the Sanctuary was an aberration.

Kaylene cringed inwardly. Some of the Senior Blessed were sympathetic to those who were not sufficiently in control of themselves to be allowed to leave. This was evidently not one of them. "We had the afternoon free. Merika has never been down here," Kaylene said.

Merika stepped forward, an open and inviting smile on her face. The stare the Guardian of Mysteries levelled at her friend was distinctly unimpressed. "This is not a place for playing. I would have thought the four of you were too old to play anyway." She made no effort to hide the prejudice. It was ironic. This woman had herself once been in a similar position to Kaylene and her friends, yet her animosity toward them was unchecked. A bubble of anger at this woman's hypocrisy began to swell somewhere in the back of her mind. She opened her mouth to give voice to an irate retort.

Suddenly, the woman froze. Even the rasp of her breath ceased. Kaylene looked in shock at Callam. The reality of what they were doing - of everything they were risking to come here – pressed down on her like a physical thing. The penalty for Callam's action if discovered didn't bear consideration. He was staring at the woman, his features strained with the effort of concentration. "She wasn't going to let any of us slip away unnoticed," he said before she had even asked her question aloud.

"Can you hold her for long enough for us to look?" Merika, always the first to action, asked.

"You'd better start now," Callam said, the strain of speaking and holding the Senior Blessed of Mysteries in place making his words clipped.

His three companions scattered, each taking a different direction. The instructions were seared in their minds; a scroll of animal hide, old, with handles of bright green rock.

Kaylene had been ready to end her life only the previous day - her birthday, although such occasions were not recognised within the Sanctuary. She had spent so many years behind its walls that she had even forgotten which birthday this was. It was amazing she remembered the date of her birth. She knew she had passed her twentieth year at least a year ago, but she didn't know how many more had passed.

The salt air had stung her lips as she approached the cliff. She could hear the water crashing against the rocks below. That water would carry her lifeless body away once she made the jump. A part of her wondered whether she possessed the courage to go through with her plan, to actually launch herself off the cliff's edge. She imagined what it would feel like to fall through the air, to have the wind caress her as she flew down faster and faster until her body met the hard rock below. There was something almost invigorating about the prospect of flight, even if it would be for only a few fleeting seconds. It was nice to think she would end her life feeling so free.

When she had reached the cliff's edge, her expectation that she would be afraid went unmet. She sat on the grass that grimly clung to the ground and stared out at the expanse of sea, watching the ships as they traced their way across the waves toward Curnith - the only way in or out of the First Country. They were tiny, almost toy-like from this distance. There was a certain serenity to the moment that she wanted to savour before she made the final leap and joined Luka. She contemplated whispering a prayer to the many-faced god to guide her to a quick death, but the words would not come and she could not be troubled to find them.

Her peace was disturbed by the abrupt appearance of an old woman with skin tanned a rich brown and deeply wrinkled. The woman sat next to her with an unpardonable air of familiarity.

Kaylene had stared at her, indignation intruding into the serenity that had settled over her. "Can I help you?"

The woman remained staring out toward the horizon. "It's a long way down. Are you sure you want to get there by jumping?"

Kaylene's initial shock was quelled by logic; few people would come right to the cliff's edge for so long simply to admire the view.

"I have my reasons." Her reply was calm. The Sanctuary would have been proud of the control she was demonstrating.

"I'm sure you do. Perhaps I can help, though."

"Nobody can help me." Kaylene spoke with no anger, no misery, only a calm certainty. Perhaps finally she had mastered herself. Oh, the irony that only when she had lost the desire to live free had she found the control which would have allowed her release from the Sanctuary.

"You seem awfully certain. Do you really think you know everything about the world around you?"

There seemed a certain prescience to the question that gave Kaylene pause. "I believe I know enough," she said cautiously.

"Perhaps you should tell me your story," the woman suggested. "My name is Ay'ash."

Kaylene blinked in surprise. It was a name of one of the Old Ones, those who claimed to be the original inhabitants of the land. They were a reclusive lot, preferring to live in seclusion amid nature rather than dwell in settlements. It was a fair preference given the treatment that had been inflicted upon their people.

She had hesitated. The Old Ones were notorious for giving advice that later came back to haunt the person who had accepted it. But such tales were likely more superstition than truth. The wizened old woman beside her radiated no air of malevolence. And she found herself wanting to speak of the pain which had wrapped itself around her and refused to let go. So she told Ay-ash about Luka, the unfairness of his death, the unbearable sense of loss that his absence left in her, and the fact that even her friends could not abate her misery. No, misery was too simple a word. She was shrouded in an inability to find any moment of joy or delight in the endless moments which filled her day. Life had become stale and unbearable in its sadness. Her story came to a halting end when she reached her decision to come here to the cliffs.

Ay-ash said nothing her face still carrying the serene as when she had first sat down. "That's one way of doing it," she agreed. "Or you could bring him back," she had added offhandedly.

READ OTHER STORIES FROM THE LEGENDS OF THE GODSKISSED CONTINENT

QUEENDOM OF THE SEVEN LAKES

"There are always those who are willing to pay for someone else's death."

Having grown up amongst the Family of Assassins, Elen-ai knows well the prices people are willing to pay to see their enemies fall quickly, quietly, and discreetly. When she is asked to preserve life rather than take it, she is surprised. Upon hearing that her charge is the Queen's only child Gidyon, who is secretly being groomed to succeed his mother, she is horrified. To ensure political stability, no man has ever sat on the throne of the Queendom of the Seven Lakes. Yet one does not easily refuse a Queen, and so reluctantly, Elen-ai accepts the contract.

Her fears only deepen upon meeting the sixteen-year-old Prince Gidyon, who treats her as no better than a petty murderer. However, following an attack on his life, Elen-ai is forced to admit that the danger of leaving this boy-prince alone maybe even worse than leaving him to his own devices. Elen-ai reluctantly accompanies Gidyon across the country to identify those within the seven most powerful families who are responsible for the attempt on the Prince's life.

Somewhere in their travels from the calm waters of Lake Tak to the looming cliffs above Lake Bertak, the two form an unlikely yet profound friendship, and Elen-ai begins to see that Gidyon has the makings of a great ruler within him. As they meet with the families of power, it becomes increasingly clear that secrets and power games run far deeper throughout the Queendom of the Seven Lakes than either of them ever suspected.

THE RUTHLESS LAND

"Lying is not simply about telling a plausible story, it's about being able to tell what someone will want to believe"

To outsiders, the Fourth Country is an unforgiving place. Under the leadership of ruthless women, powerful families regularly wage brutal campaigns against one another to increase their land and wealth, and men live in a state of complete subjugation.

Lexana, heiress to the Farwan family, is sent to the Academy, an elite institution where the daughters of powerful families learn and refine techniques to maintain and gain power. There, she finds herself attracted to Jaxen, one of the teachers who defies convention and goes about unveiled. His apparent disregard for what is expected of him leaves her both uneasy and fascinated.

Then the impossible comes to pass, and disaster befalls the Farwan family. Lexa must leave the Academy to find her mother and help restore her family to power. Jaxen insists upon accompanying her, arguing that she cannot survive without his help. Lexa can't be certain that she can trust Jaxen, but he is right; she needs his help if she is to succeed.